MOTHERTRUCKER

Journey's End

by
Wendy 'Mothertrucker' Priestley

ISBN 978-1-4710-2395-8

Published by
Lulu
For
for Mothertrucker Books

First edition printed in 2004 by Wendy Glindon Publishing

The Mothertrucker series

Mothertrucker – Starting Out.
ISBN: 978-1-4710-3383-4

Mothertrucker – Driving On
ISBN 978-1-4710-2390-3

Mothertrucker – Journeys End.
ISBN 978-1-4710-2395-8

*****

After spending over 20 years as trucker, Wendy decided to put some of her own experiences and those of her fellow truckers down on paper, so Carol Landers, our intrepid lady driver came into being. Enjoyed by a wide variety of readers from teenagers to truckers, the stories have become very popular and Wendy is always being asked to continue to write about the ongoing experiences of Carol and Gina.

To date **Mothertrucker – Journey's End** is the last in the series but who knows what the future could bring?

I dedicate this book to everyone who has read and enjoyed the first 'Mothertrucker' books and taken the trouble to contact me and tell me how much they have enjoyed the adventures of Carol and Gina.

It has given me great pleasure to receive so many letters, emails and messages telling me how much the books have been enjoyed and discovering that readers can relate to Carol and Gina, their hopes and dreams as well as their adventures.

It was wonderful to find that the books have inspired many of my lady readers to stand firm and realise their dreams, whether it be to become a trucker or to venture into other lifetime choices that they have previously been discouraged to take.   So remember – if you want something passionately enough you *can* achieve it.

My best wishes to you all.

Wendy Priestley - aka Mothertrucker

CHAPTER ONE

"Hey there Gorgeous!" The loud blast of air horns made Carol jump, spilling some of the dubious liquid masquerading as coffee from the polystyrene cup she was carrying across the lorry park.

"I thought that was you, the lovely Mrs Landers no less!" A tall, skinny young man in well-worn shorts and rigger boots swung down from the cab of a dust covered truck.

"Oh, Hi!" Carol recognised the face but could not for the life of her put a name to it. "Nice to see you," she answered warmly, pinning a smile on her face as she wracked her brain for the name. "What are you doing here?"

"Got a job with Kellerman's as you can see." The young man grinned, proudly gesturing the livery painted along the side of the cab door as Carol approached. "Never thought I would be out on the road as a working trucker. Only seems like yesterday, I was sitting at the wheel with you by my side telling me what to do and how to do it. I remember thinking, 'Kenny lad, you will never get the hang of this,' and now here I am, out on the road and not hit anything yet!" Kenny chuckled at his own witticism.

Carol laughed. Kenny - of course. She remembered now. One of her students when she had first started work with the Heavy Goods driving school. Kenny had been one of her first successes, passing his driving test first attempt and giving Carol a real sense of achievement as an instructor. "Well that was the plan, wasn't it?" she pointed out, taking a sip of what was left of the coffee. "You do the training, pass the test, then get out on the road and earn a living."

"Never have done it without you girl," Kenny continued. "I still remember everything you told me all the time I am out there on the road. It pays to be careful, don't it?"

"Sure does," Carol agreed. "So where do they send you?" She pushed back a rogue lock of auburn curl that refused to stay put in her hair-band. The late spring sunshine was unseasonably hot and the air felt heavy and humid standing amid the melee of parked trucks in the service station. Many still warm and giving off heat from their long haul down the motorway.

"Usually Newcastle area then back to base in Thurrock." Kenny told her. "Not exactly world-wide globetrotting, but it's a start and the pay's good."

"That's all that matters really." Carol replied. "A steady job with decent pay is all we can ask for."

Kenny decided to avoid getting into a debate about decent wages and rates, a subject that most truck drivers could debate until doomsday. "So how are you getting along?" He enquired. "You had just got back from Bulgaria, rescuing your mate from prison out there last time I spoke to you. That sounded a bit of a hair raiser, a real adventure!" The young driver had hung on every word when Carol had told the tale of the long drive that she and Gina had made out to Bulgaria to try to secure Jeff's release from the hell hole that was a Bulgarian prison.

"One we could all have done without." Carol replied wryly. "Let that be a warning to you, if you are ever sent abroad make sure your load is well checked all the time, and every bit of the truck for that matter. We don't want to hear of any other British drivers banged up for smuggling when they don't even know they have done it."

"Too easy to plant stuff on drivers out there." Kenny agreed. "I think I am better off staying in the UK. At least you are on home turf if something goes wrong. By the way, did you ever hear from that other character, you know, that prison guard who helped you out over there?"

"Well, no!" Carol's tone took on a conspiratorial edge. "The mysterious Mr Markov. That was all so weird. I expected him to be trouble in some way or at least have some hidden agenda or something, but he just rode with us back to the UK and left us at Dover as soon as we got into the country. Simply walked away – just like that. A complete disappearing act. Very strange!"

"No matter, he helped you when you needed it so that's all that counts I suppose." Kenny remarked, pulling a battered tobacco tin from his shorts pocket and rolling a cigarette "I reckon your mate would still be in that prison if he hadn't helped get him out."

"Yes, and we were very grateful for it at the time. I really expected to hear from him again but he disappeared like a shadow, as if he had never existed."

"Turned out to be Russian or something didn't he?" Said Kenny. "A real mystery like something out of a book - real 'Boys Own' novel stuff."

"You're right there." Carol replied. "It was all too complicated for me, I don't really do politics so I have no idea what the problems are in those countries and, to be honest, I didn't like asking too much, not that I think for one minute he would have given away any details. The man was a closed book."

"Ah well, he was there at the right time." Kenny glanced across the truck park to Carol's old Transcon. "Your company still pulling abroad?" he asked. "You and Jeff still doing OK?"

"Yes, we are getting on with it quite well now." Carol told him proudly, pushing all thoughts of Zhravko Markov out of her mind. "Not millionaires yet but the work is steady. Jeff and Tony are in full time work so that's wonderful. They both do regular runs to Italy for the olive oil, a lot of which they can haul over to Germany as well as bringing it back here and we seem to have had no trouble so far getting back loads either and we still have a solid contract shifting the waste paper."

"That brilliant – So what are you doing today?" Kenny enquired, mopping his brow with a piece of cloth he had produced from his shorts pocket.

"Well, I am still working pretty regularly for Derek at the truck driving school, but I have to be willing to be on call to do a delivery run either here in the UK or over the water when we get busy – which seems to be happening more and more these days. We got a contract last week for hauling animal feed down to Kent so that's where I have been. Dropped that load off and running back empty. Don't like running empty but the job paid well so it was worth taking. Just having this break, then another hour will get me back home."

"So you haven't married your handsome Italian yet, moved to Italy and had a dozen bambino's?"

Carol laughed. "No, nothing like that. Tony and I are fine as we are right now and as for bambinos – you can forget about that, I have certainly done my bit getting Katy brought up and into Uni. I have no intention of starting all that lark over gain." Carol's emerald eyes flashed with amusement at the thought. "And on that point I had better leave you and get on. I hope to call in and visit my friend Gina tonight. She's expecting a baby and as Jeff is away most of the time, I like to spend as much time as possible with her, although I have had a pretty long day so a phone call may have to suffice tonight."

"Is that the really pretty one that always looks like she has fallen off the pages of Vogue?" Kenny grinned. Nobody who had ever seen Gina could easily forget her.

"That's the one!" Carol replied with a grin. "She still looks good with a bump too!"

The pair said their goodbyes and Carol made her way through the lanes of parked trucks to where the old Ford Transcon was standing, emblazoned with her own livery proudly announcing 'Transcon Haulage' and the trucks own name 'The Fighting Spirit' painted along the front. Not to everybody's taste, but Carol loved the old truck and hated the idea of trading her in for a better model. They had been through too much together for that, and it wasn't as if the old girl was worked to death. A short run to Kent or Lincolnshire or up North was easy enough and that was all she was needed for at the moment. Just as well really, Carol often thought. The old truck surely would not make the demanding runs across the Continent any more. In fact with hindsight Carol often wondered how she had managed to drive the elderly vehicle over the mountains into Italy on her first run out. But ignorance had been bliss and no way in the world would she have taken on such a daunting task in the battered old vehicle now. When she did the Italian runs alongside Jeff and Tony, she hired a more up to date vehicle. At least that way she had the security of cover from the hire company should anything go amiss.

Carol unlocked the cab door and climbed in. The heat pouring through the windscreen into the cab made her clothes immediately glue themselves to her body as she settled into the driving seat. She started the engine and put the cold air blowers on full blast, spending a few minutes doing battle with her mass of thick auburn curls, trying to hold them up off her neck with the aid of a strong elastic hair band. The buzz of the low air warning system hummed in her ears as she sat patiently waiting for the tanks to build up air. It took longer each time, she believed, but when she was up to strength the old truck seemed reliable enough.

She glanced at her watch as the buzzer petered out and went silent. Air tanks full once more. Yes, she had spent enough time in the services to satisfy tacho regulations. She could make it back to the yard with ease now, providing the M25 had no incidents to cause hold-ups. She would park up, have a soak, walk Bruno when the evening got a little cooler and then hopefully call in on Gina if she had the energy after such a long hot day.

As she swung out of the slip road and onto the motorway, Carol's mind wandered back to the conversation with Kenny. It had been in the grip of winter, just before Christmas, when she and Gina had driven over to Bulgaria to plead for Jeff's release from that dreadful prison and had met the bearded giant prison guard who had helped them in their quest.

The mysterious prison guard they had first thought to be Bulgarian had arranged for Jeff's release, escorting him from the prison under cover of darkness and retrieving his impounded truck before accompanying him back to England, then disappearing like a ghost into the crowded Dover docks.

Although he had ridden a good part of the way with Carol herself after meeting up with them in Belgrade he had been far from forthcoming about his plans or indeed his past. Carol felt she knew absolutely nothing about the man at all, although her natural curiosity often made her wonder what he was doing or where he was at this particular time.

The traffic began to slow as the motorway became more crowded on the last few miles towards the outskirts of London. As usual, Carol though about Tony, her handsome Italian lover with the diamond grey eyes and kind heart. Maybe moving to the hills of Tuscany and living the simple life as Tony's parents did was a far better option than battling through congested traffic each day. But they were doing so well just now, Carol considered, to change anything before it was really completed would be a shame and she knew herself too well not to know that she would always have wondered if giving it all up now would have been a bad move.

The business partnership between she and Jeff and had gone from strength to strength in an amazingly short time. Starting out with only Jeff's Globetrotter - his beloved 'Silver Lady - and Carol's battered old Ford Transcontinental they had originally hoped that there would be enough work to keep both trucks on the road most of the time. But since buying the 'Flying Angel' for Tony to drive they found that there was enough work for all three trucks and often more.

It worked well. Tony and Jeff doing the Continental work with the two Volvo's and Carol staying back in the UK, running the business, working part time as an instructor at the local heavy goods driving school and doing short runs in the Transcon when required. She was also on hand to help Gina if needed so Jeff felt a lot happier driving abroad knowing that Carol was nearby should his adored wife need any help or have any problems while he was away. Jeff was in Italy right now. He had already dropped the load and made his way to La Casaccia, Tony's delightful family home, where no doubt he would be being spoiled to the bone with Mamma's legendary cooking.

Carol dropped a gear as the traffic crawled along the slow moving motorway. The sun was shining directly through her window, burning the skin on her arm. The old Transcon had few refinements and certainly nothing resembling air conditioning. In fact Carol suspected that the cold air blower was only just struggling to produce slightly cooler air than the air outside. Although the afternoon was beginning to cool, she felt hot and sticky and was looking forward to sinking into cool water as soon as she got home.

At last she arrived at her turn off and hauled the old truck onto the slip road towards the roundabout. Plain sailing from here she hoped, mentally crossing her fingers and wishing that 'plain sailing' had not crossed her mind and possibly tempted fate, but the traffic had now cleared enough to allow her to negotiate around the town centre with little or no trouble and continue on to the winding country lane that led to her yard and her home.

A cool breeze ruffled her hair through the open window and Carol could feel her cool bath water beckoning as she pressed the accelerator to speed her last few miles.

*****

Jeff was completely stuffed. The breakfast that Mamma Gina had confronted him with was, even to Mamma's standards, huge. Jeff knew perfectly well he had not been obliged to clear every last scrap from his plate but it all tasted so good. He had continued to cram the last few mouthfuls into his stomach, disregarding the fact that it was, especially after last evening's culinary onslaught, appealing for mercy. Jeff loved Mamma dearly although often felt secretly amused that this ample Italian lady should share the same name as his own petite wife.

"Lucky I don't eat like this every day, Mamma!" Jeff gasped. "I doubt if I would fit behind the wheel if I did!"

Mamma beamed with delight, her rotund figure immediately sweeping towards Jeff, almost gathering him from his chair and smothering him with one of her spontaneous embraces. "I like-a to see the working man eat-a well." Mamma's broken English lent more charm to her gregarious personality. "My boys and-a Poppa, they always like Mamma's cooking – always eat-a well. Nobody go without in Mamma's 'cucina!"

"I doubt anybody would go hungry here Mamma!" Jeff laughed when he had regained the ability to breathe and leaning back in the strong wooden chair as Mamma gathered the remains of the breakfast meal and clutter of plates from the huge scrubbed table.

"Mamma's lifetime ambition is to feed the world I do believe." Tony added swallowing the last of his coffee, his diamond grey eyes twinkling with amusement. As Mamma's eldest son he knew only too well that death by cooking was clearly a possibility if Mamma was left in charge of the portions served.

As usual La Casaccia was alive with children dashing in and out of Mamma's busy kitchen, accompanied by an array of dogs, cats and the odd chicken. The place had an air of constant hustle and bustle with Mamma and her three eldest daughters busying themselves with the constant preparation of food for the large family, the younger children, grubby and happy, playing in and around the huge rambling farmhouse and the fields beyond. The farmhouse was a heaven on earth to Jeff and he loved the story that it had been a tumbledown ruin that Mamma Gina had loved as a child and that Poppa had restored it for her with love in every brick when she had become homesick for her country after years of living in England.

The farmhouse seemed to radiate the love of the huge extended family and felt as though it welcomed visitors with open arms, always finding enough room despite the ever growing family that it held safe between its walls. Mamma Gina's three eldest girls shared the same striking good looks as their brother Tony. Each had the same unblemished olive skin and long dark hair that shone in the shafts of sunlight filtering through the criss-crossed grape vines that clambered over the pergola outside the kitchen windows. But whereas the flirtatious Sophia and her shy sister Carlotta had inherited their mothers deep brown eyes, Claudia, the eldest girl, had the same stunning diamond grey eyes as her brother.

"It has made a nice change to be here all together this time." Jeff remarked. The last few trips he and Tony had made over the water the runs had been staggered. Jeff loading Poppa Copeland's fine olive oil from the pack-house in San Guistino and delivering a part load to Germany before returning to England and Tony driving a couple of days behind with his loads. This particular trip had been a bonus. Both drivers had loaded their trucks on the outskirts of London and both driven direct to Italy to drop the loads. Tony had left a little ahead of Jeff to deliver in Rome and pick up a load of porcelain for the return trip. Jeff had done the regular waste paper drop in Florence before hauling the 'Silver Lady' up the rough hillside road leading to San Guistino to load drums of Poppa's fine olive oil then parking up for the night at La Casaccia. A welcome respite before embarking on the return trip to England the following day.

Tony had arrived soon after Jeff. Already fully loaded and ready for the return trip, so the two men had been able to spend a relaxing evening together, talking about the trip in hand and discussing future plans with Tony's Poppa and brother Marco. Despite marrying the lovely Guliana only last year, Marco was no less the hard headed businessman he had always been. Guliana calmly took his long absences from home in her stride and quietly went about helping Mamma Gina and the girls about the house while she waited for her husband's return from his business dealings' in the city. Jeff often wondered exactly what Marco's business dealings were – as they had never been made perfectly clear – but decided long ago that it was perhaps better not to ask.

"Paulo, Georgio get yourselves ready for school – now! Carlotta is waiting to take you down to meet the bus!" Commanded Poppa Copeland, his distinctive Stoke-on-Trent accent never having being tinged with any Italian dialect even though he had lived in Tuscany for what seemed like forever. A short stocky man of indiscernible years, a shock of white hair and distinctive diamond grey eyes that had been inherited by his eldest son, Poppa lived amongst the organised chaos of his Anglo-Italian family with calm and ease. "Sophia, go and find Christo and Maria – they are out with the donkey and the dogs and will stay there all day unless we catch them!" The two smallest children seemed to run happily wild with no fear of any harm every coming to them in this idyllic place, but Sophia happily went out in search of her younger siblings to check on their well being.

A flurry of preparation and a mixture of Italian and English protestations followed as the nine year old twins gathered their books and unwillingly left the comfort of the friendly cluttered kitchen to make their way to the small village school. "Those boys are so much like I was at their age." Remarked Poppa, "Too much of interest going on to want to be cooped up in a schoolroom all day. Although Paulo still is keen to be a vet when he grows up so he is starting to realise that passion alone won't get him the job – he will need exams with high pass marks as well."

"I always enjoyed school." Tony put in, rising from his chair and taking his empty dishes over to the big brown earthenware sink where his sister Claudia was about to start the task of washing up and putting the crockery away before the preparations of the next meal took place.

"I enjoyed my young days in school in England and also when I was older and we were living over here in Italy. There was no keeping me at home. Unlike Marco who always had something better to do!"

"Ah, my Antonio!" Mamma ruffled Tony's mass of black curls. "Always-a the good boy – no trouble to his Mamma and Poppa, and now getting himself the beautiful bride!"

Tony planted a kiss on Mamma's cheek. "Hush, Mamma, I haven't asked her yet." Tony reminded his mother. "Carol may not want to get married – well not yet at least. All I can do is ask her you know." Tony's spoken English was almost without inflection. Having being born and brought up in England through his early years, it was pretty much his first language. Jeff loved to hear the family chatting. The easy switch from English to Italian was seamless although Jeff had always noted that, apart from Tony and Marco, when any of the younger brood spoke in English it was always with a charming mixture of both Italian and Poppa's Stoke-on-Trent accent.

"Carol is lovely girl and very much in love with-a my Antonio." Mamma stated firmly. "She will be happy to be wife to such a handsome boy!" Mamma could never have been expected to grasp the possibility that any woman would be happy being single and spending a life without a cluster of children around her feet and a warm husband to curl up with at night.

Poppa smiled at Mamma's obvious faith in her son's ability to woo any woman and sweep her off her feet, but he too, knew Carol well for the independent woman she was. "Well son, all you can do is ask. You never know, she may have been waiting for you to ask. Carol is a strong lady but even strong ladies like to be asked and not have to do the asking, you know lad."

Tony nodded, appreciating his father's attempt at paternal wisdom, gathering up his bag and checking that all his necessary paperwork was safely tucked away. "Well don't any of you let anything slip should you speak to Carol before I get the chance to ask her." He warned, his eyes meeting his sister Claudia's with a firm glance and privately hoping that Carol would not telephone La Casaccia before he arrived back in England and speak to Claudia who was notorious for her chatter.

The younger Carlotta smiled at Tony as she nudged her elder sister. "Claudia is too much in love herself to think about other romances!" She smiled wickedly as Claudia's cheeks turned a pretty shade of red. It had certainly not gone unnoticed that a certain young man had been paying more visits than usual to La Casaccia of late and that Claudia was always on hand to greet him when he strode up the long drive towards the veranda. In fact Vincenzo was becoming a bit of a fixture it seemed.

"That is one thing that will not slip out." Claudia remarked starchily, tossing her glossy black hair back from her shoulders as if the very idea of any secret passing her lips was unheard of. "I am for ever discreet!"

Tony decided not to pursue that last remark. He loved Claudia dearly and would have trusted her with his life, but sometimes she forgot herself in her eagerness to chatter. "Good." he answered firmly. "You ready Jeff? Time is getting on. We had better get these trucks on the road."

Jeff unwillingly got to his feet and gathered his belongings. "Well, Mamma, thank you once again for the wonderful food and for putting me up for the night."

Jeff braced himself as Mamma advanced towards him, arms outstretched. "You are like-a my family Jeff, you always welcome in Mamma's house." She treated Jeff to a huge kiss on the cheek, enveloping him once more in one of her enthusiastic hugs before releasing him and turning her attentions to her firstborn and enveloping him as though they were parting forever.

"Safe journey lads." Poppa gripped Jeff's hand and slapped his eldest son on the back. "You will hopefully get to England by early Friday all being well, is that right?"

"Yes, Pops that's the plan." Jeff replied. "Should be able to spend a nice long weekend with my lovely missus and also give Tony time to pluck up the courage to pop the question to Carol."

"Ah, belissima, a huge wedding with all-a the family, the biggest cake, dancing, singing, lots of-a food!" Mamma sounded ecstatic.

"We will see Mamma." Tony replied gently. He had a strong idea that a huge wedding would be the last thing that Carol would want, if indeed she wanted a wedding at all. Mamma Gina made her customary lengthy and tearful goodbyes to the two drivers before allowing them to walk out of the warm farmhouse kitchen into the cool morning air.

Stepping over the group of dogs lounging on the vine-covered veranda, hoping for goodies from Mamma's kitchen to come their way, Jeff and Tony made their way across to the pair of Volvos standing by the barn. One of the young dogs scampered after Jeff, leaping about his ankles. Jeff bent down and rolled the youngster over. "These pups have sure grown fast!" he remarked, glancing over to the young mother dog lazing by the barn door.
Tony smiled. "It does not seem so long since we took the mother in when Carol and Gina found her on the road." He said. Hard to believe that was the first time Carol and I met. I feel I have known her for a lifetime." Jeff untangled himself from the young dogs' attention, clapping his hands and sending it scurrying back to its litter mates so that he could walk without the hindrance of a pair of teeth pulling at his boot laces. He always felt he was greeting an old friend as he walked over to his well-loved 'Silver Lady' and unlocked the cab door. Tony's 'Flying Angel' may be a newer and more up-to-date model but Jeff had no desire to upgrade his reliable truck.
"You boys take it steady out there, you hear." Said Poppa, standing back while Tony and Jeff climbed into their cabs and made preparation to leave. "With a bit of luck you will get a good run with no hold-ups and be on the boat quick smart.... and Tony, don't you go getting yourself worked up about what the lovely Carol will say. Just be yourself Boy and all will be well I am sure." Poppa gave his son a conspiratorial wink and a thumbs up of support as the Volvo engines roared into life. A pleasant, and hopefully uneventful, two-day run would bring the small convoy to the boat then directly home. Jeff to his beloved Gina and Tony to Carol – with his hopes and dreams tucked into a tiny box in his jacket pocket.

*****

CHAPTER TWO

"Let me get through the door, boy!"   Carol staggered under the greeting of the big German Shepherd as she tried to close the heavy oak door behind her. Bruno made one more attempt to leap up and reach her face with an enthusiastic tongue before turning and dashing across the polished wooden floor of the hallway into the kitchen and the direction of his food bowl.

Carol kicked of her trainers in the hallway and carried them across the polished parquet floor as she followed Bruno into the cool shady kitchen at the rear of the rambling old house. She flung the window wide and opened the door leading to the garden. It was like two way traffic, Carol thought with a smile, as two cats shot in through the door into the kitchen, scrambling between Bruno's legs as he, totally ignoring them, shot out, bounding across the grass area that Carol hoped could one day be called a lawn, and disappeared into the cluster of trees at the far end, tail wagging with delight, nose to the ground in search of hidden delights.

"Starving again, Thomas O'Malley?" Carol laughed as she pulled a packet of cat crunchies from the cupboard, the label proudly announcing that most cats preferred this particular brand, and sprinkled some into the pretty china bowl on the floor that the young ginger and white cat was trying his best to lick the pattern from. "Come on Digger, don't be left out now." She scooped up the quieter black and white cat and pushed him into place next to Thomas. The young cat, hardly more than a kitten sniffed casually at the food then strolled languidly back out into the garden and wandered off in the direction of Bruno. Hard to believe those two are litter mates, thought Carol with a silent chuckle as she filled the kettle and clicked it on to boil before picking up a note that was lying on the scrubbed pine table.

'Cleaned out most of the old workshop and finished the service on Jeff's car. Tony rang and said he was on his way back and would 'phone around 7

tonight.   Katy rang too and said would you ring her back when you get in (probably out of credit again ha! ha!)   Fed Bruno before leaving so don't believe him if he tells you he's hungry. Fed the cats too so don't believe Thomas either if he pretends to be starving! See you in the morning.'

No name, just a small spider on a web ended the note: Spyder's usual signature. He was a real treasure. Carol had never regretted taking him on as mechanic, painter, decorator and general handyman. In fact Carol often wondered how she would manage without Spyder and his surprisingly endless supply of skills, helping her to renovate the once crumbling old house and bring it back to its former glory. Still a little way to go as yet, but what had once seemed a daunting and impossible task was now beginning to feel and look like an elegant and comfortable home.

Spyder was also pretty much a genius when it came to mechanics too. He kept the trucks in good running order and was always happy to check out Carol's and Jeff's cars whenever the need arose. Of course he always enjoyed working on Carol's classic Chevy Impala. As she had bought it from him in the first place, he felt almost obliged to keep the huge American car purring like a kitten at all times. Carol sometimes felt guilty if she had forgotten to clean out the interior and polish the metallic paintwork to a high sheen, not to mention keeping the large expanses of chrome in mirror-like condition. Both she and Spyder loved the old 1960's American car and in fact Carol used it as her daily driver, completely disregarding the looks of amazement when she parked in supermarket car parks or wended her way down the narrow country lane towards her home.

Carol made herself a coffee and carried it into the shady garden in her bare feet to sip the strong liquid and relax for a moment. She had plenty of time to wind down, take a bath and relax before Tony's call. She could then take Bruno for his walk and visit Gina. The garden always made her feel at ease, the birds singing in the trees and the buzz of bees going about their daily routine. Early mornings and late evenings were her favourite times for the garden in the summer with the dew settling on the grass and the smell of lavender and jasmine drifting through the warm air.   Right now it was a little early in the season for jasmine and lavender, but the scents of spring still warmed Carol's heart as she sipped her coffee, luxuriating in the last rays of the fading sunshine. In a few hours the woodland area would be alive with rustling sounds of wildlife and the scents would be stronger in the cool evening air, reminding her of Tony's Tuscany farmhouse. She had planted a grapevine to grow over the old building that had once housed an outside privy in the corner. She had decided against demolishing the weather-worn crumbling building, loving its quaint old-fashioned look, in keeping with the rest of the old rambling house with the huge walled garden. Apart from that, the half-wild mother cat had taken up residence there, having never plucked up the courage to come inside the house as her kittens had done, so Carol had decided to keep it as a feature. There was plenty of room in the huge garden anyway and she certainly did not need the extra space that the small building took up.

She glanced down the pathway that led directly into her haulage yard. The old Transcon was parked near the ivy-covered wall next to her beloved Chevy Impala. The big American car's metallic blue paintwork and huge expanse of chrome, gleaming in the late afternoon sunshine and further back a row of driving school vehicles were lined up neatly at the far end. Derek insisted on paying her a small rent for keeping the overflow of buses and trucks in Carol's yard although she insisted that there was plenty of room and that they were of no inconvenience to her. She remembered that she had promised to call in to see Derek the following day, find out if he needed her for any work and chat about life in general. He had become a close and trusted friend since she had ventured into trucking well over a year ago. A year in which so much had happened Carol herself found it hard to take in at times.

Since taking the step into trucking she had driven across the mountains to Italy, met and fallen in love with Tony, returned to England and bought her own house and haulage yard. Of course, the fact that Tony's family had offered a permanent contract to haul their fine olive oil from Italy had been a positive and promising start, so setting up a partnership with Gina's husband Jeff had been a good move for both of them as the work was certainly not in short supply. Carol had even been confident enough to go ahead and buy another Volvo, her lovely 'Flying Angel', the perfect truck for Tony to use on his regular trips between his father's vineyard in the Tuscany hills and Carol's home on the outskirts of London.

The 'Flying Angel' had certainly been tested when she and Gina had driven the arduous journey across to Bulgaria to secure Jeff's release from that evil stinking prison, helping to return them all safely to England to resume their budding haulage business. A business that was taking off well with lots of promise for the future. Things looked good right now and Carol was content.

She tossed back the remains of her coffee and peered through the bushes to see Bruno and Digger rolling about together before making her way back inside and heading for the bathroom. She would treat herself to a long soak to rid herself of the road dust that was sticking to her mass of auburn curls and damp skin. A half hour of luxury after a hard day on the road.

*****

Zhravko Markov pulled aside the grimy piece of tattered net curtain covering the filthy window and stared out over the rooftops. From his vantage point in the cramped attic room he could observe the daily comings and goings in the street below, although nothing taking place down there was of any interest to him.

The cries of market traders, shouting their wares to the multi-cultural passers by, their stalls filled with a multitude of bargain goods, spewing into the walkway between the two lines of stalls. The constant stream of shoppers, edging their way through the goods, pushing past the opposing stream of foot traffic and manoeuvring shopping bags and trolleys with the expert skill of the seasoned bargain hunter.

Markov dropped the limp rag of curtain and turned his back on the spectacle. The tiny room was stuffy and airless but, despite the unseasonably warm day, he had not bothered to switch on the dust covered fan standing against the wall opposite the single bed and chest of drawers. Pushing the ancient single bar electric fire with its frayed cable out of his way, the huge man crossed the pokey room in two strides and filled the kettle from the wash basin sink, setting it to boil and spooned coffee granules into a cracked cup as he waited.

Things had not gone according to plan since his unorthodox entry to England some months earlier. He had expected to be welcomed with open arms by those names that he had known for many years while holding his high position in Moscow. But this had not been the case. Politely, but coldly welcoming him to England, they had made it perfectly clear, in the language of politicians, that his presence would not be acknowledged, nor required by any government body, but if he wished to remain in England then that would be arranged, avoiding all the usual red tape under the circumstances, and he could settle and earn his living in whichever way he wished.

Earn his living! It was not a question that Markov had considered would arise. He had, of course, contacted his one friend that he knew in this strange country, one that he had known from the old days, but he found this man to be of little help. Not for want of effort, but because of declining health and age. He had recognised Markov and greeted him, taken him into his home for a brief stay but beyond that could be of no assistance. The man's daughter had suggested he rent an inexpensive room until he 'got on his feet' so he had taken the slum of an attic that was, for now, his residence. The bearded giant clicked the kettle switch off as steam poured from the spout, pouring the boiling water into the cup and stirring in two heaped spoons of sugar. The room was stuffy and smelt of old, damp plaster. The sort of room that would feel damp and cold even in the height of summer: not an inviting residence at the best of times, but Markov had lived, if that is what it could be called, within the four small walls for some months now, lying low and pondering his next move.

He knew he could not spend the rest of his life like this, stepping outside only to buy his meagre provisions and pay the extortionate rent to the owner downstairs. His cache of money would not last long even so. He needed to organise his life, find himself employment and learn to blend into this new country.

After spending all his adult life in a strictly regimented regime this would be alien to him. He was no longer a young man so what sort of employment would he be fit for? After approaching the names that he knew in high government, those who knew who he was and who he had been, all he had been offered was leave to stay without the usual red tape and long waiting lists. Arrangements were being made for his registration as a UK citizen in a name that had not been decided upon as yet. But all this took time – time that Markov felt was running out. He had been given a cash sum of money for 'past services'. He had at first thought the amount generous but, after only a few weeks of living in England, he realised that the cost of living was far different from that which he was used to and the sum of money was not as generous as he had first thought. He soon realised he had to be frugal to survive. No further help, financial or otherwise, had been offered, although he knew that arrangements were being made for a small 'pension' that he would be able to claim when the necessary red tape had been successfully stamped and sealed. This he suspected was the government's way of keeping him happy and out of their way. He was an embarrassment to them, this he knew and he also knew it was wise not to push too hard in these matters and to be grateful for anything at all. In fact he was pretty sure that he would have been totally ignored and all knowledge of his name denied had it not been for his one old friend.

He drained his cup and glanced once more out of the window. Cash in hand work doing manual labour on the market may be the answer. But that would be a last resort. He would speak to his old contact once more. Tell him he needed to work and the relevant paperwork that would allow that. Surely that was the least they could offer him.

Disregarding the bright spring sunshine outside in the market place he reached for his long black overcoat and made for the door. He would telephone from the public box on the corner and arrange a meeting. He was beginning to feel like a caged animal in this tiny cell. He would make the call then go for a long walk. He needed fresh air in his lungs. Making his way through the bustling throng of the street market, he found his progress blocked temporarily as a delivery truck, reversing klaxon buzzing monotonously, reversed slowly into a small side road, edging slowly back towards the loading doors of the shop.

Markov stood for a moment between the narrow streets, the tall buildings clustered closely together completely shading the sun's rays from the pavements so allowing no warmth to find its way down to the street. A gust of chill spring wind swirled discarded newspapers and food wrappings around his feet, finding its way through the thick beard and bringing colour to his cheeks. The sudden chill meant nothing to him. He had lived through Russian winters for many years. This was simply a warm breeze in comparison. Idly waiting until the truck had reversed far enough to allow him to continue, a vague thought slipped into his mind. A driving job maybe. That would suit his purpose. Alone out on the road there would be no one to question him. No work mates to indulge in idle conversation, asking questions that he would feel uncomfortable in answering. Why he should feel the need for silence, after all these years, even he could not understand. He was in England, far away from anyone he knew or who had known him. Even so, old habits die hard and Markov had spent too many years watching his back and telling nothing to anyone unless it was absolutely necessary. Yes, a driving job would be the answer.

He continued on his way, striding past the public telephone box and heading into the newsagent's shop on the corner. He sieved through the selection of newspapers and selected one that had a large section of employment advertisements. He would sit in the comparative comfort of the steamy corner café and study the section advertising for drivers. He felt that he had made a firm decision and his spirits lifted a little.

*****

"Hi Mum! How's you?" Katy's voice sailed cheerfully down the telephone line.
"Hi Darling, I'm fine of course." Carol replied curling her feet under her as she settled back into the big comfortable armchair in the spacious living room. She felt cooler and fresher after her long soak and change into fresh cotton trousers and T-shirt. The sun was shining through the open French doors of the adjoining sunroom, flooding the early evening rays across the tiled floor and into the living room where Carol was sitting. "It's been really warm today but I left home at the crack of dawn to miss most of the traffic and got back nice and early.
Parked up and flung myself into a nice bath to relax before calling you. And how are you Honey? Busy, busy, as usual I suppose?"
"Oh, you know me, Mum," Katy giggled. "Never stuck for something to do. I am dashing off out in a minute with Claire and Jane, we are going for a walk on the hills and will be stopping at a nice country pub for a pie and a pint before walking home. The evening is lovely for going on the hill."
Katy was a serious hill walker and loved nothing better than striding over the hills and dales regardless of the weather.
"I thought you were nose down studying for your finals." Carol reminded her daughter. "Not long until graduation now, is there?"
"Oh, don't nag Mother!" Katy scolded her. "I have swotted until I am cross-eyed, so I reckon a break will do me good."
Carol secretly wondered exactly when Katy did find the time to study. She was always hill walking or rock climbing or out somewhere or other with friends, but Carol was not the sort to be heavy handed with her daughter. She always believed that Katy had a mind of her own and would do what she knew was right.
"As long as you're enjoying life." said Carol "After all, that's what life is about, being happy."

"Well, I sure know that you're happy Mum. I have never known you so laid back and relaxed since you met Tony. How is he, by the way? Will he be home with you at the weekend?"

Carol laughed. "Yes, I am laid back as you call it and yes, Tony will be here at the weekend. He and Jeff will be travelling over together on the same boat I believe so should be here any time after lunch on Friday."

"Oh, that's nice." Katy sounded genuinely pleased. "Last time they didn't get in 'til around lunchtime Saturday did they? Sure cuts down the time you guys get together doesn't it?"

"Hmm, yes it does, but it seems to be working out OK for us. We are still happy so that's all that matters."

"I will be home on a flying visit before long." Katy announced. "Tell Spyder the Mini is running perfectly and is such a boon. I don't know how I ever managed without it before, and just *so* economical – unlike that tank of a thing of yours, Mother dearest!"

"Watch it cheeky!" Carol laughed. "My 'tank' as you call it suits me fine and is not as bad as you think petrol wise. Anyway I don't use it to go that far so I may as well have something I am happy with – just as you are."

"By the way, I met up with the guys last night too." Katy remembered. "They said to say hello to you and thank you again for putting them up. They had a ball 'doing' London and think you are really cool!"

"Well thank you." Carol's tone was amused. "I suppose being 'really cool' is good. Sounds better than red hot Mamma anyway!" she teased.

"Mother really!" Katy giggled. She asked about Gina and Spyder, Bruno and the cats then said her goodbyes, eager to dash out and meet her friends for their walk on the Yorkshire hills.

Carol replaced the receiver and picked up her coffee. Maybe it was because she had brought her daughter up alone that she and Katy had always been so close. Even with Katy away at Leeds University and Carol living on the outskirts of London, their tie was still strong. Carol always looked forward to her daughter's whirlwind visits and made a mental note to keep the week of her graduation free so that she could be on hand to join in the celebrations and be there to see Katy collect her awards. The phone rang again. "Transcon Haulage." Carol answered.

"Hello Cara Mia, so you are home already." Tony's voice as always sent a tingle down Carol's spine.

"Hi, Darling, yes I have been home a couple of hours. I left early this morning and made Gillingham in good time. Dropped the load and picked up the re-load in record time, hardly any waiting which was good. It was pretty hot this afternoon on the drive back but I've just had a relaxing bath and wound down a little and just this minute put the phone down from Katy."

"That's good, it doesn't hurt to have some time out now and again." Tony remarked. "I believe that relaxing is a very important part of life."

"Well, yes I know you do!" Carol replied. "Your whole family have made relaxing into an art form." She laughed happily. Tony's Parents were the most laid back of people she had ever met. Always happy and smiling in the organised chaos of their huge family, almost overflowing the rambling farmhouse nestling in the Tuscany hills.

"And how is the dynamic Miss Katy?" Tony enquired. He and Katy were firm friends and Carol was glad of that. "Still dashing about up mountains and across waterfalls?" Carol could hear the amusement in his voice.

Carol laughed. "Something like that." She replied. "But why not? She is young and enjoying life so bless her for getting so much out of it. And how are Mamma and Poppa and the kids?"

"As always Poppa is busy working in his vineyards and Mamma is cooking. Is she ever doing anything else?"

"Little wonder with all those mouths to feed. It amazes me how she copes and always happy to do so." Thinking of Mamma bustling around her wonderful farmhouse kitchen, cooking up a storm for the family with her eldest daughters helping with military precision made Carol feel a little guilty as she contemplated making herself a sandwich for her own dinner, or maybe a bowl of cereal. "I miss her cooking." said Carol wistfully. "And am looking forward to my next visit."

"I hope that may be very soon, Cara Mia, but at least I will be with you in a couple of days. Jeff and I have set off already, so all is well this end. We should be in England by mid-afternoon on Friday so we will get tipped and come straight on to the yard. Will you be in?"

"Yes, of course." Carol replied. "I have promised to go and see Derek at the driving school for a chat, but I can fit that in tomorrow and I have nothing pressing for Friday, so will of course be here." Carol always arranged her life to make sure she missed not a moment of Tony's company. "I was planning on a quick visit to Gina's this evening but I think I will just 'phone her later and see how she is and go and see her tomorrow I think. Today has been a pretty long day so all I want to do is walk Bruno then curl up in bed with a good book so I had better get myself together before I get too relaxed and won't want to do anything."

Tony laughed. "I doubt that you will ever be too relaxed to get things done my love, I know you too well!"

They said their goodbyes and Carol gathered up her cup and walked into the kitchen, dropping it into the sink and calling to Bruno who was still out in the garden playing with Digger. "Come on you – Walkies!" Carol slid her feet into her trainers as Bruno, tongue lolling happily in anticipation of his walk, bounded through the door, closely followed by the little black and white Digger. Thomas O'Malley, always the adventurer, was nowhere to be seen.

Carol clicked the lock onto the back door and reached Bruno's lead from the hook. She was in a particularly good mood, as she followed Bruno out of the front door and down the wide stone steps leading towards her haulage yard and the country lane beyond. The air was beginning to cool and Carol was looking forward to her stroll along the river. But not as much as she was looking forward to Friday and the thought of seeing Tony again.

***

CHAPTER THREE

Zhravko Markov sipped his coffee, idly glancing out of the steamy café window at the market traders as they began to pack their wares and close down the stalls. The general hubbub of the market had eased down to a trickle of last-minute bargain hunters, hoping to get cut price goods as the traders packed away. Litter galore blew down the narrow market road, totally ignored by those who had left it behind.

Markov wondered if he could lower himself to pick up some vegetables left behind in boxes by the greengrocer who had just loaded his van and driven away, leaving behind some unloved and unwanted greens and some carrots that appeared to have lost the first bloom of youth. Still edible though, Markov noted and his mind for one moment fled back to his youth when there would have been no question as to his picking up such treasure. Not that anything like that would have been discarded in the first place back then.

"Hello Zhrav." Markov started at the sound of his name.

"Oliver! I did not expect to see you here my friend. This is most unexpected!" The last person Markov had expected to see, standing behind him in the little market café was Oliver Carter, the retired Civil Servant, his only friend and certainly the only man Markov had ever felt any form of trust for. He rose to his feet and pulled a chair across from an adjacent table for the frail old man. "Sit down my friend I will get you a coffee."

"Tea for me, Zhrav, coffee does not agree with my prostate these days." The old man looked pale and tired. Not the man that Markov remembered from many years ago. Markov gestured to the bored waitress to bring a mug of tea and replenish his coffee. "Should you be out on this hot day old friend?" he enquired, his concern for the frail old man genuine.

"No choice, Zhrav." Carter coughed violently, clutching his chest. "I had to see you straight away, there have been developments."

A cold chill ran through Zhravko Markov's body. Developments. If they had been good developments then he would have been notified by letter or telephone. This did not sound good at all. "What sort of developments, old friend? What is so important that you come out to see me? You could have sent for me, I would have come to you."

"Not safe, my friend. It seems word has got out about your being here. I don't know if they know exactly where you are but they know you are in the UK. With luck they will still be sniffing around in Edinburgh, that's the first place they looked."

Markov knew exactly who 'they' were. "They are in Scotland? How do you know? What happened?"

"There was an incident – an accident, or so it appears. An electrical fault caused a fire in the house and both the occupants died in the ensuing blaze." They both knew exactly what house and who they were talking about. "As soon as I heard about it, I sent out enquiries to see if the accident was – well exactly that – an accident. After getting some feedback I doubt it. Too many things did not add up."

Markov was silent. Mr and Mrs Sanderson had seemed like any other middle-aged Scottish couple, living in quiet retirement in the small village outside Edinburgh. To the casual onlooker an elderly retired businessman and his wife. "I have made no contact with the Sanderson's Oliver." Markov remarked quietly. "There was no need. I am not working in those circles anymore and as it had been so many years past, I did not deem it necessary, or prudent." Markov stared thoughtfully out of the window. "What have the British police discovered?" He enquired, although the reply was exactly as he expected.

"The police can only act on the evidence they are provided with." Carter coughed violently again. "Accidental death due to faulty wiring will be the outcome I assure you. Trouble is, we don't know who – or how many – were involved. We do believe there was only one.

Strangers in small Scottish villages are soon spotted, but of course as you know, it only takes one good man to get a job done."

Markov remained silent. What had exactly happened to the couple would forever remain a mystery. The shadowy people, those that the Government would never admit to having any knowledge of, would certainly see to that.

But he had a very good idea. The type of person that had visited Mr and Mrs Sanderson was the very type that he had grown tired of dealing with. He had become sickened and disillusioned with the whole corrupt and violent system and had quietly left Moscow telling nobody of his intentions. All had been well for a number of years until recently. First the two men arriving in Sophia. How the hell had he been tracked to Bulgaria? He had told no-one of his past. He was far too experienced to have let anything slip by mistake.

"What I do not understand my old friend," Markov mused, stirring his cooling coffee, "is why they are even bothering with me after all this time. I have nothing to tell them – or your people for that matter - that could be of any interest. Anything I ever knew is so out of date and in the past it would be laughable to think it important any more."

"You slipped their net Zhrav, that's all it is from what I hear. Times have changed as we all know. Those who were once enemies are now allies and friends but the fact still remains. You left them – deserted if you like – and that is something they can never forget. It would encourage others to do the same if they just let you drift into oblivion and they did nothing to make you pay."

Markov nodded, he knew that was, indeed, the case. There was nothing he could do to make amends. Justice had to be seen to be done and they would hound him to his grave, literally. "But it has been so many years since I left." Markov ran his fingers through the rough mass of beard. The course hair springing back to exactly where it wanted to be.

"It's cat and mouse, my friend." Carter continued. "They have had all the time they needed to wait and lull you into a false sense of security. Tell me Zhrav, have you any family over there. We have known each other for many years, but I know nothing of your family or your life – strange isn't it?" Carter coughed again, thumping his chest and taking a mouthful of the almost cold tea to try and ease retching in his body.

"We never had the need to discuss personal matters." Markov remarked, trying not to embarrass Carter by mentioning the obvious ill health. "But no, I have no family – not now." For a moment his memory flashed to a beautiful face framed in silver fox fur, smiling up at him through the biting wind of a Moscow winter, holding the tiny bundle of a child close to her body for warmth. The memory was painful and cut like a knife: he pushed it back where it belonged in the recesses of his mind.

Carter, watching his face with the trained eye of the interrogator, decided not to pursue this line any further. "Well, that's just as well then." He said quickly. "They have no hold on you that way, but from what I hear it is nothing more than a direct hunt to find you and eliminate you. Nothing more, nothing less. Just get the job done, finish you off and go back and tell the others that is what happens to deserters. Trouble is, they won't stop 'til they get the job done – so the question is what the hell are we going to do about it?"

"We?" Markov raised an eyebrow. The British Government was suddenly a little more interested in him now things had started to take a nasty turn. "Why is it your worry? And I thought you had retired old friend?" Markov reminded Carter.

"Ah, we never really retire do we?" Carter replied leaning back in his chair and trying to take a deep breath without sending himself into yet another coughing fit. "I got the call as soon as the Scottish incident happened. They know where to come when they want something doing properly!" The old man tried to laugh but the coughing returned.

A slight chill ran though Markov's spine. He knew what the old man had been in his prime, and even now, in ill health and elderly, his reach was long. "Are you going to throw me to the wolves, old friend?" His coal black eyes looked directly into the hooded gaze of Carter. "We have always been honest with each other, I hope that still remains."

Carter returned the gaze for a moment. "If I was going to do that I would have done it last week directly after the 'incident'. One 'phone call is all it takes as you well know."

Markov nodded. Of course it was. Times don't change that much in the circles in which they had both lived and worked. "So what plan do you have, if at all you have one, old friend? You know I have great respect for you and trust your judgement."

Carter nodded. "The perpetrator of the 'incident' is no longer in or near, Edinburgh. At least we don't think so. From what I can gather, there was only one man, working alone. He showed up in the Sanderson's village then was gone directly after the fire. But I have heard since he has been seen in the Dumfries area somewhere near Lockerbie or thereabouts. It was a little vague – more so as we don't know who the hell we are looking for."

"What was the description?"

"Tall, wiry, late forties, wire rimmed spectacles, grey hair – thick silver grey hair. Mean anything to you?"

Markov stayed silent for a moment, staring into the bottom of his coffee cup. He looked up and gestured to the waitress hovering nearby, obviously hoping to close early, for more drinks. "I know him." he said simply.

"Who is he?" Carter smiled at the sullen waitress as she plonked two mugs in front of them – no pot of tea this time. The false smile fell from his face as he turned back to Markov. "Who the hell is this guy? Do we know him?"

"Maybe," Markov returned. "As for his name, that changes to suit the year, the country, the time of day. I don't even know if the official name he gave on his papers in Moscow was correct. But it mattered little at that time. He was given many different names to suit the work he was assigned to. I myself assigned him to more than one task. I have not seen the man for many years but I would know him."

Oliver Carters face showed no surprise. So, Markov had been this man's superior at one time. Interesting. This vendetta could be personal.

Markov gazed out of the steamy window. So they had not sent a young man. They had sent one of the old school: an equal to Markov himself, probably more dedicated to the old cause than the new recruits. A well thought out move. A man who could think along the same lines as his quarry. But also one that Markov himself could understand: Understand his moves and possibly out-think him, maybe.

"Well, you may not have to do anything as yet." Carter's voice cut into Markov's thoughts. "The only contact you ever had over here was the Sanderson's – and you made no contact with them at all since arriving this time you say."

Markov shook his head. In a way he regretted not contacting them. At least they would have had something to tell the assassin when he 'called' on them. Not that giving the man the information he wanted would have saved them, it was too late for that the moment he stepped into their home, but it would have eased the end for them a little he was sure of that. "I contacted nobody except you," He told Carter. "You contacted the necessary people to have me get my papers. I have spoken to nobody except through you."

"Well, somebody has blabbed." Carter said briskly, a glimmer of his old self shining through as his mind tried to kick itself into gear and pick up the quick thinking of yesteryear. "Trouble is Zhrav, there is too much bloody paperwork, and these flaming computers, well anybody can get hold of pretty much anything if they have half an ounce of brain these days. Well at least nobody in the department knows your address exactly."

"But we have to presume he knows by now I am in the London area." Markov pointed out. "That at least must be written somewhere, but that is not my real worry. The same people that allowed this leak also know my connection with you. This man will come to you next."

Carter was silent for a moment. He knew this of course, had known it since the first word of the fire had come to his ears. Not that he cared much for his own safety, he was an old man and was a fatalist about life. He had lived in these underground circles and if he were to die in them then so be it, but his daughter, that was a different matter. She had two children – his grandchildren – and he would fight to his last breath to protect them. He would even give up Markov if he had to, although he felt at this stage that this would make no difference to the safety of his family. This assassin was not human. All human emotions had been trained out of him years ago. He was more machine that man – a robot programmed to do the job with no question or thought. Carter had met those types before and knew there was no pity or reason in their souls, if, indeed they still had souls.

"And there is, of course the small matter of the truck driver that you used to cover your exit from Bulgaria." Carter looked Markov directly in the eye. "I doubt it very much if our friend has not already got the full name and address of this man and can find him at any time he wishes, although if my judgement is correct he will want to deal with your first. I doubt he will want to make too many waves before he has reached you, his primary target. But after that...." Carter did not have to voice the words.

Markov felt a great weight on his soul. There were too many people involved in this mess. Too many innocent people who could be killed on account of him. On account of him and what he was, or had been. It had to be ended.

"There is only one option." Markov's voice broke through Carter's thoughts. "I, or we, have to find him first. Find him and deal with the situation once and for all."

Carter nodded. It was true. He had known that all along, that was why he had come straight to Markov. There really was only one option. The old man hauled his aching bones out of the chair. "Meet me here tomorrow at the same time Zhrav." He said simply. "Just be ready my friend." Markov clasped the old man's hand. "Always ready old friend. Always ready."

*****

"I don't know. Really I don't, it's a big step!" Carol took the mug of coffee from Derek and leaned back in the big leather swivel chair.

"Of course it is." Derek replied taking his place behind the desk and stirring his coffee. "That's why I said give it some thought. You have to be sure about it. It's an opportunity but like you say, with every investment there is the added responsibility, so yes, you are right in giving it time to think it over."

Carol looked out of the window into the driving school yard. The vehicles neatly lined up for the night, locked and fuelled up and ready for the following day. Yesterday's warm sunshine had not given a repeat performance and a dull cloud hung over the yard. "It certainly has expanded this last twelve months hasn't it?" She remarked. "There is no shortage of work, that's for sure."

"Especially since I took on the coach contract." Derek nodded. "I couldn't have done that so easily if I hadn't been renting that space in your yard. There isn't the room here for all the vehicles we need right now. But that's not why I asked you if you wanted to buy in. Just thought you may be interested, that's all."

"Well, I'm certainly not *not* interested." Carol replied. "In fact I am pretty tempted, it's just that I don't want to get out of my depth and run too far too fast if you know what I mean. It was only a year ago that I didn't have a job or a heavy goods licence, now I own a haulage company and am thinking of getting involved with owning a driving school as well. It's all a bit much when I think of it like that!"

Derek Laughed. "That's your trouble girl, you have started thinking. You didn't have this problem when you just jumped in both feet!"

"Oh, yes I did!" Carol laughed. "The problems were still there, I just didn't know about them. Too busy jumping in!"

"Busy is the understatement of the week with you!" Derek raised one eyebrow. "You never seem to stop, girl, which reminds me, how are all the home improvements coming along?"

"Very nicely thank you." Carol replied. "Of course Spyder's a real treasure and has got most of the house well under control. One bedroom at the back of the house is still a bit of a storeroom, but at least the walls and ceiling are plastered and ready for finishing off. The other four bedrooms are all done out very nicely now. Two still need furnishing but I can take my time with them and chose stuff as and when I see what I like."

"I certainly thought you had overstretched yourself with that great big old place." Derek was amazed that the neglected old house had not fallen down years ago. "But you sure took the bull by the horns and licked it into shape. I admire your tenacity, I really do – but don't you get lonely in there all by yourself?"

"Lonely!" Carol threw her head back and laughed. "What chance do I have to get lonely? I am far too busy for that. Anyway, Spyder is there most days and I have just had a house-full of Katy's friends staying for the week. They were 'doing' London so my darling daughter kindly announced that they could camp out at my house!"

Derek raised an eyebrow. "Were they any bother?"

"Not at all. I hardly saw anything of them really – just noticed that the food cupboards looked like there had been locusts passing through." Carol raised her eyes. "But I did tell them to help themselves so I only have myself to blame I suppose – but at least I don't have to check the cupboards for any out of date foodstuffs now – there's nothing left!"

Derek laughed. "It's lovely to see how you and Katy have such a solid relationship. You will certainly never be lonely with her in your life. She never thinks twice that you wouldn't welcome her friends at any time, I think that's great."

"Yes, too great sometimes." Carol replied jokingly. "But no, I never get a chance to get lonely – not that I am the lonely type. Even when I am alone I just enjoy my own company. I never really feel lonely or needy or anything like that. I can't understand these people who can't live alone or are desperate for a husband as they think they can't manage as a single person. Weird if you ask me." Carol drained her coffee and placed the empty cup on the cluttered table. "But busy or not, I will give your suggestion some thought, and thank you for thinking of me."

"Well, no rush, girl. You have a think and let me know. The offer isn't going to run away overnight. I hadn't given much thought about having a partner until recently and you are about the only person I could trust to work alongside, you take as long as you want – no pressure." Derek got to his feet and cleared the coffee cups into the small sink, swishing the last of the hot water from the kettle over them before standing them to drain. He wiped his hands on a rather grubby tea towel and returned to where Carol was sitting. "Right now I think it's time we called it a day. Tony going to be home soon is he?"

Carol smiled. It sounded cosy when anybody referred to Tony as being 'home' when he arrived in England. "Yes, expecting both trucks back by Friday afternoon. A lot better than Saturday morning and, as they are tipping locally we should have some quality time together. Gina is sure looking forward to having Jeff home for a couple of days."

"How is the lovely Gina?" Derek enquired.

"Oh, Gina's fine. She is sailing through this pregnancy with absolutely no trouble at all." Carol pulled a face. "Most of us ladies suffer from one or two problems but Gina is making it all look like a walk in the park!"

"Better than making hard work of it." Derek replied cheerfully with the typical ignorance of any man when confronted with anything to do with women's ailments or pregnancies. "Well, all I meant....." he continued, noticing the wry look on Carol's face. "Was that it is a lot easier on you if she's fit and well and must be a lot less of a worry for Jeff too."

Carol laughed. "You wriggled out of that one quickly enough! But yes, you are right. Gina has not had any emergencies or ailments since the morning sickness went away so that's a good thing. I can't even see her giving up work as yet. She enjoys herself so much in the boutique I reckon she will hang on in there until her waters break!"

Derek pulled a face, opening the portacabin door. "Oh, *too* much information." He laughed.

"Wimp!" Carol giggled, slipping on her denim jacket as the two walked from the small portacabin office, Derek locking the door securely behind them. "Oh well, I had better get back and get all the paperwork sorted out and make it look like I have been doing my bit before the boys get home." She pulled a face at the thought as she unlocked the door of her big blue Chevy and slid into the driving seat.

"So tonight will be all girls together!" Derek grinned.

"Yes, that's the plan. I did not have time to go round last night so we decided that tonight we will have a nice dinner and a girly night in. Manicure, pedicure and a facial I think."

"Well done girl, you enjoy! Give my regards to Gina and I'll see you Monday!"

Carol waved and flicked the ignition. The big block Chevy engine leapt into life as she waved to Derek and knocked the column change into gear, cruising through the yard gates and heading towards home.

*****

CHAPTER FOUR

Gina swished the bright yellow duster through the open window, making sure that the brisk spring breeze did not waft any specks of dust back into her newly cleaned living room. She carefully re-arranged the snow-white net as she pulled the window closed and checked that all the ruffles were neatly and evenly spaced before turning back to her duties.

The elegant room was a peaceful haven of tranquillity as Gina carefully checked that each lamp and piece of china was exactly as it should be after her dusting spree. She took great pride in her home and, with her natural flair for understated elegance the room mirrored Gina's own personality. Being six months pregnant had not diminished Gina's sense of style. Her home was, as always, in pristine order, the only change being in the smallest bedroom. Now newly decorated in pastel mint green with daffodil yellow curtains at the window and a brand new white cot standing proudly in the corner. There was also a small white chest of drawers, already holding baby items in preparation for the coming arrival. Gina had disregarded the old wives' tales of bringing bad luck into the house by having the cot in place too early. She liked to have everything ready well in advance and the baby's sleeping arrangements had been arranged almost as soon as she had confirmed her pregnancy.

Gina made her way into the bright spacious kitchen and set the kettle to boil. She had not been to work at the Boutique today and had made the most of her day of leisure, by thoroughly cleaning the house from top to bottom. Not that her home ever looked particularly in need of a clean, but Gina liked to make sure that it never would.

She glanced out of the back door and called for Phoebe, her spoiled tortoiseshell cat. A flurry of fur shot past her legs depositing a swathe of multi-coloured hairs onto her black crepe trousers. "Thank you madam!" Gina admonished her pet quickly taking a clothes brush from the cupboard and briskly removing the offending hairs. Pheobe ignored the protests and made her way directly to her food bowl, freshly filled with pink salmon, the remains of the tin that Gina had opened for her lunch. "I'm off for a shower sweetie." Gina remarked to her pet. She ran her hand over Phoebe's soft fur and was greeted with a feline chirrup before making her way to the bathroom. She felt satisfied with her day and was looking forward to treating herself to a long shower and shampoo. Having Jeff away most of the week had its compensations when a girl could spend time doing exactly what she wanted to do at any time she fancied doing it.

She kicked off her satin pumps and tucked them under the cream chaise longue in her bedroom. She slipped out of her clothes and tugged off the velvet hair band, allowing her long pale blonde hair to tumble around her shoulders made her way into the en suite shower room. She would prefer a long soak in the bath but having a bump to contend with, felt it was more prudent to take showers if she were alone in the house.

The sharp tring of the bedside telephone stopped her in her tracks. Disregarding her nakedness, Gina bolted back into the room and sprawled across the bed, reaching for the receiver. "Hi Darling, you just caught me starkers and about to step into the shower!"

A second's silence then "Ah, Gina. You are at home then – for a change!" Her mother! Damn! Why the hell had she not switched on the tap a moment sooner and been unable to hear the phone for the rushing water.

"Well yes, I am home. I was just about to have a shower but thought the call was probably Jeff!" Gina had no idea why she felt she had to explain herself to her mother and mentally kicked herself for doing so. She heard her mother sniff almost inaudibly into the receiver.

"As you have not called or visited for so long, I thought I had better make the time to speak to you Darling!" Her mother's clipped tones always seem to hold an air of reproach. Gina was tempted to remind her that they had in fact not been on speaking terms lately but decided to hold her tongue.

"Thank you Mummy." Gina's best attempt at sarcastic tone was not quite as biting as she had hoped. "How are you – and Daddy, of course?"

"Oh, you know quite well how your father is, you do see quite a lot of him, Darling, so please don't make small talk. I am as well as can be expected under the circumstances............."

"And what might those be?" Gina sighed – knowing full well that her mother wanted her to think some dreadful happening had occurred. "You are not ill or anything are you?"

"Well, it would be a small miracle if I was not ill the way things are. What with you expecting a baby at any time right now and the area going so terribly downhill, Daddy is beside himself with worry and insists that we sell up and move to somewhere more suitable!"

Ah, so that was the point of this out-of-the blue call. Her mother had decided to move. Her father, Gina was pretty sure, did not want to, and Gina had been called upon to make Daddy see sense. "I can see that you probably fancy a move Mummy, but I am quite sure Daddy is far from 'beside himself' as you say he is. In fact I have never seen Daddy get into a state so are you sure you're not exaggerating a little?" Gina winced and held the receiver a little way further from her ear in preparation for the expected outraged tirade from her mother.

"Gina! I should have known better than to try and appeal to your judgement, and you with a baby on the way you really should learn something about maternal feelings!"

Gina's eyes widened. Maternal feelings! Coming from her mother that was rich, but before she could reply her mother swept on. "I think you should give serious consideration to coming to live closer to us. You never know when you will need your family around you. I have it from a very reliable source, my friend's husband is a councillor you know, that there will be council houses built here soon!"

Gina's eyes widened. Good grief, her mother certainly had not improved since their last heated conversation. Gina opened her mouth to ask what the inference was to her needing her family around her but decided that she was not in the mood to hear her mother's thinly disguised hints about Jeff being an unreliable work-away husband. Instead she focused on her mother's greatest horror. "Council houses you say?" Gina tried hard to disguise the slight amusement in her voice. "Well, you had better get the house valued before they are built and prices plunge below rock bottom!" She regretted her words the moment they were spoken. Poor Daddy was probably perfectly happy to stay in his own home with the garden he had tended with loving care for many years, but Gina knew well her mother would get her way in the end so what the hell.

"Oh I have already done that Dear." Gina's attempt at sarcasm had been lost on her mother. "Daddy took me out almost at once to view other more suitable properties. It's a crime that decent people should be all but driven from their homes!"

Gina sighed. Whatever her mother wanted she would get in the end. No use she, nor anybody else trying to dissuade her from her chosen path.

The conversation, if it could be called that, with Gina's mother doing most of the talking and Gina losing track of most of it, ran along the same lines for a short while. Eventually Gina managed to excuse herself, reminding her mother that she was still in a state of undress and needed to get into the shower.

Replacing the receiver Gina shivered and dashed into the shower room, spinning the taps onto full power. Hearing from her mother was always the guaranteed way to dash any happy mood that Gina was in and cast her into a state somewhere between frustration and anger. She had never forgiven her mother for her lack of support when Jeff had been taken prisoner through no fault of his own and locked in the Bulgarian prison. Her father had been a true rock and had supported Gina wholeheartedly, never for a moment questioning the possibility that Jeff may ever have been guilty.

Gina stepped gratefully under the hot water, pulling the clip from her hair allowing the water to wash it in golden streams down her back. The hot water running down her body was welcome: Even though the day had been bright and sunny it was not the ideal weather for lounging around in the nude and Gina had felt decidedly chilly by the time she had finished the call with her mother.

She was still rather taken aback that her mother had called at all. The last time they had spoken was when Gina had turned down her mother's invitation – no command – to attend Christmas dinner and endure the intolerable after-dinner conversation with the collection of pseudo upper crust acquaintances that her mother liked to gather around her. She lathered her body with luxury moisturising shower gel (guaranteed to make your skin feel ten years younger, according to the label) and pondered the reason for her mother's call.

It was certainly not her father's doing. Daddy was wonderful, kind and understanding and had supported Gina in every way. Although it saddened him, he fully understood his daughter's reasons for wanting to distance herself from her mother. Although she knew all about Gina's pregnancy, her mother was hardly likely to turn into a doting and loving grandmother overnight. Flying pigs were a more likely occurrence, Gina grumbled to herself. No, it was probably the fact that she had decided to leave the area and thought that if she pointed out the horrors of council estates within a short drive which would surely in turn be followed by a huge rise in muggings, robberies and probably murder, then Gina would come around to her way of thinking, be eternally grateful that her mother had pointed out the fact that she had been so blinkered thus far and immediately move to the same area as her mother. Very handy, Gina thought. Not for herself or any hope of help with the baby, but very handy for her mother to have Gina on hand to help deal with every tiny crisis, real or imagined that her mother managed to thrive on.

Gina switched off the shower and reached for a large fluffy towel, wrapping it around her and winding another around her hair. She had so far had a satisfactory day and the call from her mother had put a dark cloud on the horizon. How on earth did her mother manage to make her feel guilty every time they spoke? Guilty about what for heavens sake?

Sitting at her dressing table she stared hard into the mirror. Well, one thing was sure. Having a mother like hers certainly had given Gina one good solid piece of information. When her baby was born she would do her best to be kind and understanding, giving the child plenty of room to develop its own personality. She swore on all that she held dear that her baby would grow up in a loving and close environment, with a mother who loved it and supported it in every way. Yes, every experience in life was a lesson well learned and Gina would make sure that the lessons she had learned from her mother – on how not to treat your offspring – were well worth remembering.

*****

Zhravko Markov watched the frail figure of Oliver Carter disappear amongst the diminishing foot traffic of the market place. Many years ago Carter had been a man to reckon with and his brilliant mind had outstripped any who thought they could put one over on him. But now, to the casual onlooker, just an elderly man in poor health.

The bearded giant turned to make his way back to his shabby room. Carter had met him as arranged that morning and the men had spoken in length. The problem would not go away by itself – it had to be dealt with and only he – or they – could deal with it. Good God, he thought he had moved away from such goings on years ago, but the past had a nasty habit of creeping up behind a man when he least expected it, creeping up and haunting him, dragging back memories that were better left where they were.

At least he could travel light, that was a blessing. Years of experience had taught him that only the bare necessities were worth carrying at any time. Reaching his room at the top of the stairs Markov let himself in and stared around. There was nothing that he needed that would not fit into a shoulder bag. Oliver Carter would provide the other items he required. Markov glanced at his watch. He would hear from Carter within hours, by that time Carter would have everything in place. All the information they needed would have been gleaned from Carter's contacts and any information they wanted to leave behind would be planted in the correct quarters.

Oliver Carter did not trust this new regime that was now running what had once been his department. If any 'leaks' had taken place while he was in charge they would have been plugged immediately and the perpetrator dealt with at once. Times change, things were slacker and he hated it. But his motto had always been 'use what you have' and this he intended to do. If there were gossips around, then he would give them something to gossip about. Give them exactly what he wanted broadcasting. He was old and retired but his lifetime before him had been one of cunning and wile - things like that never change.

Markov pushed his hand into his overcoat pocket and pulled out a brown envelope. The envelope contained a piece of paper with a name on it, Stefan Marek. A vaguely Eastern European name, not suggesting any particular country but satisfying the British curiosity of Markov's heavy accented English. It did not have to be precise. To the untrained British listener, one foreign accent sounded pretty much the same as the next so he could manufacture a sketchy background to suit. There was also a one-way ticket to Scotland, a slim bundle of bank notes and a cell phone. The cell phone was a cheap pay as you go type, unobtrusive and fairly untraceable. There was only one number stored on the 'phone, another cell phone number. His one contact: Carter.

Carter had started the groundwork. Things were being put into place. Markov threw the overcoat from his shoulders and hung it on the nail behind the door. He would be out of here tonight. He owed rent, but that was not something that worried him. He would be gone and would not be returning so had no intention of wasting the small amount of cash that he had at his disposal. He threw his considerable bulk onto the creaking single bed and reached for his cigarettes, lighting one and inhaling deeply. Two spiders crawled across the stained ceiling as he lay staring but not seeing. He would wait for the call from Carter. Knowing the old man so well, he knew things would move quickly.

The only puzzle that Markov's brain would not, or could not, grasp was the area in which his enemy had been sighted. Why Lockerbie? Markov himself had never visited the area - he was sure of that. His mind trawled through his memory banks, desperately trying to dredge up the sharp thoughts of many years long gone and forgotten. He had to think. Had to get his mind working like the steel trap it had once been. Think as his opponents thought, out-think them and outwit them. Stay one step ahead. The years had taken the edge off somewhat, but he knew it was all still there – he just had to find it, sharpen it and use it. His mind was his best tool. It had kept him alive so far and hopefully it would continue to do so.

A pang of painful memory flashed through his brain. His razor-sharp mind had kept him alive, but had not been able to offer his wife the same protection. The car crash had been unexpected. Brake failure, that was the official finding. Markov knew the brakes had not failed. The car was in perfect order and no way would the brakes have failed so suddenly, and also he knew his wife would never have been driving at such a speed as was recorded in the paperwork. He had been able to protect his son – but at what cost. The ensuing enquiry into the accident had reported that both mother and child had been killed instantly and the funerals of both had taken place together, their coffins carried from the church and laid side by side in the ground. Nobody had asked to look inside the coffins at the disfigured bodies so there was no suspicion that the tiny coffin of the one year old could be empty. Everyone knew that Valentina Markov went nowhere without her child at her side so no-one had considered the possibility that the child had been so sick that his mother had been forced to risk leaving him alone while she went for medicine.

Little Sasha had been spirited away to a far-off town and left with trusted friends. Markov had never visited, never wanted to put his son in danger. He had received messages now and again that the child was well and growing strong. The boy had a good heart and a happy, although poor life, growing up in the countryside and believing that the elderly couple who had brought him up were his parents. Markov was just grateful that the boy had survived and no connection to his real father was traceable. He often wondered what his son looked like, what sort of character he had grown to be, but twenty years was a long time and some things were better left to drift into the mists of time.

He closed his eyes. There would be a lot to do very soon and he knew the value of rest. He was getting no younger but his body and mind were still the tools of his trade and had to be well serviced to give him the maximum output and gain him the advantage that he knew he would soon need. Right now he was safe and would sleep. God knows, after this day, would he ever feel safe enough to drift into a deep slumber.

*****

"Oh, that looks so much better!" Gina leaned back onto the soft cream sofa and admired her newly painted toenails. "It's such a wiggle to try and lean down and paint them myself with this bump in the way."
Carol replaced the top of the nail varnish and put it back into the small tartan vanity case along with a multitude of other brightly coloured bottles. "At least it's not a huge bump," she remarked. "When I was carrying Katy I looked like the side of a barn and certainly felt like one too!" Carol placed the small vanity case on the polished glass coffee table. "I'll take that up for you in a moment and put it away. Is there anything else Madame will be requiring while I am in Beauty Therapist mode?"
Gina laughed. "Oh, no thank you Kiddo, it is just the toes I have a tiny problem with, apart from that nothing else is a bother. I can't believe how good I feel with only a few weeks to go before baby arrives."
"How long will you keep on working do you think?" Carol called over her shoulder as she made her way to the immaculate kitchen to make coffee, closely followed by Phoebe, who always considered a move towards the kitchen meant waitress service.
"No point in giving up yet." Gina called after her, lifting her dainty feet and wiggling her toes to help the varnish to dry. She did not want any of the bright pink polish accidentally coming into contact with her pale green carpet or immaculate cream sofas. "After all, I only go in three or sometimes four times a week and that's only for a few hours, and what would I do cooped up here all day if I wasn't there? Just end up doing housework and cleaning and the like which is harder than selling a few stylish dresses, isn't it?"
"The way you go about housework I have to agree." Carol remarked, leaning on the door frame to speak to Gina and keep an eye on the kettle at the same time. "Your place always looks like a showroom advert – I don't know how you do it!" Carol stepped back into the kitchen and poured the

freshly boiled water onto the coffee grounds in the glass cafetiere and pressed down the plunger.

"Did Tony ring you today?" Gina called. "Geoff rang a couple of hours ago, they were doing well and heading for an overnight stop at Nancy. He said they were booked on the midday ferry on Friday and, with a bit of luck, would be back here in time to tip the load late Friday afternoon rather than having to do it Saturday morning."

"Yes, that's just what Tony said yesterday. If they can get back in good time they can tip the loads straight away and then we will have a lovely unbroken weekend together. Well, a super-long weekend actually as they don't go back out 'til Monday evening, so that's a lovely long time together. 'Course all those plans depend on traffic as usual. All they need is to be stuck in a jam halfway from Dover – and you know what that can be like on a Friday – and the warehouse will be closed by the time they get here so it may well just have to be Saturday morning after all." Carol pulled a face at the thought, reaching down a packet of cat food from the cupboard and tearing off the top of the foil pack. Phoebe made the usual encouraging motions, weaving in and out of Carol's legs as she tipped the 'Finest Quality' tasty chunks into a china bowl and setting it down on Phoebe's personal place mat. "Do you want anything to eat yet?"

"Oh, absolutely!" Gina replied enthusiastically. "I just can't seem to stop eating these last couple of days. What do you fancy for dinner? Kebabs and rice? I bought some chicken breasts yesterday and had them marinating overnight." Gina waddled into the kitchen behind Carol, her toes still encased in the pink sponge toe separators that she had worn for her nail painting.

Carol giggled. "You look like a duck walking like that!" she laughed, peering into the fridge "You go and sit down and I'll throw some rice into a pan. Oh, those kebabs look good – they won't take more than a few minutes under the grill – yummy! Shall I grill these red peppers too? I love grilled peppers!"

Gina ignored Carol's instructions to sit and relax and set about finding some part-cooked bread rolls hiding in the freezer. "Had a call from my Mother today." She remarked casually – almost too casually.

"Ah." Carol was not sure what to say in reply to this announcement. "Is this the first time you have spoken since Bulgaria?"

"Not since Bulgaria, but definitely since we refused to spend Christmas dinner trapped around the table with all her awful snobbish friends." Gina replied. She had never really had a good relationship with her mother and the remarks about Jeff being a criminal, a drug runner and a disgrace to the family had been the last straw for Gina.

"So what prompted this call?" Carol enquired.

Gina shrugged. "Well, I think she is pretty peeved that I haven't gone grovelling back to visit her – and also she hates it that I speak to Daddy on a regular basis." She mused. "And don't forget, Mother can't possibly be left out of anything and will no doubt want to try to influence me over the baby. Not that I will allow that to happen!" Gina's eyes flashed with determination. "If she can't accept Jeff for the good man he is and accept the fact that I love him and have no intention of 'bettering myself' for her benefit then that's her problem. She has never got over the fact that her only daughter is married to a common trucker!"

"Common trucker!" Carol snorted. "Well, for a start there is nothing 'common' about being a trucker – it is a well respected and highly professional career. Anyway, Jeff is far more than that. He is not only an owner driver he is also co-owner of his own haulage company!"

"I know that and so do you, but to my mother a truck driver is a truck driver and pretty much one of the lower classes, manual labourer and all that and nothing else. To be honest I would not care if we never met each other again!" Gina replied with a sigh.

Carol poured a measured amount of rice into a large pan of boiling water and began preparing red peppers for char-grilling with the kebabs. "What does your Dad have to say about all this?" she enquired tactfully, not really wanting to give an opinion as to whether Gina should cut her mother out of her life or not.

"Oh, you know Daddy – always the diplomat." Gina absently studied the advertising blurb on the discarded cat food pouch. (Only the Highest Quality for the Most Discerning of Cats). "He is delighted about the baby of course and can't wait to be a Granddad, and loyal as he is to Mummy he won't say anything directly against her, but he knows exactly what she is like." Gina's father had spent so many years tolerating his wife's ideas of grandeur that he had learned to turn both a blind eye and deaf ear to most of her ranting's.

"The latest saga is that she has decided to move house. Apparently the neighbourhood is 'not what it used to be' and is going down hill fast so Mummy has decided - all by herself of course - that they should up sticks and move to a more suitable area. More suitable that is to her idea of what constitutes a decent upper class residential area for the likes of herself and Daddy!" Gina snorted with derision and tossed the foil cat food packet into the small chrome pedal bin.

"And where would that be exactly?" Carol enquired. As far as she could remember Gina's parents lived in a very nice area a few miles out of town.

"The other side of Epping is the plan." Gina replied. "Or should I say Mummy's plan. Daddy doesn't seem to have been consulted on the matter. Simply informed that their area was fading fast and they had to move. Fading fast, that is, due to the impending plans to build some council houses a few miles down the road."

"Council houses? Well that should do it!" Carol laughed. "Can't have your mother living anywhere near council house people can we?"

Gina giggled. "The funniest thing is that she forgets that she was born in a council house herself and Granny Greenwood lived in the same house until she died, and very happy she was there too. Mummy, of course, conveniently forgets that fact or – if pushed on the matter – prefers to reason that the new kind of people inhabiting council properties are not in the same league as the original tenants of the same." Gina sighed. Her mother had laid claim to upper crust living many years ago and was not going to change now. "Trouble is Kiddo, and I hate to admit this, I have been so much happier since I have not had Mummy breathing down my neck than I have ever been." Gina admitted. "It's like being set free. To be honest I love seeing Daddy and would be devastated to lose contact with him but if I never saw my Mother again I would not care – does that sound awful?"

Carol gave the rice a quick swirl in the pan and came and sat on a kitchen stool next to Gina at the breakfast bar. "No, of course not. I am in no position to speak having never known my Mother – well I suppose I did know her but I was far too young to remember her when she died – but from an outside point of view nobody should be forced to accept someone into their lives if they don't want to. It should be done out of love or not at all."

Gina sighed. "Biggest problem is that I don't want to hurt Daddy."

Carol nodded. She understood the dilemma her friend was facing. "So anyway, what exactly did she say – or more to the point what did you say?" The last conversation Carol could remember Gina having with her mother had been very volatile. Gina had stood her ground when her mother had maligned Jeff for his incarceration in the Bulgarian prison. That had been altogether too much for Gina and she had told her mother exactly what was in her mind and had refused point blank to spend Christmas with her parents and their upper class friends, an almost unforgivable slur in her mother's eyes.

"Oh you know what she is like." Gina sighed. "She chirped down the phone as if nothing untoward had happened and that we had spoken only yesterday and parted as the best of friends. Of course she managed to sound like Joan of Arc when telling me all about the fact that she and Daddy were being driven from their home and forced to leave the area due to the amount of undesirables that were about to be shipped into the parish. And what is more," Gina s voice rose a pitch. " She also started to make plans that we too move out too before the baby is born so that the poor little mite should not be subjected to a lower quality of life due to being brought up in such squalid surroundings!"

Carol spluttered with laughter. Gina's home was far removed from any suggestion of squalor and the wide tree-lined avenue in which she and Jeff lived was perfectly acceptable to any respectable family. "And were these plans to include Jeff as well?" Carol enquired wickedly.

"Well, that's the other thing, absolutely no mention of Jeff whatsoever," Gina replied indignantly. "I know Mummy has always looked down her nose at Jeff. After all he is only a common truck driver and I should have known far better than to marry him but she magnanimously acknowledges him – when she has to – and as far as that is concerned it just is not good enough! Jeff is my husband and my baby's father, and as far as I am concerned we are better off without her!"

Carol raised an eyebrow. "Do you really feel that strongly about it kid?" she asked. "The decision is yours of course but if you could possibly steer a middle course it may be best – you do have your Dad to consider."

Gina nodded. "If it wasn't for Daddy I made a conscious decision to cut mummy out after all the disparaging remarks about Jeff last year, but as you say, there is Daddy to consider. I did have a good long chat with Daddy after I spoke to her and, although he would rather we all be friends, he does realise that it will never happen. All he wants is for me to be polite now and again to Mummy, let her see the baby here and there and try not to rock too many boats. Oh, Kiddo, I could do without all this right now, and I don't want to meet Jeff with all these problems the minute he walks through the door tomorrow evening!"

"No, of course not and I agree you don't need this right now – or at any time really." Carol replied. "I sure don't envy you that quandary. But look on the bright side. If and when your parents do move house – and, knowing your Mother, I am sure they will – then they will be further away and you won't have to put yourself out too often to go and visit will you? After all your Dad often calls here and I know that won't stop happening so you will be able to see him as often as you want and knowing him as I do I am sure there will be no keeping him away when the baby is born. He will want to be around to do his share of spoiling him/her rotten as often as possible but of course you can choose your moments when – or if – you want to visit your Mother."

Gina gave her friend a spontaneous hug. "I knew you would come up with the sensible answer." she laughed. I couldn't see the wood for the trees but you, my friend, as always come up with the logical answer. Very simple. I think I will just see how things go and cross each bridge as it comes. I will do whatever feels right for me. And I do mean feels right for me – not my conscience, or what Mummy thinks is dutiful or right but what I think is right. So that's that!"

"Good!" said Carol, checking under the grill that the chicken kebabs and peppers were charring nicely. "That's that sorted. Thank goodness I don't have any complications right now or momentous decisions to make. Life is nice and even with no sign of anything about to rock my boat. Pass the plates will you? Dinner is almost served."

*****

CHAPTER FIVE

Carol rolled over lazily, wallowing in that last moment of bliss and comfort in the warm bed, as she opened one eye to catch the time on the small digital clock on her bedside table. Seven twenty five. Why was it that the bed always felt extra comfortable in the mornings when it was time to get up and set about the business of the day?

Stretching lazily and stealing an extra few moments snuggled under the soft duvet, Carol felt a thrill of anticipation. Today she would see Tony. With luck he and Jeff would be sailing towards Dover right now and then only a few hours and they would be together again.

She flung back the duvet and sat up, swinging her legs out of bed and reaching for her bath robe. The early morning light flooded into the room. Her bedroom window at the front of the big house overlooked the haulage yard which was in turn surrounded by a high brick wall and tall trees affording complete privacy, so Carol had never bothered to draw the heavy brocade curtains over the window and always enjoyed her early morning view of the world outside.

She flung the window wide and inhaled the fresh morning air. A spider had spun its web across the window pane, the early morning dew clinging like tiny diamonds onto each intricate strand. The predatory mistress of the web sitting silently in the centre, reminded Carol of the virtue of patience, a quality that Carol herself often lacked.

Carol curled her toes into the deep pile of the mint green carpet as she padded barefoot to the bathroom. Only a matter of months ago the whole house had been a sorrowful run down shell but, with hard work and a vivid imagination, Carol had almost finished transforming it into a home worthy of a fashionable magazine photo shoot.

The huge master bedroom was a haven of comfort and style. The pale ivory of the walls acting as a foil for the deep crimson curtains, tied back with tasselled ivory cords. A beautiful Victorian chaise longue, restored to its former beauty and re-covered in the same material as the curtains, lay in splendour under the tall sash window, near the delicate rosewood dressing table left in the house as old and unworthy of rescue, now gleaming in the morning sun. Carol had spent hours cleaning and re-polishing it to reveal fine gold inlay edging the beauty of the grain. She had topped it with finely turned triple mirrors to finish the genteel and elegant effect.

Carol had scoured the auction houses and second-hand shops in search of suitable wardrobes and had installed old, intricately carved, wooden ones in keeping with the feel of the rest of the room. Carol always believed that older furniture had more style and character than the modern mass produced ones, and delighted in the deep drawers and ample storage they offered as well as the elegance they gave to her rooms.

The bathroom, another huge room with ball and claw bath and original marble fireplace was one of Carol's favourite retreats. Yet another room left in a state of neglect by old Bill Winters, the previous owner, Carol had once again worked her magic and, with very little alteration, had transformed the room into a haven of rest. She had used a professional to replace the enamel on the old bath but the rest of the work had been done by herself and the invaluable Spyder. The only concession to the modern age being the installation of a power shower, arching elegantly over the bath. The cast iron fireplace was a wonderful luxury in the midst of winter. Carol would pile it high with logs and spend a decadent hour soaking in the tub with the crackling flames warming the room.

This morning was not cold, so no need for a fire as Carol spun the taps and waited for the steaming water to fill the tub. She examined the contents of the corner cabinet for small luxuries. Tony would be home later today and she wanted, as always, to look her best. Skin softening body wash to pamper her during her soak and luxury shampoo for her unruly auburn curls would fit the bill nicely. She gathered the bottles from the cabinet, placing them by the side of the bath as she swished the water around and added some cool to the steaming tub.

She had known Tony for almost a year now but time had not dampened the passion she felt for the softly spoken Italian with the diamond grey eyes. She slipped out of her robe and sank into the warm water, sliding down into the deep bath until the water lapped around her shoulders. She had at least an hour with the house entirely to herself before Spyder arrived to get on with whatever odd jobs that he had planned for the final day of the working week and Carol wanted to make the most of her time alone, enjoying the peace and quiet of the early morning before Spyder's energetic arrival. As much as she liked the outspoken young man, she still valued her own space and always enjoyed her moments of solitude.

Lazing in the water, Carol daydreamed about Tony's imminent arrival, her plans for completing the restoration of the rambling old house and her plans for furthering the future of Transcon Haulage.

Already the haulage company had improved more than she or Jeff could ever have dreamed of. Starting out with only her old Ford Transcon and Jeff's Globetrotter, they had hoped to make a modest living and, with luck, a little more business for something a little more than a modest income. But, after meeting Tony's family and being given the olive oil, contract things had taken off big style.

Jeff's contacts had landed them the waste paper contract and so far it looked like the work they had coming in was more than enough to keep two households in good pay on a year round basis. The olive oil contract from Poppa Copeland was a truly wonderful stroke of luck for them and as Tony had wanted to do the driving job it proved to be more lucrative than they had imagined. Transcon Haulage was paying its way well and things right now looked pretty good. Good enough for Carol to chance buying the 'Flying Angel' and increasing the fleet.

But Carol was never one to take things for granted or at face value. She needed to find an hour or two to have a serious talk with Jeff about the company's future. Although it was looking good right now, she felt that they could not afford to rest on their laurels and that they had to get together regularly to check up on progress and to discuss further investments and ideas for the future. Carol knew that only by keeping a strict eye on how Transcon Haulage was progressing and keeping an ear to the ground for how British haulage, in general, was doing, was the sole way to keep the business healthy and in profit.

The terrible events of Jeff's arrest in Bulgaria before Christmas had threatened to bring the company to its knees. The memory of the whole event was more like a bad dream. Carol could remember Tony's shocked tones as he told her of Jeff's arrest on the Bulgarian border and the stunned look in Gina's eyes when Carol had the unenviable job of explaining to her that her husband had been locked in a foreign jail.

The reckless drive that she and Gina had taken to Bulgaria to visit Jeff in that awful place was never far from Carol's mind even now and she would never forget the expression of total desolation on her friend's face when she thought that her husband could not, or would not, be released. That trip had been an eye opener for Carol. She had discovered that Gina had hidden strengths that she could never have imagined. Discovering Gina had secreted a large amount of cash in the cab of the 'Flying Angel' in the hope of buying Jeff's release had been a surprise to say the least. And when they had been attacked by robbers on the road from Nis, driving towards the Bulgarian border, it had been Gina's quick wits and instant reactions that had saved them. She had taken charge of the situation and shocked Carol into action: shocked her into gunning the engine of the 'Flying Angel' and driving the cab straight at the bandit's car. Gina surely had hidden depths.

Carol spun the hot tap and swirled the water with her foot, the new burst of heat warming the now cooling water in the tub. She slid down further, throwing her head back and soaking her mass of auburn curls, then pulled herself up, reaching for the shampoo and massaging it liberally into her hair. Maybe it was the earlier conversation with Kenny that was bringing it all back but somehow she could not manage to stop thinking about Zhravko Markov. Maybe it was natural feminine curiosity, but as she lay in the warm water she could not stop herself from wondering what on earth had happened to the man after he melted into the crowd at Dover without so much as a goodbye. Very strange behaviour, she thought briskly, trying to shake him off her mind and plunged back under the water to rinse the rich shampoo from her hair before sitting back up, wringing most of the wet from her hair and wiping her hands over her face. But whatever had happened to him, he had been there when they needed him and, regardless of Jeff's rather sketchy explanation that the big Russian had helped them for his own benefit, they were grateful for his intervention just the same. As Jeff had said at the time, to hell with the reasons why, just let's be happy with the results. It was highly unlikely that either of them would ever see the huge bearded man ever again, so a mystery he would always remain.

Carol climbed out of the tub and slipped on her bath robe, wrapping her soaking hair in a towel and making her way back to the bedroom. She could hear Bruno pacing around downstairs in the hallway, his claws making clicking sounds on the polished wooden floor. He was getting impatient for his early morning walk and would no doubt let his enthusiasm get the better of him and bound up the stairs to keep her company as she dried her hair and dressed for the day.

Clean blue jeans and a crisp white shirt – that would be the dress code for today – with a little subtle make up and her hair brushed to a burnished glow. Tony would be with her soon and there was plenty to do before he arrived.

*****

The unmistakable throb of a V8 engine drew closer as Carol pulled on her boots. Bruno dashed to the kitchen door, tail wagging in delight and woofing softly in anticipation of Spyder's impending arrival.

Carol glanced at her watch. Spyder was early this morning. She threw the door open and Bruno dashed through, making his way down the side of the house and through the small side gate into the yard as the lime green pick-up truck, loudly emblazoned with orange flames down both sides, crunched over the gravel. Spyder came to a halt beside the brick workshop next to the gate, parking neatly alongside the wall and pulling on the handbrake.
"Hello you!" A young man with a definitive retro teddy-boy haircut and rolled-up jeans climbed out of the brightly painted pick up truck and ruffled Bruno's ears. "Where's your Mum then Bru, not still lying in bed is she?"
"No, she is not!" Carol called, walking down the path. "She is up and dressed and about to take the hound for his morning walk. Why are you here so early this morning? Bed catch fire?"
Spyder laughed, struggling to get through the small gate with Bruno alongside. "Well now, it is Friday isn't it, and lover boy will be arriving today, so I thought I would get here early and leave early – give you a bit of quality time together."
"Oh, you know that's not a problem." Carol replied, although secretly she appreciated the fact that she and Tony would be able to spend a little more time alone. Their time together always seemed to be so short with so much to do on their few days together. "But thank you anyway for being so thoughtful. What are the plans for today – anything specific?" Carol walked back into the kitchen with Bruno and Spyder following.
"Well, yesterday I cleared most of the big workshop out and sorted the tools and stuff, so that's taking shape nicely. It will be something we can call a workshop soon. Good for all the vehicle maintenance when its all neat and tidy. So much better when you can find stuff and everything in its place. But I collected the rest of the emulsion we ordered from the shop on the way

home last night, so might as well get the paintwork finished today in the last bedroom. The woodwork is all done now and so is the ceiling, so it's just a case of a couple of coats on the walls and that will be all the upstairs pretty well sorted."

"Great!" Carol smiled. "I know we did get held up on that with Katy's friends descending the other week. Can't go knocking out walls and sloshing paint round when the rooms are full of sleeping bags and bodies can we?"

Spyder laughed. "Wouldn't make 'em feel welcome would it?" he agreed.

Carol raised her eyes skyward. "Maybe that's where we are going wrong – making them feel welcome 'cos they keep coming back." she remarked wryly.

"You know you would not have it any other way." Spyder laughed. "But now we have got the place back to ourselves I can get it finished off. Then it's just the finishing touches to do – and that's your department."

"I can't believe we have got so much done is such a short time actually," Carol filled the kettle and clicked it onto boil. "Tea and toast?"

"Oh, yes please." Spyder rarely refused tea and toast before he began his daily round of jobs. "I did really want to speak to you if you have a minute to spare."

"Of course – what is it?" Carol detected a slight undertone in Spyder's voice as she loaded the toaster with thick slices of bread and laid the butter and plates on the table.

"Well, the house is nearly finished, restoration wise." Spyder slid of his padded body warmer and sat down on one of the sturdy wooden chairs, leaning his elbows on the big scrubbed table. "So I was wondering – sort of – what else is there for me to do here – apart from the general maintenance on the trucks and stuff."

"Hey, you're not worried that I am going to give you the sack the minute the house is finished are you?" Carol turned to face Spyder. "You don't have to have any worries on that score, you're almost part of the furniture by now and I never for a minute thought of you leaving – unless you want to that is!"

"Oh, no!" Spyder sounded relieved. "Err yes, well maybe....Well it was just that.....err.... well, you did only take me on to do the house up originally didn't you."

"Ah, that was back then." Carol replied, a mischievous glint in her eye. "That was before I found out you had so many hidden talents," she laughed. "And anyway, who else would look after Bruno and the cats if I have to dash off to Italy or anywhere for a day or two?" The toaster clicked and Carol caught the pieces of golden brown bread as they leapt out of the slots. "Seriously Spyder, I love having you around. And that's not just because you have got so much done in such a short time. You are a real treasure and a good mate and well worth the wage I pay you anyway, there is always something to be done here. All the trucks need attention after each trip, not to mention the Transcon that needs nursing on a daily basis. And of course, there is the work you do for Derek on his training vehicles, so there is work here for you as long as you want it as far as I am concerned."

Spyder grinned. "Well now, that's a relief. I did hope that you wanted me to stay on here but, what with having the kids and missus to consider it just makes sense to make sure that the job is as permanent as any job can be. Sure makes me feel better hearing you say it."

"Spyder, I would be lost without you!" Carol passed more toast over the table.

"Well, now you say that, there was something else I thought about." Spyder glanced at Carol over his piece of buttered toast.

"Oh, yes, and what would that be I wonder?" Carol asked warily, she had long since learned to decipher Spyder's tone of voice.

"Well, like I said, I was thinking, as you have five bedrooms upstairs, why only have one bathroom? You could really do with another small one or at least an en suite."

"Can't think why I would need another bathroom." Carol raised an eyebrow. "I do live here on my own remember?"

"Yes, I know that but I was just thinking that under normal circumstances, most people who have five bedroomed houses have big families and would need more than one bathroom. Yes, I know what you mean about being alone." Spyder ploughed on before Carol could reply. "But thinking logically, it would be the obvious way to put extra value on the house should you ever consider selling in the future and also – and most importantly - it would save queues when you have visitors, it was a bit crowded the other week wasn't it?"

Carol considered for a moment. Yes she did technically live alone but it always seemed that there was a house full for one reason or another and Spyder was usually irritatingly right on such things. "Yes, I do see your point, but would we not lose a bedroom that way?"

"No, not really. I had a good look at the walls the other day and the one dividing your room from the next is only a studded partition wall so will come down pretty easily. Just a case of stealing a piece off each room to create a nice space for an en suite for your room and that will solve the problem the neatest and most inexpensive way."

"Seems a shame seeing as we have done all the decorating." Carol pointed out, secretly reluctant to go through any more mess just as things had begun to look better.

"Only emulsion on the walls." Spyder pointed out. Nothing that I can't put right and you would only be losing a couple of feet off that wall you don't have anything standing against anyway and as both rooms are so flaming big you would hardly notice."

Carol laughed. "You are right of course. It was chaos the other week with all Katy's friends here. The queues for the loo always seemed to form at the same time and were getting a bit out of hand!"

"That was what gave me the original idea." Spyder admitted. "Had to wait for ages to get in there. Was tempted to use the old one outside at one point!"

"I had considered getting that done up." Carol said thoughtfully. "Although it actually it does work fine, even with the old 'thunderbox' and chain, but I just like the old fashioned feel to it, and it's very handy when I am doing anything in the garden just to nip into and save trailing muddy boots through the house. Not to mention the fact that Mother Cat lives in it most of the time!"

"Her own personal Throne Room!" Spyder laughed at his own witticism. "I suppose that was originally the one and only facility when the house was first built." Spyder mused. Picking up his mug of tea. Funny when you think about it. This must have been six bedrooms originally with the maid's rooms in the attic and no bathroom at all. Probably a hole in the ground privy before the flush one was installed."

"Yeuww!" Carol shuddered. "Hardly bears thinking about on a cold winters night does is? We are truly spoiled these days, we have everything going for us."

"Yep, that's true." Spyder agreed with his customary grin. "And no worries about rats leaping up the U bend!"

"Oh rats don't bother me like they do some people." Carol cast her eyes skyward. "I can't see why they are so hated. It's just bad press I think. To me they are just another species of our British wildlife."

"Hmm, they do carry diseases thought don't they?" Spyder wasn't fully convinced about Carol's casual attitude.

"Yes, they do." Carol agreed ruffling Bruno's ears. "But so do dogs and cats and we don't persecute them do we? The only reason rats are so hated is that it was always believed that they carried the Bubonic plague. But for a start we don't have the Bubonic plague here anymore and for seconds it has been proved beyond doubt that no way the rats could have carried it as it's a bit outdated to hate them I think."

"Well, you certainly have a good way of putting things." Spyder admitted, still not fully convinced and passing two large mugs over towards the kettle. Carol laughed. "I can see you are not going to turn into a rat lover overnight, but just thing of them as our own personal Wombles. They clean up all the mess that we humans leave behind. I honestly think that without our busy rats we would be knee deep in discarded burgers, pizza's and left over chips that people dump in the streets!"

"Well I do agree that people are the worst offenders when it comes to making a mess and causing pollution." Spyder conceded.

"But right now I am happy to know my job is pretty secure so that makes me a happy man."

"Good," Carol replied firmly as she poured steaming tea into the big china mugs. "Now we have that out of the way I will leave you to scoff your toast and get on with whatever needs getting on with, while I take Bruno down the river. Then when I get back I am off to the supermarket to get something nice for dinner tonight for Tony and me. We have a nice long weekend together and I intend to make the most of it."

"Good for you! I get on as much as I can today before clearing off early and leaving you in peace." Spyder replied, his mouth half full of buttered toast. "I am going to spend the whole weekend in my garage. I have some work to do on Suzie's car."

"And what would that be?" Carol enquired, slipping on her jacket. She vaguely remembered Spyder telling her that he had picked up an old Cortina for his wife that he intended to restore and customise.

"Suzie fancies it all de-badged and lowered, so that's this weekend's mission." Spyder launched into enthusiastic descriptions of the job in hand. "And then later on, getting the bodywork back to perfection and primed for painting as she wants it deep purple with ghost flames on the sides." His enthusiasm for the new project was obvious.

"Sounds good," Carol agreed, reaching for Bruno's lead. Six months ago Spyder's explanation would have been like speaking a foreign language to her, but after living with his tales of hot rods and customising she now knew at least enough to understand what he was on about. "What plans for the interior?"

"Strip it right out of course," Spyder stated firmly without a second's hesitation. "Sort out any rust that's lurking and seal the whole shell, then get the seats re-upholstered in cream leather with purple trim. Matching steering wheel and dash too, we think, but see how it goes as we get into it."

"On that thought I will leave you to ponder." Carol smiled. "We're off. See you when we get back." Bruno galloped ahead as she headed for the gate. She glanced at her watch. Not long now. Time to walk Bruno then drive to the supermarket for tonight's dinner and by then she would probably have heard from Tony telling her he was off the boat and on his way to her. She lengthened her stride across the yard, stopping to clip Bruno's lead to his collar before reaching the lane. The river bank was just a few yards away, across the road and through the small copse of woodland. She loved walking there, the atmosphere reminding her of her old home in Derbyshire. Moving to the city had been a big step but one she had never regretted. She had made a good life for herself and the business was showing much promise. She was happy and contented right now. She enjoyed every moment of her life and wanted it to stay like this forever. She just hoped that nothing would come along and spoil it.

*****

CHAPTER SIX

"I was ready for that!" Jeff pushed his empty plate away from him and relaxed back into the dining chair, reaching for his coffee cup.

Tony nodded as he mopped up the last of his gravy with the remaining piece of crusty bread. "Me too." he agreed. "I always enjoy a meal on the boat, it sort of rounds off the trip does in not?"

"Not a bad trip either," Jeff added. "A good clear run and the luxury of tipping so close to home." It wasn't often the two were able to tip so close to home.

"We should be docking pretty soon," said Jeff, glancing at his watch. "So – have you decided what to say to Carol – how to make your proposal?" He grinned at the younger man sitting opposite him. "Any romantic words spring to mind or are you just going to go for it?"

Tony's diamond grey eyes shot Jeff a slightly embarrassed glance. "No idea," he admitted sheepishly. "In fact I keep getting cold feet and wondering if it's a good idea at all."

"Why the hell shouldn't it be?" Jeff retorted. "You two are obviously besotted with each other so why not make it a complete commitment. Your family seemed happy enough about the idea when you mentioned your intentions – and for an Italian family that should go a long way." Privately Jeff had been surprised at the delighted response from Tony's family. Although he knew they loved Carol dearly the thought of their eldest son marrying a woman seven years older with a grown daughter could have been something of a stumbling block. "Nothing like the blessings of Mamma and Poppa to give you a bit of courage my lad!"

"Well they are not the ones doing the asking are they?" Tony pointed out, "and you know how fiercely independent Carol is. I don't want her thinking I just want her because she runs the business – and pays my wages don't forget."

Jeff leaned forward in his chair. "Now you listen to me, Tony me lad. You and Carol fell for each other long before Carol and I started Transcon Haulage didn't you?" Tony nodded. "And just because she runs the business – and runs it bloody well I may add – don't forget that you are not exactly penniless are you? Your family owns one of the biggest olive oil businesses in Italy and as for Carol, she is not the type of girl who gives a flying fart about who has money and who hasn't – it's the person inside that counts to her and you should know that by now!"

Tony looked suitably sheepish and nodded in agreement. "Of course I know that. Carol's character is above reproach in all aspects – it's just me that feels …err….well... worried I suppose. I have been going through everything in my mind and thinking up a thousand reasons why she would turn me down!"

"What ARE you like!" Jeff laughed. "I would put a week's wages on her being delighted with the idea."

"Really?" Tony still felt out of his depths with what had, back in Italy, seemed the most logical decision he had ever made.

"Well, all you can do is ask the girl." Jeff remarked sensibly. "You will never know until you do will you? And have some faith in her – and yourself too for that matter."

The robotic voice of the ferry tannoy cut into their conversation, reminding passengers that they were about to arrive at Dover dock and telling all drivers to return to their vehicles in preparation for leaving the boat. Jeff and Tony got to their feet and made their way out of the truck and coach driver's restaurant and headed for the stairs. "I'm going to ask her at the first possible moment." Tony sounded determined. "I won't be able to stand three whole days with it playing on my mind. Oh, and Jeff, please don't tell Gina what I have in mind until I do it will you? I don't want any loose talk spoiling it."

"My lips are sealed, my old son." Jeff grinned. He knew for sure that Gina would never break a confidence but also knew that having to keep a secret such as this would certainly cause her sleepless nights.

*****

The two Volvos rolled off the ferry into the afternoon sunshine and made their way slowly towards the customs. Jeff crossed his fingers that for once, the boys from Vosa would not target the 'Silver Lady' for a spot check. It was usually his luck to be singled out and pulled from the long line of trucks for a safety inspection. Jeff knew the 'Silver Lady' was in good order and well maintained and had no worries in that department, it was simply the wasted time that irritated him. He wanted to get home to Gina. He always missed his beautiful wife when he was out on the road, but accepted that it was all part of the job. It was the added and, to Jeff's mind, unnecessary, delay's that really niggled at him. He glanced sideways at the group of hi-viz yellow jackets and noted with satisfaction that this time he had been ignored.

Tony, sitting tight to Jeff's trailer, was still pondering his decision to ask Carol to marry him. It was not a sudden spur of the moment thing. He had thought long and hard about it for some weeks now but Carol had always seemed so happy the way things were that he felt a tiny niggling feeling that she would not want anything to change. "If it's not broke then don't fix it." She had often said when things were going well. Tony wondered if that adage applied to their relationship but, as Jeff had pointed out, he would never know until he actually asked her.

He patted his chest, the tiny ring box was still safely tucked away in the zipped breast pocket of his padded denim jacket. As soon as he had seen the ring he could imagine it on Carol's finger. The most beautiful quality Italian diamonds, not too big to be ostentatious but big enough to catch the light and flash their fire across the room. Five perfect stones in a gentle curve to span the finger. Once again his brother Marco's contacts had come in handy. The jeweller who had designed the beautiful ring had given Tony a huge discount due to the family connections. Tony had learned long ago that there were not many businesses that his brother Marco was not involved in, he certainly had a wide range of contacts throughout a diverse range of businesses from catering to farm machinery and now, it appeared, jewellery as well.

Tony was certainly not complaining. The ring was stunning and, although he had no way of knowing Carol's finger size, he had made a wild guess and decided to hope for the best. Maybe it would be a fate sort of thing. If it fitted it was meant to be and if it did not – well if it did not then he would just get it altered and make sure that it did! He smiled at his own way of twisting fate. It gave his confidence a boost and he felt a lot better about the whole thing as he handed in his paperwork and prepared to set off for the final leg of the journey back to Carol's home and the warm welcome of her waiting arms.

*****

The gentle patchwork of fields and trees of the English countryside flew past the train windows in a monotonous blur, as the Edinburgh express sped along the lines towards its destination. Open moorland blended seamlessly into arable fields and banks of woodland. Grazing farm animals occasionally looking up from their constant feeding routine to glance idly at the speeding passenger train, showing only little interest before lowering their heads once more and continuing their dining. It was a sight that they knew well and held no novelty for them.

His considerable bulk cramped in the grubby second class seat, Markov stared out of the windows, equally paying little attention to the pleasant moving scene passing in front of his eyes. The habits of years made him take note of particular landmarks. Remembering them and where they stood but, whereas the average traveller would have been enjoying and admiring the view, his main objective was simply committing to memory exactly where he was in relation to any point of reference that may be useful to him in the future.

He glanced at his watch, an old but reliable wind up type that had journeyed many miles on his wrist. Not long now. Another hour would bring the train over the border into Scotland and to the station where Markov would leave the cramped confines of the carriage. He felt no need to check the piece of paper in his pocket with the address of the small back-street hotel. He had read it once and had no need to double check. All he had to do was pick up the car that had been left for him in the station car park and make his way to the hotel. He would book in as agreed for a few days, just long enough to make his presence known in the area but not long enough to be obvious. Then move on to the 'safe house' where he would sit and wait. Wait for as long as it took to be found. And found he would be – of that he had no doubt.

Oliver Carter had done as much as was humanly possible in the short time given to clear the way for Markov's journey. Both men knew that the assassin could not be allowed to roam free and that one way or another this whole situation had to be brought to a close. What had been unspoken between them had been well understood. If Markov disposed of his enemy he would have to cover his tracks well. Carter was a dying man. How much time he had left had not been discussed, but his time was short, they both knew that although the words had been left unspoken. Carter was his only contact in this affair and the only man on whom he could rely to offer help, but only if he was still alive. With Carter gone, no help or assistance would be forthcoming from Carter's old department or any other. By the same token, if Markov lost his life nobody would ever own up to having known him. He would be an unknown man who met an untimely end. No relatives or friends would ever come forward. Zhravko Markov was on his own – again.

'Welcome to Scotland'. As Markov caught sight of the sign he realised that he had just passed into another country. It was a long time since he had passed over the border from England to Scotland. A long time, almost another lifetime and he, Markov, had been another person leading a totally different way of life – or was it. Was it different. A wave of sadness ran through his soul as he realised that it was no different. No different at all, except in one small way. This would be the end. The end of that life and that lifestyle – one way or another.

The train slowed and pulled into the station. Markov thankfully unwound himself from the cramped seat and stood up. The journey had been fraught with hold ups. Rubbish on the line, signal failure, a small fire on the track, another train broken down and waiting to be moved. All these inconveniences had dragged the journey time out to almost double what it should have been. A disembodied voice apologised for the delay and hopefully wondered if the passengers had had a pleasant journey all the same and hoped that they would travel with this rail line on many more occasions.

Going by the amount of grumbling coming from the disembarking passengers, it was a highly unlikely hope unless it could be avoided. Markov had taken the problems in his stride. He was in no hurry to reach his destination. Timing was not of any issue on this particular trip so sitting in the railway carriage was no different from sitting and waiting anywhere else to his way of thinking. He had spent many years of waiting one way or another in his lifetime and a hold up on an English railway was nothing to him.

Markov slung his small bag over his shoulder as he made his way down the platform towards the exit. The air was fresh and cool after the stuffy confines of the railway carriage. Markov took deep breaths as the crowd of passengers thinned out, filing away in different directions, some to the exit and others to the various choice of platforms to await further confinement on other, equally stuffy trains.

Markov strode directly to the exit. The late afternoon traffic was busy on the main road but nothing in comparison to what he had experienced in London. He stood for a moment getting his bearings. The car park was only a short step away and he made his way towards it, glancing at the lines of cars, looking for the number plate he had been told to memorise.

Tucked into the corner a faded blue, unobtrusive Ford caught his eye. Markov checked the number plate. This was the car that had been left for him. Around ten years old and nothing that would stand out in the crowd or catch any admiring glances from onlookers. There must be thousands of identical cars within a mile radius, all with similar signs of neglect, all belonging to middle of the road owners with little ambition and even less desire for a finer model with no leanings towards flair and panache.

Markov glanced unobtrusively around before crouching down and running his hand along the ground behind the rear tyre. His fingers caught on loose metal and he grasped the cluster in his fist, straightening up, shaking the loose dirt from the small bunch of keys, and opening the driver's door. The big man folded himself into the driver's seat, pushing it back as far as it would allow. The seating arrangement in the small car was cramped but Markov was used to this. Few cars had been built that accommodated a man of his size and bulk, but he cared little about this right now. It would do him service in the days, possibly weeks, that lay ahead. He had used the last few days sharpening his mind. Thinking ahead and trying to recoup the fast reasoning of yesteryear. He had surprised himself on how quickly it all came back to him. Remembering how to blend into the background. Even for a man of his size that was possible given the right circumstances. By the same token, making himself prominent was also a serious consideration at the right time.

If he were to come face to face with his old adversary he had to allow himself to be found. This, of course would be playing the cat and mouse game of old. Markov knew that he could stay undercover pretty much for ever. His skills had been honed to a fine art. He could blend into the background of any situation and as he knew more or less where his enemy was he could have moved to the furthest possible point to avoid contact. But if he wanted to be found, and made life too easy for his opponent, allowing himself to stand out and be easily seen, his old enemy would immediately know that he really wanted to be found and smell a trap. This game had to be played with the utmost care. Both men were evenly matched and both could read each other's minds. Markov could not afford to be blasé about any aspect of this. Only one of them could survive it and Markov knew exactly how it would end. At the end of this round of combat, the life of Zhravko Markov would be over for ever.

*****

The big blue Chevy Impala dwarfed Spyder's brightly painted pick up as Carol manoeuvred it into position and parked up, hauling three laden carrier bags from the back seat and making her way to the garden gate. Bruno was no help as she did battle with the latch, struggled through with her burdens and kicked the gate closed behind her. "Oh, do get from underfoot you silly hound!" she admonished her pet as she made for the kitchen door. Bruno totally ignored her pleas and eagerly harried her steps into the large roomy kitchen where she deposited her load.

Thomas O'Mally and Digger had sensed the arrival of food replenishments and had joined in the fray, winding themselves around her legs as she unpacked her shopping.

"Here you go – now scram!" Carol threw a bone-shaped biscuit at Bruno who snatched it delightedly and ran outside to enjoy his treat. Carol ignored the two cats for a moment as she picked the groceries from the bags and put them away in the fridge and cupboards. Minted lamb cutlets with tiny new potatoes, baby carrots and peas for dinner or herself and Tony with a bottle of Chardonnay to help wash it down. Luxury ice cream for afterwards with tiny rataffia biscuits to sprinkle on top. Simple but tasty, just as she liked it. Tony was used to large portions of his Mamma's pasta and to-die-for sauces, so Carol always tried to ring the changes when she cooked for him in her own home. Although she enjoyed cooking Italian dishes she always remembered that it was a treat for Tony to eat a typically English meal every now and then.

"Spyder, you still busy?" She called down the hallway. No answer. Spyder was obviously engrossed in his work at the top of the house. Carol opened a couple of packets of cat food and emptied them into the dishes for the eagerly awaiting felines.

"Spyder! Yoo Hoo!" She made her way to the foot of the wide curving staircase and called louder.

"Up the ladders," Came the faint reply from afar. Carol bounded up the stairs and along the landing to the bedroom where Spyder was working.

"Well, hey, this is looking good!" She commented with pleasure upon entering the room. The large bedroom at the back of the house was stripped bare of furniture, making her voice echo. The big room had been completely re-plastered, the walls now silky smooth and the floor stripped of the age worn carpet that had managed to adhere itself to the floorboards. On one wall a huge sash window overlooked the garden, and on the side wall the original white marble fireplace stood resplendent. The intricately carved ceiling had been painted in toning shades of white and cream with some of the artwork picked out in palest lemon, as were all the ceilings in the big house. Spyder was atop a tall ladder, roller and tray in hand, sweeping pale magnolia emulsion onto the walls.

"Nearly there with this room now," he remarked cheerily, his quiffed hairdo speckled with paint. Then all we have to concentrate on is the landing and the job is pretty much done up here – apart from your en-suite of course."

Carol looked around with admiration at the transformation of the room. In her mind's eye she was already furnishing it and adding the finishing touches. Five bedrooms to furnish and decorate had been a monumental task when she had first moved into the rambling run-down house, but she had enjoyed every minute of it. Having Spyder to do the main building work had been a godsend and had speeded the process up beyond all Carol's expectations. Her own bedroom had been the first one she had concentrated on but each room had now been completed and all that there was left to do was the finishing touches.

"I thought that big 'gentleman's dressing unit' in the workshop would look brilliant against that far wall," Spyder remarked, gesturing with his roller. It's a bit tatty at the moment but I have a mate who does stripping and, if he takes it and strips off the old lacquer and we polish it up with beeswax, it will look great just there."

Spyder always seemed to have a 'mate' who could do, or come up with any number of things that needed getting or doing. Carol cast her mind to the sorry-looking wardrobe that she had pushed into the workshop. It was large and sturdily built as was all old furniture with big double doors and three large drawers underneath, the wood carved with fleur-de-lys. One of the hinges was broken and hanging but obviously not beyond repair to Spyder's way of thinking. "Are you sure it will do up OK?" She queried doubtfully. "I thought it was a bit far gone myself."

"Nah! Not at all." Spyder swiped the final stroke of paint onto the wall and climbed down the ladder, standing back and admiring his handy-work. "Get it all stripped down and polished up and put some new hinges and handles on and it will look great – believe me."

"OK, whatever." Carol had learned that Spyder's foresight on such things was usually impeccable. "I saw a lovely cast iron bedstead in the second-hand shop window the other day. That would look good in here, with a new mattress of course." She was already picturing the finished effect. A big jug of dried flowers in the hearth of the fireplace, the cast iron bedstead topped with a soft duvet. The big carved dressing robe along the far wall and a smaller chest of drawers under the window. She remembered the big ornate mirror that was also stored in the workshop and pictured it above the fireplace. She intended to follow through the whole of the upper rooms with the same aqua green carpet, sweeping it down the stairs to the polished wooden hallway. All each room needed was a different accent colour to ring the changes. She had chosen brilliant crimson for her own room. A vibrant colour to reflect her personality. Not everyone's choice for a bedroom but Carol loved it. The smallest bedroom was to have soft lilac cushions and throws and in this room, east facing for the morning sun, Carol could picture rich royal blue accessories.

"So are you happy with it, Boss?" Spyder's voice cut into her reverie.

"Happy? I am delighted." Carol replied enthusiastically. "Now the top floor is finished, I feel we have broken the back of all this work. Glad we found the hole in the roof and plugged that before we went any further though." She laughed.

"You don't want roof leaks on new paintwork." Spyder agreed, gathering up his rollers and trays and wiping up the spills from the tin. "Now we have this all under control I can leave the fancy girly stuff in your capable hands!"

"Flaming cheek!" Carol threw a paint covered cloth at the cheeky grinning face. "And here was I just about to offer you a beef sandwich and a mug of tea!"

"Ooh, that's sounds wonderful oh, Lady of the Manor." Spyder bowed his head and began wringing his hands. "Very grateful m' Lady, very 'umble I am for your charity – very 'umble!"

Carol laughed. "Oh, DO shut up and get yourself back down to the kitchen peasant! A nice cuppa and a beef sarnie is the least I can offer my slaves!"

Spyder grinned and flung his arm around Carol's shoulder. "Best boss in the world you are you know?"

"Yes, I know!" Carol laughed. Today was a wonderful day. The upstairs was finished and Tony was coming home. No wonder her spirits were soaring.

*****

CHAPTER SEVEN

Gina gathered up the sheets of paper as they spewed from the printer. She checked each one and shuffled them into order before fastening them together with a staple and placing them in a folder and folding down the lid of her laptop.

Gina always kept track of the incomings and outgoings of Transcon Haulage and meticulously printed out the details for when Jeff arrived home so that they could go through it together. She had noticed a small downward turn in the rates of late and had made a mental note to keep a strict eye on the finances. It was only a small decrease, and probably just a tiny glitch that was the norm for most transport companies and small enough for her not to have immediately worried Carol about it, but decided that it should be mentioned sooner than later.

Gina's bookkeeping skills were thorough and Carol left most of the paperwork for her friend to deal with, knowing that, apart from the books being in safe hands, it also gave Gina a bigger sense of being involved in the family business.

The smell of roasting vegetables drifted from the oven as Gina carefully re-arranged a stray flower that had dared to fall awry from the others in the crystal vase, carefully placed on the highly polished coffee table and trotted back into the kitchen to check on dinner. Jeff would be home soon and she always greeted him with a special meal.

She glanced at her reflection as she passed the mirror in the hallway. Dressed in ballerina slippers, black calf length cropped trousers and loosely fitting white blouse, her long fair hair tied up in a chignon, she felt neat and tidy without being overdressed for an evening at home with her husband.

"Off there you pest!" Gina waved a spotless, white linen tea towel at Phoebe who had taken a calculated chance to creep up onto the worktop to appreciate the tantalising aroma coming from the cooker. The indignant tortoiseshell hopped down and began to circle Gina's feet as her owner finished the wiping down of her already pristine worktops and emptied the dishwasher, placing all the crockery back in place in the cupboards with the exception of two plates left under the grill compartment to warm.

Gina glanced at the clock on the wall. Jeff should be pulling up at any time now and she was eager to see him. It had not always been that way, she remembered with a twinge of guilt. She had gone through a period of self doubt about their marriage and had entered into an affair with Mark Cameron, the suave solicitor, who she thought she had fallen in love with. Jeff's homecomings had been an inconvenience to her then. But she had soon found out that Mark had not been the true love she had thought him to be. She had discovered that he was simply a charming womaniser and had felt hurt and betrayed when she had found him wining and dining his secretary.

Looking back on those days she felt a pang of guilt. It was only when Jeff had been arrested and she thought he would be locked away in that awful Bulgarian jail for years, did she realise how much she truly loved her husband and had gone to great lengths to rescue him. Any feelings that she thought she had ever held for Mark Cameron had immediately been dashed from her mind as her only thoughts were for Jeff. She and Carol had raced to Bulgaria in the 'Flying Angel' and Gina had been prepared to pay any amount of money, use bribery or any method in her power to obtain her husband's release.

It was strange twist of fate that her ex lover, Mark Cameron, had been the only solicitor who would take on the case and for that she was grateful, although she no longer held any feelings for the smooth talking man who had lured her affections from Jeff for that short time.

And now, much to her delight, she and Jeff were expecting a baby. Gina had wanted this baby so much, discovering she was pregnant during the gruelling and frightening trip to Bulgaria. Carol had supported her friend with all the strength she could muster as Gina's eyes had filled with dread at the thought of Jeff being locked away for years and she left alone to bring up their child. A child that may never get to know its father if they could not have managed to effect his release.

Gina shuddered at the thought and made a conscious effort to push those dreadful memories from her mind. Jeff was back with her and she knew that she loved him dearly and knew that he loved her. Gina knew the strength of love and believed in it totally.

Phoebe suddenly shifted her attention to the front door and unhurriedly paced down the hallway, tail waving gracefully aloft. Gina glanced up. The sound of the 'Silver Lady's' engine throbbing in the road outside had reached Phoebe's ears before Gina's. Jeff was home at last. Gina gave her kitchen a last glance to check that it was totally in order before following her pet to the front door and flinging it wide in time to see Jeff cut the powerful engine and swing down from the cab.

"Hello Darling!" Gina hurried down the short garden path to meet her husband at the gate. "Home at last!"

Jeff's face cracked into a wide grin at the sight of his delicate wife standing at the gate of their home waiting to welcome him. He dropped his canvas bag and swung Gina off her feet, depositing a kiss full on her lips. "Hello Bumpy!" He lowered his wife onto her feet and patted the small protrusion of her tummy. "And how are you two doing my darling?"

"We are both doing very well thank you much!" Gina answered primly, holding Jeff's free hand as he retrieved his bag and made their way back into the house. "I had my check-up at the clinic last week and they say I am doing perfectly well and no problems at all – and I feel wonderful – absolutely full of energy!"

"Well, you are always full of energy my darling. You are a little Dervish, I'm sure." Jeff gazed fondly at his lovely wife. He always felt such a sense of pride whenever he came home that this beautiful woman was his and always there to greet him after a long trip over the water.

Jeff followed Gina into the kitchen and threw his bag into the laundry cupboard. "Nothing that can't wait in that lot, Darling." He announced, closing the door firmly, slipping off his jacket and heading towards the hallway to hang it in the closet. "What's cooking? It smells wonderful." He sniffed the air like an advert for gravy granules.

Gina giggled. "Salmon en Croûte with sauté potatoes, side salad and crusty bread rolls," she announced, peering through the steamy glass door of the oven. "And I have made your favourite, sponge pudding with cream, too."

"You spoil me – as always." Jeff returned to the kitchen, standing behind Gina and wrapping his arms around her middle as she clicked the kettle on to boil. "Have I got time for a shower before it's ready?"

"Of course." Gina replied. "Half an hour will be fine; coffee first?"

"Yes, thank you, that's great." Jeff perched on one of the breakfast bar stools. "That was a good straightforward trip." He remarked as Gina poured boiling water into the glass coffee jug and pressed down the plunger. The smell of fresh coffee filling the room, almost drowning the aroma coming from the oven. "Would be nice if all the trips were so easy."

Gina poured a mug of steaming coffee and stirred in cream and sugar. "I have been thinking." she mused. "It may be a good idea to look into more UK runs. The rates may be just as good if not better than the European trips at the moment. I don't mean give up the Continental all together of course, we cannot do that obviously as we have the olive oil contract and the waste paper on regular runs, but I thought it may be worth looking into the UK runs a little more and getting them to play a bigger part.

"Is there a problem do you think?" Jeff knew Gina kept her ear to the ground and kept a strict eye on the profit and losses of the company. He was under the impression that Transcon Haulage was doing extremely well, but hearing Gina mention this made him wonder. It also crossed his mind that maybe with the baby coming, Gina would prefer to have him closer to hand in the future.

"No, not at all." Gina was quick to put him at his ease. "But what with so many Europeans driving over here now and also working from UK bases, some rates are dropping. I do think we should all get together and have a chat about the future don't you?"

Jeff smiled. Gina certainly took the business side of things seriously and kept her eye on the ball where the rates were concerned. "I agree that the rates have fallen a little just now." He replied. "But that is normal in the haulage industry. They go up and down all the time and don't forget we are pretty sound with the olive oil and the waste paper contracts." He reminded her. "Even if we lost the waste paper I doubt that the olive oil would dry out. I can't see Poppa Copeland giving the contract to anybody else can you? Not with Carol and Tony ...err... well... being so close." Jeff bit his lip to stop Tony's secret from slipping out. "But even so, as we run a small concern, we only have to keep ourselves don't we? I think it's the bigger companies that have the problems. More trucks to keep on the road with drivers wages to find, it's pretty obvious that they will need a lot more runs to break even and to make a profit. Also the smallest drop in rates makes a big difference when there are more trucks on the road. It's all relative you know Darling. There is a lot to be said for keeping it small and simple you know."

Gina smiled. Yes, Jeff was right about that. They only had the three trucks to maintain and keep on the road and they certainly were earning their keep. Maybe she was just being over-keen.

"I agree we should have a chat with Carol and Tony about it." Jeff conceded, although he had no real worries about the matter. "Just to keep on the ball so to speak, but not tonight Darling, maybe tomorrow or Sunday. Let's just spend some time together right now – just you and I, yes?"

Gina planted a kiss on his cheek. "Of course, Darling, that will be lovely and we have plenty of time to talk about business – a full three days before you ship out again. Wonderful!"

Jeff smiled and drained his cup. It was true that he was looking forward to spending some quality time with his lovely wife but he also had Tony's secret to keep and wanted to give his friend enough time to pluck up the courage to make his proposal to Carol. Secretly Jeff was a romantic at heart and was looking forward to hearing the outcome. Not being able to tell Gina would not be easy, but he had given his word and would keep his friend's secret. But he could hardly wait to see Gina's reaction to the impending news. That was, if Carol actually agreed to Tony's proposal. Women could be very unpredictable!

*****

Markov signed the register in the bright friendly reception hall of the tiny family run hotel on the outskirts of town. Little more than a bed and breakfast house, the owner, a small and friendly woman with a strong accent chatted cheerfully about the benefits of staying at her establishment and assured Markov that his holiday would be one to remember. There would be little doubt about that, Markov decided, although holiday was hardly the word for what he had in mind for his stay.

He paid for two nights, signing the register in the name of Stefan Marek and producing the driving licence, provided by Carter, to prove his identity. He had considered using his real name but, had he done that, then his adversary would be immediately wary. Only a fool would make it easy to be found, and the man Markov had in mind knew that he was no fool. There was a fine line to be trodden here. Enough subterfuge to be believable but not enough to make himself impossible to be found.

He would make himself noticed in the village, in an understated way. Speak to the right amount of people and drop enough crumbs of information to possibly reach the ears of the assassin. It was a dangerous game but one that had to be played and, in a strange sort of way, one that Markov wanted to play. If anybody was to come face to face with this man then Markov wanted to be the man to do it. Maybe fate had planned this all along. Maybe this was fate's way of giving Markov the chance to rid himself of this evil once and for all and, in doing so, lay the memory of his wife to rest.

Markov summoned a smile for his landlady. "I am looking forward to exploring your beautiful country." He remarked pleasantly. "I doubt if many of my countrymen have had the pleasure or privilege of doing so."

"Oh, I don't know about that," Came the cheerful reply. "We get all sorts here from every corner of the world. "Scotland is a beautiful country and almost everybody starts here before travelling further up to the Highlands for even more scenery, although personally I think you canna beat the rolling hills of these parts for beauty." Mrs McTavish smiled proudly. "Only last week my cousin had a gentleman stay with her for a full week that seemed to be from your part of the world. Very nice man he was too."

"Ah?" Markov's black eyes flashed for a second before adopting the less interested gaze he was more used to wearing.

"Yes, a lovely young man. On his gap year from college in Holland and touring the British Isles while he had the chance!"

Markov nodded politely, a half smile touching the corners of the heavily bearded mouth. Obviously not the man who had for years been Moscow's most prized killer, but at least Carter's assurance that in general one foreigner was just the same as the next to the general member of the public certainly held true.

After settling himself into his small but scrupulously clean and tidy room, Markov returned to Mrs McTavish's reception and asked for directions to the nearest shops. He needed a grocery store and a chemist. His plans were set in his mind and he needed to be prepared.

As Markov paid his landlady the few shilling she required for a small visitor's guidebook of the local area Mrs McTavish's natural curiosity was apparent. "Where exactly is it you are from Mr Marek?" She asked. Under normal circumstances Markov would have fielded such questions with the expertise he had honed over the years but now things were different.

"Originally from Russia, Mrs McTavish," he answered, "But I have travelled many countries and am now settled in the south of England." After so many years of telling no-one the slightest scrap of information about his life, speaking in this way felt alien to Markov but he knew he had to sow the seeds in order to reap the required harvest. And besides, it was hardly the truth. He was far from settled in the south of England and, in fact he was far from settled anywhere.

"Oh, that's nice for you now, isn't it?" His landlady made a mental note to remember that to pass on to her friends the next time they met for tea, buns and a gossip. Russia! Now that was surely one up on Mrs Stuart's

Americans and Dutch visitors. "And what is it you do Mr Marek? Business is it?"

"Computers," Markov answered, trusting that the bland reply would cover a multitude of possibilities and be too complex to have to explain thoroughly."

"Ah, computers!" Mrs McTavish's expression glazed over. She had little time for such modern fancies and much preferred trusted pen and paper to keep her accounts. "My grandson has one of those contraptions and uses it for all sorts of this and that, but oh, dear me, not for the likes of me!" She laughed loudly, casting her eyes to the heavens and gesturing helplessly.

"They are not for everyone, I agree, dear lady." Markov inclined his head in a modest bow, ending the conversation politely and heading for the door. He hated having to answer even the most innocuous of questions but realised that the need to do so was paramount on this venture. He had broken a little ice and now he would make himself seen around the town.

The small town of Lockerbie was pleasant enough. The afternoon sun shining down on the red sandstone buildings gave the whole town a welcoming glow. The general hustle and bustle of the townspeople going about their daily business mixed with a handful of visitors to the area lent to the friendly atmosphere. Markov strode out towards the main street. A strikingly beautiful sandstone building with a high bell tower announced itself as the town hall and seemed to dominate the area. Guide book in hand Markov made his way towards it. He was supposed to be a tourist after all, so showing an interest in the local culture would stand him in good stead. Apart from that, he had always had a real and abiding interest in the history of the places he visited.

He stood for some time admiring the architecture of the nineteenth century building and noting the three strips of stained glass windows, commemorating the disastrous air crash that had made the small town a household name in more recent times. The national flags from all countries involved in the tragic disaster were forever stained on the glass panels and also on the hearts of those who gazed upon it.

As he turned away from the building his eyes fell upon a large bronze statue of an angel atop a white base with the inscriptions of those lives lost in the Second World War. More useless loss of life. More innocent lives caught up in other people's useless causes. More killing in the name of ....what?

A small voice in Markov's mind whispered quietly to him. Whispered things he did not want to hear and had ignored for many years. He too had been a perpetrator of 'causes' for many years. He too had been brainwashed into believing that any means would be justified to achieve the end required. But who had benefited from such ends. These last years he had questioned himself on many occasions. Who was he to say who was right and who was wrong? He sighed. It was as though the weight of a thousand years had landed on his shoulders. What difference would it make to the world if the assassin cut him down today? Who would mourn his passing? Sadly there was not one person that sprang to mind. A chill ran through his body and for the first time in his life Zhravko Markov felt entirely alone.

*****

CHAPTER EIGHT

The original Victorian conservatory at the rear of the house almost spanned the whole breadth of the building. With huge arched windows overlooking what had once been a spectacular garden, it was a room that Carol adored and had spent many hours restoring and furnishing into a restful haven.

The original black and white marble tiled floor had been cleaned of years of ground in dirt and the diamond pattern now gleamed in the shafts of sunlight that filtered through the trees, abundant in the still overgrown garden. The huge expanse of windows were an ongoing cleaning mission for Carol and she tried to make a point of polishing at least some of the many panes of glass each day to keep the job under control – if she could find the time.

She stretched up on her toes to reach the top of the tall window as she wiped the cloth over the wooden frame. While waiting for Tony's arrival she had decided to use the time to wipe the glazing bars clean of dust. Even weeks after Spyder had finished the mammoth task of sanding down all the floors in the house, the dust still managed to appear from thin air and settle along the newly painted white frames.

Carol wiped the cloth over the final piece of framework and stood back to admire her handiwork. She had ordered specially made drapes to hang across the roof. They would be ready for collection soon and would shield the inside of the spectacular sun room from the magnified glare of the mid-summer sun, giving the room a more shaded and relaxing ambience. She had been delighted to find some discarded wicker furniture in one of the many sheds and had sprayed both the cane chairs and settee a pure and startling white. She had used white broderie anglaise to cover the cushions, following the theme through by spraying a small chest of drawers to match along with an old gate-legged table, also found discarded in the workshop. The once sadly neglected table now stood elegantly in the middle of the large airy room, a white lace cloth thrown casually across it and topped with a dramatic arrangement of scarlet roses displayed in a huge jug 'n basin.

When Carol had first bought the old house in its sadly run-down state, she had decided at first sight that this room would be an all white affair. Working on the theory that the strength of the sun would fade any colours she chose to use anyway, she decided that working with nature would be the easiest route and had kept to the all white theme, a simple theme, but one which had a startling and stunning effect. The only splashes of colour where provided by displays of the vibrant red or gold flowers that Carol loved to display in the huge jug in the centre of the table.

Both kittens had crept in behind Carol and had taken up a comfortable position on a woven rug by the garden doorway, basking in the warmth of the sun's rays, magnified by the full-length glass doors.

Carol's gaze swept the room making sure that all was neat and tidy. As each room was refurbished and completed, she made a point of keeping it clutter free, banishing any might-come-in-handy items to the workshop in the yard. She had worked hard to get the old house this far and took great pride in her home, making sure that, although it was homely and welcoming, no clutter was allowed to creep into the newly decorated rooms.

The sound of the 'Flying Angel's' engine caught Bruno's ears before Carol's. The big German Shepherd pricked his ears and dashed down the hallway, his claws slipping on the wooden floor in his eagerness to reach the front door. Finding it closed, he about-turned and dashed back through the kitchen and out the back door, tearing down the pathway and leaping up onto the wrought iron gate, tail wagging furiously. Tony swung the road dust covered Volvo forward then selected reverse, manoeuvring the unit and trailer neatly into position against the ivy covered wall and killing the engine.

"Ciao Bruno, come stai oggi?" Tony flung the cab door open and dropped down, pulling his bag off the seat and throwing it over his shoulder.

Bruno seemed fit to burst with excitement as Tony approached the small side gate and ruffled the dog's ears before attempting to struggle past despite being hindered by the weight of his bag and the large dog leaping at him with glee.

The noise of Bruno's commotion carried through to Carol in the conservatory, making her give the cleaning cloth a final shake and hurry through the hallway and back into the kitchen to stow the cleaning utensils out of sight in the cupboard.

"Bruno! Move it!" Carol called sharply as she stepped out of the kitchen door and saw Tony trying to manoeuvre his way past her pet. "Come out of it – Now!" Bruno adopted a crestfallen demeanour and slunk away from the gate, passing by Carol and disappeared into the garden to sulk.

"Hello, Cara Mia." Carol ran towards Tony and flung her arms around his neck. He kissed her firmly on the mouth then nestled his face into her neck for a moment. "I fear you have offended Bruno, my love, he is ignoring us." Carol laughed, taking Tony's hand as they walked back into the house together. "Oh, he will get over it in a minute no doubt. He is just so in-your-face when you try to come in."

"Only because he loves us, Cara Mia." Tony pointed out kindly, dropping his bag on the kitchen floor and flopping onto a chair.

"Yes, I know he does, bless him, but he is a bit over enthusiastic sometimes the big idiot!" Carol felt slightly guilty about being sharp with Bruno as she clicked the kettle on to boil and walked over to Tony, standing behind him and draping her arms over his shoulders. "You are such a kind and patient man." She observed, nestling her face into his mass of thick black curls. "Which is probably why I love you so much." She planted a kiss on his cheek. "It's always lovely to have you home, and for a nice long stay this time too – Coffee?"

Tony nodded. "Yes please. Then a long soak I think. Jeff and I set out really early this morning and tramped for the earlier boat. We were lucky and got placed on it but the traffic around the North Circular was solid when we went to drop the loads so it has been a pretty long day. All done now thank goodness so we can relax for a few days."

A more subdued Bruno peered tentatively round the open door before boldly stepping back into the kitchen and taking up position slumped against Tony's leg, appreciating the ear ruffling that Tony was happy to provide. It reminded Carol of the first time she had met Tony. She and Gina had found a pathetic abandoned dog in the Tuscany hills, obviously starving and heavy with pup, and she remembered how kind he had been to the unfortunate animal, gently scooping her up and taking her to his home where she and her pups would be safe and well cared for.

"I told you he wouldn't sulk for long!" Carol reached for a crunchy dog treat and handed it to Bruno. "I spent the evening with Gina yesterday," She changed the subject as Bruno crunched happily, all bad feeling forgotten and forgiven. "She has been checking the books and wants us to have a get together this weekend to discuss progress of the business – a sort of power meeting to make sure things are keeping on track." She poured the boiling water onto the granules and reached for the milk. "As far as I can see, everything is going great don't you think?"

"It certainly seems to be running smoothly, Cara Mia." Tony took the steaming mug from Carol's hand. He could see no immediate problems with Transcon Haulage and certainly did not want to spend too much time with Jeff and Gina when he had other things on his mind. "I don't suppose that there is anything to talk about other than just reaffirming that all is well – or at least let us hope so."

"Well, we won't worry about it today anyway. I just want to spend some time alone with you, my darling, and I am sure Jeff and Gina would appreciate some quality time alone together too." Carol came and sat next to Tony, her hand resting on his knee. "I have been looking forward to this long weekend together, three whole days, wonderful!"

Tony leaned over and kissed her. "Yes, wonderful, and have you any plans for these three whole days, my beautiful flame-haired lady?"

Carol smiled. "Oh yes, you can be sure I have!" Her emerald eyes flashed as she looked into Tony's. "As soon as you have finished your coffee I will run you a really deep bath and offer to scrub your back. Spyder has left early so I intend to make the most of our hours alone, starting right away!"

Tony was not about to argue. "That is the best offer I have had since the last time we were together, Cara Mia." He replied, gulping back the last of his coffee and getting to his feet. A whole evening just the two of them. Surely tonight was the ideal time to make his proposal. But first things first. The offer that Carol had laid before him, no red-blooded Italian would turn down.

*****

Carol reached into the tall cupboard and pulled out a large fluffy towel. "That's two baths I have had today!" she laughed. "I must be the cleanest person in the vicinity now!" She wrapped a towel around her wet body and handed one to Tony as he stepped out of the tub.

"I think you enjoyed this soak more than the first one I believe, Cara Mia." Tony's diamond grey eyes sparkled mischievously as he spoke, rubbing his hair with the towel before throwing it around his back and rubbing himself dry. "I know I enjoyed every moment!"

Colour rushed to Carol's cheeks as he spoke. "You bring out a side of me I never knew existed you wicked man," she answered primly, throwing her damp curls off her face and turning to the large bathroom mirror to check her appearance. Her hair was damp and hung in tendrils around her flushed face. Her mascara had run a little under her eyes and her lipstick was gone, but her eyes shone and her unblemished skin was glowing.

"You look beautiful – as always my darling." Tony assured her. Although younger than she, he had a self-assured manner that belied his years. Carol had always been surprised by his confidence, but loved the way that he made her feel treasured and protected. Tony's outward confidence at this moment belied his inner feelings. He dearly wanted to whisk Carol off her feet with the most romantic proposal ever and hear her delighted acceptance but secretly wondered what her answer would be. Carol was a very strong woman despite her love for him. She had brought Katy up alone and had bought her own house in Derbyshire before re-locating to London. Then she had managed to pass her heavy goods driving test and land herself a job running to Italy before moving from her rented flat and buying the huge rambling house with the haulage yard attached. It was she who had taken the lead in getting Transcon Haulage off the ground and up and running as it was today.

Tony well knew that this feisty, red-headed woman with the sparkling emerald eyes was the driving force behind the enterprise, and although she had Jeff as her business partner, neither he nor Jeff had any doubts that she would have gone it alone without a second thought. Tony also knew that Carol was not the sort of woman that needed a man just for the sake of having one in tow. She was perfectly self contained and the only reason she would give her heart to a man was for love, not for need of security or company.

Tony silently said a prayer to those on high that Carol would not refuse his request that she become his wife. He was totally in love with her and wanted nothing more than to become her husband, but, as he had told himself a hundred times on the long drive from Tuscany, she was, on paper, his employer and hoped that this small fact would not make a difference.

*****

Tony dressed in clean clothes before going back out to the truck and pulling out two bottles of fine wine from the cab. This evening was to be one to remember, one way or another, so he had purchased the best wine that Italy had to offer. He made his way back to the living room where Carol had lit the fire in the marble fireplace, bathing the room with a warm and sensual light. The evening sun was setting behind the trees and soft music played from the stereo in the corner. The room was comfortably but sparingly furnished with two large settees either side of the fireplace with side tables playing host to the elegant table lamps on their surfaces. An intricately inlaid Chinese cabinet stood along one wall and a television set and stereo stood unobtrusively along the other. Along one wall, a pair of large sliding doors led directly to the dining room which in turn led out to the conservatory. In the summer the doors were flung wide allowing the light and warmth to flood through, but this evening Carol had chosen to keep them closed and provide a cosy feeling of intimacy.

"I have dinner on the go," Carol announced walking into the room and curling up on the couch close to Tony. "We have time for a glass of wine, if you fancy one, or a cup of tea. Which is it to be?"

"Well, I am in the mood for wine," Tony replied getting to his feet. "I want this evening to be very special so wine is a must." He got to his feet and stepped over to the oriental cabinet and chose two tall glasses. "This wine comes highly recommended from those who know their wines," he announced, bending down to peer in the cabinet in search of the corkscrew. "Mamma says it is the vino la'amore – the wine of love!"

"Vino la'amore! Well, I declare!" Carol effected her best Scarlett O'Hara impression? "Really Mr Copeland Sir, I swear you're insatiable!"

Tony laughed. "Not at all, Cara Mia. I just want tonight to be special and as for the la'amore, please give me time to recover from your bathtub, Senora!"

Carol flushed slightly but kept her composure and smiled. "Of course Darling, I don't want to wear you to the bone after just one evening." She took the glass from Tony's hand. "Salute!" she announced raising her glass and taking a sip. "Oh, that is lovely, a really good choice, my compliments to the lovely Mamma Gina."

Tony plumped down onto the couch beside her. His nerve was slipping a little as he tried to think of reasons to postpone the moment when he would speak of his intentions. He kissed her lightly on the lips. "To us, Cara Mia." He raised his glass. "You know I adore you absolutely don't you?"

"Yes, sweetheart I know you do." Carol replied, running her finger down his cheek. "And I adore you too. In fact I can't remember feeling this way about any man. Not really. Not so completely and trustingly as I do with you. I feel I have known you all my life and could trust you with the world if I had to."

"That is good to hear, Cara Mia, as I have something of great importance to ask you."

"That sound ominous!" Carol observed with a slight sinking feeling. The awful thought flashed through her mid. Tony was Italian and had her family decided that he should marry an Italian girl as Marco had done. Would she never be able see him again. No, don't be ridiculous that could not be it – could it? For a moment she wondered if Tony was in some sort of trouble, if he needed her help, although she could not think of any problems that warranted the serious expression on her lover's face. "Whatever it is, if I can help you in any way you know I will." They were the only words that would come out.

Tony reached into the pocket of his denim shirt and secreted the tiny box in his palm. "Carol, Cara Mia, my darling.............. " His throat began to dry, it was now or never. "Will you do me the great honour, I mean would you ever consider...... Cara Mia, will you marry me?" The words that he had for so long planned had vanished into infinity right now and he felt he was stammering like a schoolboy, clutching for straws. It had not come out as he had wanted it to, rushing the most important few words in a gabbled torrent.

"Marry you!" Carol's emerald widened as she stared at him. "Marry you!" She repeated as rational conversation failed her completely. In her moment of fear it was the last thing she had expected to hear. She snapped her mouth closed to stop herself from babbling like an idiot and repeating the words 'Marry You' like a stuck record.

"I'm sorry, Cara Mia." Tony felt his heart sink as Carol's amazed eyes held him captive. "I know you have so much and that you have little need of a husband, but I love you completely and hoped that you would find it in your heart to love me in the same way..... but of course if you want us to stay as we are then that is OK with me – we will go on as before..........."

"Tony!" Carol regained the power of speech. "Oh my goodness this is just so.... well.... err... unexpected!" She gulped hard and at last managed to turn and place her wineglass down on the side table before she drowned Tony in wine spilled from her shaking hand.

"You don't have to answer me right away my love." Tony felt the desperate need to make a bolthole for both of them. For himself in wishing to play for time before hearing the words of Carol's refusal and also giving Carol time to possibly rethink her attitude against marrying him and to maybe allow herself to give it some thought. "All I ask is that you consider what I have asked and not to turn me down at once. I know you have much in your favour and all I have is my work on your trucks and the olive groves but…………."

"Turn you down! Oh, Tony, you idiot, of course I am not going to turn you down. I love you, love you, LOVE you and of course I will marry you!"

Tony's face lit up, the worried expression clearing into bright-eyed delight. "You will? You truly will?" Cara Mia, that is wonderful, I did not think that I would be good enough for you….. I thought that…….. well I wondered." Once again the handsome young man's words trailed off as he lost all track of rational thought.

Carol saved him from trying to think what to say next by cupping his face in her hands and kissing him on the lips. "Idiot!" She murmured softly, kissing him again. "Not good enough indeed." She kissed him once more. "If you don't know by now how much I love you then you really are a lost cause!"

Tony sat back a little and took Carol's hand in his. "Oh, I almost forgot!" He sat back and unclasped his hand to reveal the ring box. "In the vain hope that you would accept me, I came prepared!" He snapped open the lid to reveal the ring nestling in the dark blue velvet inside.

"Tony!" Carol gasped. The row of diamonds curving over the ring were like nothing she could ever have imagined. Five evenly matched stones, flashing a myriad of colours across the room as the light caught them, the quality standing out even to the untrained eye. "Oh, Tony it's beautiful!" It was Carol's turn to catch her breath and struggle to find words to express her feelings. She was completely taken aback with the beauty of the ring, the size of the diamonds. It must have cost a fortune! Carol would have been happy with a small inexpensive token, this ring was beyond anything she had ever expected in her life.

Tony took the ring from its nesting place and slipped it on to Carol's finger. "It fits! How on earth did you know my size?"

Tony laughed, once more finding his composure. "It was a wild guess my love, but a truly lucky one, it fits you and looks wonderful in its rightful place." He kissed the ring on Carol's hand and told her of the silly superstitions he had invented as to the ring fitting her or not.

"Aha, so if it fitted then the wedding was meant to be and if not then it was still meant to be as we could get it altered, is that right?" Carol laughed.

"Absolutely!" Tony agreed.

"Well top marks for being Mr Cunning I have to say." Carol held her hand at arm's length to admire the ring. "Katy will be gobsmacked I'm sure. I can't wait to tell her, and Gina and Jeff too." Carol's delight was obvious.

"We will tell the world if you want to, Cara Mia!" Tony was floating on cloud nine with happiness.

Carol swung her legs off the settee. "But in the midst of all this excitement I think we just may have burnt offerings for dinner." She hurried towards the door to rescue her cooking.

Tony did not care. He was the happiest man alive and if he had to starve this night he could not have cared less.

*****

"Zhrav?" The gravel voice of Oliver Carter was unmistakable. "Are you alone?"

Markov was lounging on the bed in the pleasant bedroom of the small hotel. The TV was switched on but the big man had been paying little or no attention to the events of the soap opera cast and their family dramas. "Yes, my friend, I am alone." He spoke softly, holding the small cellphone to his ear.

"Good." Carter coughed wretchedly for a moment then paused to catch his breath. "Right. How many nights have you booked in for Zhrav?"

"Two, as agreed."

"Extend your stay." Carter's words were more of a statement than an order but Markov knew that all the old man's plans would have to be followed without question. "Book a further five nights to give me time to put things into position this end. I have already 'leaked' your whereabouts – or roughly your whereabouts, basically that you have gone to the Dumfries area, a fairly wide spectrum. We can't make the hunt too easy for this guy!" Carter controlled the urge to chuckle at his own joke and paused for a moment. Markov could hear him breathing heavily, trying his best not to convulse into another coughing fit. "If my calculations are correct, and my suspicions about who has a big mouth in the department are as I suspect, then it should take no more than a week for the news of your location to reach the ears of our pyromaniac friend. Stay put where you are for now. Spend some time getting to know the area, travel around and see the sights, speak to the locals and get yourself noticed a little. I will contact you and tell you where to go next. You used the new name of course?"

"Yes, Stefan Marek." Markov confirmed. "And of course I have already started to make myself discreetly known in the vicinity."

"Good. Using your own name would have been far too obvious and our friend would have smelled a rat five miles away. Stephan Marek is enough to attract his attention but also enough to make him think you don't want to be found."

Markov knew all of this. Years of experience had made cunning and wile second nature to him. He had already laid an almost invisible trail for his enemy to discover. Invisible to everyone except a man well trained in the art of discovery. This man was no amateur. His mind was as good, if not better, than either his or Carter's. But what difference did it make in the fine scheme of things? Markov would be found, had to be found, one way or another: that was the plan. But the outcome would be the same whichever way he looked at it. One of them would have to die.

"Have you discovered if he is working alone?" Markov needed to know this much at least although he doubted that the man would be anything other than alone.

"As far as I can find out, the man is alone. Our people thought there were more to begin with, but that has been discounted now. Just one man it seems: that, at least is something."

If it was indeed the man that Markov had known from the old days, then he being alone was no comfort. This man had no need of back up. "Depending of course on who that one man is." Markov pointed out, lying back and stretching out on the bed, staring at the ceiling.

Carter knew of course that he was right. "Yes, my friend, depending on who that man is and if he is the one we believe him to be, one man is enough." They both had enough experience not to underestimate this lone assassin: a short silence then. "Be straight with me Zhrav, do you believe you can match this man?" Carter's thoughts were with his daughter and his grandchildren. Markov was the only barrier between them and this cold minded killer.

Markov reached for his cigarettes and lit one, totally disregarding the 'No Smoking' notice displayed prominently on the wall. "You want the truth, old man?" Markov watched the thin spiral of smoke drifting up to the ceiling and dispelling into the air. "I don't truly know. Only at the time will we know, but I will assure you, old friend, that I am the best man, the only man for the job. If I lose this confrontation then no-one else will stop him."

A shudder ran through Carter's body. It was exactly as he had thought all along. If Markov could not dispose of this man then no other could. In the back of his mind, he had hoped that when Markov and the assassin met, then the job would be completed: finished and done with forever. If Markov were killed, then maybe, just maybe, the killer would consider his duty done and return to his home land. But a dark voice in his brain told him that this would not be the case. Carter was a loose end that needed tying up. Markov had been in his home and all who had been in contact with Markov would have to be silenced. Even those drivers who had innocently brought him into the country. He had no doubt that the killer knew everyone who had been involved with Markov since his flight from Bulgaria.

"I will promise you this old friend." Markov spoke as though he had read Carter's thoughts. "I will do my utmost to come out of this the victor – have no fear on that score. I know it is not only my own life that is at stake here."

Carter did not reply but Markov could hear his laboured breathing and knew the old man was putting his life in his hands. Trusting him with not only his own life but the lives of those he held dear. It was no longer the hard, cold businesslike dealings they had been used to many years ago. This time it was different. "Tell me, have you heard any news from Bulgaria? I was there for some years and had friends." Markov felt that under these new circumstances he could ask questions such as this.

Carter had not wanted to mention this right now, but as Markov had asked. "Yes. Governor Balenko was found dead in his apartment. I'm sorry Zhrav, I know he helped you."

It was what Markov had expected to hear, but had hoped not to. His friend, the prison governor had taken a big chance in allowing Markov to take the job as head guard in his prison, but things had run without incident for years. They had almost forgotten that Markov was in hiding, or at least began to think he had been forgotten, but then things had changed. They had been discovered and so things had to change – again. It had been a twist of fate that the Englishman had been imprisoned there and so had given Markov the means to silently leave the country. The governor had helped him and now had paid with his life.

"I will be ready for this man, old friend." Markov's tone was low. He had more than one score to settle with this hunter.

"Then all I can wish you is God Speed, my old friend." Any religious beliefs that Carter had ever held had left him many years ago, but right now a little divine intervention would not go amiss. "I will pray for you, and also for myself." Carter clicked off the call.

Markov pushed the small 'phone back into his pocket. Carter was right. Maybe spiritual assistance was the only way that he could have any hope of surviving this encounter. But Markov knew there was one other, more abiding, spirit that would give him the edge.

Hate. A pure, abiding intense hatred. A hatred that Markov had carried in his heart for many years: since the time that his beautiful wife had been laid in the ground and his infant son, taken from his life. If any emotion ever drove a man to greater strengths then it was hate – and Markov had that in abundance.

*****

Carol lay in the darkness, staring out of the bedroom window at the night sky. The moon hung low behind the trees, casting a ghostly light into the room and behind it a million stars flashed their lights in competition for her attention. Carol was wide awake, sleep, for her, was not an option right now, her mind was racing.

After the heady events of the evening it had been well past midnight before she and Tony had collapsed into bed, Tony had fallen asleep almost at once. Carol had watched him for a while, lying beside her breathing steadily, his back turned and an arm flung out to his side, but sleep was the last thing Carol could manage right now. A multitude of thoughts were fighting for attention in her mind. She knew she loved Tony, adored him totally, but his proposal of marriage had knocked her sideways. Her first reaction had been immediate acceptance then the evening had continued in a celebratory fashion with glasses of wine flowing freely as the couple enjoyed each others company in the glow of the firelight. The thought that Tony loved her enough to want to spend the rest of his life with her was something she had never dreamed of, but lying here, in the silence of the night, the magnitude of the situation hit her.

In the happiness of the evening they had not discussed anything about the future. What, she wondered, did Tony expect of her. Did he expect her to move to Italy and take up residence with his family and become one of the women of the house. Carol's heart sank. That was not an option, not for a moment. For the life of her she could not imagine spending her days cooking for the men of the family and keeping house. No. That just was not going to happen! But would Tony want to move to England and leave his family? And what about children? Did Tony have any desires in that department – Carol certainly did not. She was thirty six and had no intention of having babies. Now, that would have to be a huge obstacle. Surely

Mamma Gina imagined her eldest son to provide any number of bambino's for her to spoil and surely Tony would want to please his family. After all, Tony was only twenty nine. Would he be happy to live without children? Carol had Katy and had never considered, or been in the position to consider, adding any others.

She glanced over at Tony, sleeping peacefully by her side, and slid, as quietly as she could, from under the covers, creeping barefoot out of the bedroom. She gently pushed the door closed behind her so that Tony would not be disturbed as she clicked on the landing light and padded downstairs. Bruno lifted his head from his slumbers as Carol passed him in the hallway and made her way to the kitchen. She wanted a cup of hot chocolate to help her to sleep.

The blackness of the night was like velvet clinging to the wide kitchen window as Carol poured milk into a small saucepan and put it on to heat. She was vaguely aware of an owl sitting high up in the branches of the tall oak, but had too much on her mind to show her usual interest in the wild life that frequented her garden.

She wondered if she was putting obstacles in the way that were not there. Tony had said nothing about his expectations of the future. They had simply basked in the closeness of each other's company that evening and Carol had been the happiest she could remember being for a long time. Why then, she asked herself, were all these doubts and fears creeping in.

She carried her cup of steaming chocolate into the living room and clicked on the table lamp. Bathed in its soft glow, she curled up in the big comfortable couch and hugged her mug. The main problem was that she was happy with the way things were right now. She could not remember any other time, when her life had been so full and happy, waking every morning with a feeling of complete contentment. She had not envisaged any change other than the business improving by the day and had not put any thought into changing any aspect of her life.

But Tony meant more to her than she had realised. She certainly did not want to lose him, but she knew in her heart of hearts that she could never revert to being the little housewife while he played breadwinner.

It just was not in her nature. She had spent too many years of independence for that. Her first marriage, if indeed it could be classed as such, to Katy's father had been a short-lived affair ending when Katy was only eighteen months old. Since then she had kicked and clawed her way through life, bringing Katy up the best she could and buying her own house in Derbyshire before moving to London. And now she owned this fine house and her own haulage company, all obtained by her own hard work.

For many years she had been totally responsible for herself, mistress of her own destiny. She had worked hard and struggled to make ends meet when bringing up her daughter. Working on farms and behind bars to make the money that was needed to keep Katy clothed and fed and herself with enough money to keep her home the way she liked it. She had spent so many years on her own before making the move to London after meeting the irresponsible Nick, she had become frighteningly independent. As for relationships, she could hardly count the few months that she had lived with the womanising Nick: that could hardly have been called a solid partnership, as even then Carol had fended for herself while he was away on the road. Marrying Tony would be completely different. She and Tony were totally in love with each other and she trusted him wholeheartedly, but she was so happy in her life right now she worried that making any changes may spoil it.

Bruno padded into the living room and laid his head on Carol's lap. "What do you think Bru?" She whispered. "Is your mum being silly do you think?" Bruno flapped his tail, lifted his head and plonked a paw on her knee. Carol absently ruffled his ears, staring without really seeing, through the tall French windows and across the conservatory into the blackness of the garden beyond. Maybe it was because things were happening so fast. She hardly had time to adjust to one situation before another came rushing up to surprise her.

After spending so many years alone and short of money, suddenly things had improved so dramatically that at times she could hardly believe it was happening. Since breaking off with the unscrupulous Nick things had moved at breakneck speed. Transcon Haulage had taken off well and she was proud of the way the company was progressing. No way was she willing to consider giving it up, or even taking a back seat in the running of what was originally her brain child. But to be fair to Tony, he had not suggested that she should. Maybe she had better stop letting her mind run riot and talk her fears and worries over with Tony. After all, she had always discussed her problems with him. He was her friend as well as her lover. She felt slightly guilty about sitting here alone going through all these questions in her mind, while Tony lay asleep, blissfully unaware that the woman he loved was struggling to come to terms in her own mind with what was also his future.

Eventually she realised that the darkness was beginning to lift. She could see the trees in the garden more clearly, their stark branches making ghostly shapes against the sky behind them which was fast losing its velvety depth. One or two early risers in the bird world had already started to call tentatively to each other. It would soon be dawn. Suddenly she felt very weary. She drank the last of her now cold chocolate and got to her feet. Maybe now she could sleep and things would be clearer tomorrow. But one thing was sure. She and Tony had a lot of talking to do.

****

CHAPTER NINE

"Good morning Cara Mia." Tony's voice seemed to be coming from far away as Carol attempted to open her eyes. It felt like the lids had been glued down. "Wake up sleepyhead, I have brought you some tea."
Carol managed to drag her eyes open a little and shake her head. She still felt decidedly groggy through lack of sleep but managed to pull herself up into a half sitting position. "Ah, good morning." She managed to string the words together, still waiting for her brain and body to start functioning in unison. "What time is it?" She didn't really care what time it was, it was simply the first thing that she could guarantee as being coherent.
Tony came slowly into focus, wearing a dark green towelling robe and holding a large mug of tea in his hand. "Not late, so don't worry." Tony knew Carol hated to waste time by being a late riser. "But you were so sound asleep I did not wish to disturb you my love, so here, have your tea."
Carol hauled herself into a sitting position and took the mug from Tony's hand. The tea was strong and tasted good to her parched throat. "Thank you Darling, that is so kind. I think I was out for the count, I certainly didn't hear you get up."
"I heard you though – in the night. Tiptoeing out of the room and down the stairs. I waited, but you were gone some time. I was going to come and join you but thought you may wish to be alone. Is everything all right?" Tony's diamond grey eyes met Carol's. "You are not worried or unhappy are you Cara Mia?"
Carol returned his gaze. She could see that Tony was worried. She could almost read his thoughts. He wondered if she had changed her mind about accepting his proposal. Wondered if she was going to retract her acceptance and turn him down. Carol looked into his eyes. They were the eyes of complete honesty and trust. There was no guile in Tony. He was the most open person that Carol had ever known and right now she could feel what he was thinking. He was imagining that she did not want him and inside he was frightened that is should be so.
"I am not unhappy Darling." Carol could not bear to see that look on Tony's face. "But I do have some silly little worries about things, but now that you

are here we can talk them over and I am sure they will fly straight out of the window." She heard her words and surprised herself by how reassuring they sounded. But it was true. They could talk everything over together and be honest about how they both felt. They could find out what plans, hopes and dreams each of them had for the future and possibly, discover that they were both hoping for the same kind of life. She took another sip of the strong hot tea, it helped to clear her head. "Thank you Darling, I needed that."

Tony pulled the covers back and slid in beside Carol. "What's troubling you Cara Mia?" he asked gently. "You haven't had second thoughts about becoming my wife, have you?" His piercing grey eyes met Carol's. She took a deep breath and leaned against him.

"No, not as such." she began. It was better to voice her doubts right away. Carol was not one to let things simmer. "I just had an awful night of wondering what the future would hold. What you had in mind for us when we were married. Would you want me to give all this up and move to Italy? Would you want me to change my life completely for you and settle down to being a little wife, and children..........." her voice trailed of as she looked Tony honestly in the eyes.

"Children!" Tony laughed out loud. "Good grief, you are looking far into the future. But I never thought you would want any!"

"I don't!" Carol blurted out. "I don't want to move to Italy either, or give up this house, or Transcon Haulage!"

"Cara Mia, I did not for one moment think that you would!" Carol went to speak again but Tony put his finger to her lips. "Listen, I had only considered that I wanted to be your husband. I honestly had not thought much further than that. But I had not planned on anything changing other than you become my wife. A wife that I could love and treasure. Of course I don't want you to give anything up. I love you just as you are, this is who you are and this is who I fell in love with. To expect you to change would be wrong. You would not expect me to change would you?"

Carol had not thought of it that way. "Well, no, of course not." It sounded a bit limp but it was all she could muster after all the turmoil and anguish that she had gone through in the still hours of the night.

"I had presumed that, if you wanted to be my wife, we would be married and carry on pretty much as we are, except that we would be man and wife. I don't expect you to become an Italian Mamma with loads of bambinos around your ankles." Tony laughed out loud at the thought. "I don't think that would really be your style would it Cara Mia? But of course if you change your mind I will be just as happy." He continued to chuckle at Carol's panic-stricken thoughts.

Carol felt a flood of relief run through her. She should have known. She should have had more faith in Tony and trusted him not to have such ideas. "But what about your family?" She had to ask. "Mamma will surely want her eldest son to provide her with grandchildren."

"Trust me, mia dolce metà, Mamma will have more than enough grandchildren running around with all the ones that Marco and Guliana intend to provide and Claudia, Sophia and all the others. Rest assured she will have enough to spoil and cook for without us adding to the crowd."

"And what about you?" Carol had to ask. "I don't suppose you set out in life expecting to take on a woman with a grown daughter and not have any of your own."

"Who knows what fate will throw in their path, Cara Mia?" Tony said philosophically. "Who could tell that you and I would meet and fall in love. Maybe it was meant to be. Not every man can follow the same path. We are all different and follow the different paths in life. Who can say what is right or wrong? Each of us in this world live different kinds of lives and travel different journeys. The world would be a very boring place if we all followed the same set of rules."

Carol was a little taken aback at Tony's words. So sensible and matter of fact. Wise beyond his years. Nothing seemed to be insurmountable. She felt more relaxed and at ease. She leaned over and kissed him. "I am so sorry, Darling, for ever doubting you. I feel guilty now!" She buried her face in his shoulder. "I love you and you love me and we will be happy – I know it. Of course there is lots more to talk about and plan but the bottom line is, yes, I still want to marry you – if you still want me, that is, after all this fuss!"

"Don't be so silly, Cara Mia, of course I do." Tony hugged her tightly. "Come now, drink your tea and come downstairs. Bruno is waiting for his morning walk, we can take him together, then I am sure you will want to telephone Gina and tell her the news. I know you ladies cannot keep any secrets from each other for long!"

Carol laughed. "Maybe." She flashed him a mischievous smile. "Or just maybe I will keep it our secret, just a teeny weeny bit longer. I'll come down and 'phone her now though and tell her we will go over later. I want to see her face when I tell her." Suddenly Carol wanted to tell the whole world that she and Tony were to be married. Right now she felt the happiest woman alive.

*****

Jeff relaxed in his favourite chair and lit a cigarette. He had enjoyed an extra hour in bed then a refreshing shower before breakfast. He had demolished a large plate of bacon and eggs, washed down with plenty of tea followed by marmalade on toast. Satisfied and fit to burst, he decided to spend the next half hour perusing the paperwork Gina had printed out.

"I think I will give Carol a call after I have tidied up in here." Gina's disembodied voice came from the direction of the kitchen. "Maybe we can all get together this evening for a 'power meeting' and see which direction it is best to go in."

Jeff peered over the top of the papers. "Let's leave it until later shall we, Darling? Give those two love-birds a chance to surface. You know what they are like!" He was not sure if Tony had managed to ask his all-important question as yet and did not want to throw a spanner into the works at the wrong moment.

"Why wait?" Gina, dressed in cream cropped trousers, a simple pale green cashmere top and ballerina slippers, trotted in to the living room, her pale blonde hair tumbling over her shoulders.

Jeff smiled. He never tired of admiring his petite wife and loved the thought of having three full days to spend with her. "Why rush?" He countered, waving the sheaf of papers at Gina. "Let's just spend a few minutes going over these together then we will know if we have any problems before we call."

Gina shrugged, accepting the argument and went about plumping cushions and searching for any stray specks of dust. "Well, as I see it, the rates for Continental work have fallen a little. Nothing to worry about particularly, but just a slight downward turn. Of course the regular runs are on contract so they stay steady, but the stray ones we pick up are not quite what they were six months ago, whereas the UK runs that Carol has been doing seem to be pretty healthy rate wise, see for yourself." She leaned over Jeff's shoulder and turned one of the papers over. "This run is new, and if we can get a regular run with these people that will be great. First one next week, see?"

Jeff studied the papers. "Wow! That company is a good one to get a contract out of. They usually give you a couple of runs before putting anything firm on paper, so well done you!"

"Well, I was considering the rates and running costs of the Continental runs against the UK ones and hedging bets a little." Gina replied casually, but feeling secretly pleased with herself.

"I see what you mean, Darling, but don't forget there are lots of factors involved, how far the drop is, what sort of load and what sort of company the work is for, not to mention time of year etc. I don't see anything here to get us worried right now." Jeff sifted through the papers again.

"No, not worried as such." Gina plonked down on the sofa. "Just worth keeping an eye open and an ear to the ground though, don't you agree? It is foolish to think that we can rest on our laurels and just plod on. We have to explore further avenues if, and when, they open up."

"You really do have the mind of a business woman, my love." Jeff said admiringly. "You and Carol are a good team aren't you."?

"Oh, we are." Gina replied quickly. "We both keep our ears open and Carol agrees that we should make sure we keep up with any movement in the industry to keep ahead of the game. The haulage industry can be notoriously fickle as every trucker knows, but Carol always says she prefers to listen to your advice on that side of things."

Jeff nodded. After spending most of his life as a working trucker, he knew only too well how the ebb and flow of the haulage industry impacted on both businesses and the employed driver. "When Winters Haulage went to the wall, I presumed it was the bottom falling out of haulage in general, but in hindsight I can see it was just old man Winters letting things slide. He was always so busy ducking and diving for an extra few bob and running bent half of the time. I think keeping on top of things sort of passed him by."

"Well, we certainly don't want anything passing us by," Gina replied, "and we are certainly not going to start with that running bent lark! Both Carol and I make sure everything is run completely to the book. The accounts are up to date and every single receipt is kept safe for the accountant and the tax man. We have no intention of getting any nasty surprises at the end of the tax year. Even yours and Tony's wages are accounted for to the penny."

"Yes, I know the firm is in good hands with you and Carol looking after the books." Although Jeff spoke with a teasing tone he knew it was true. Who would think that this pretty china doll of a lady could have such a good business brain. "I am sure Tony and I would have run it into the ground by now!"

Gina was not fooled by that remark for an instant. "Well you know what they say." She smiled sweetly. "If you need the right man for the job then get a woman!" She stuck her tongue out and pulled a face.

Before Jeff could think of a suitable retort to her sassy remark, the ring of the telephone cut him short. "Saved by the bell." Gina laughed, reaching over the arm of the sofa and lifting the receiver. "Hi, Kiddo, we were just talking about you!" She settled back down, nestling into the cushions. "You sound terribly bright this morning..... of course, yes, that's just what Jeff and I were talking about........ Yes, absolutely, that's fine........ Ooh, that sounds interesting........... You have made me curious now..... I can hardly wait.........Any time that suits you...... Sevenish? ....yes that's great. See you then."

"That was Carol," she announced rather unnecessarily. "She sounded extra bright this morning, being with Tony certainly brings out the best in her." Jeff tried to look casual. "She and Tony are coming over tonight around seven. No need to fuss as they are eating first but they will bring some wine."

"Well that's OK then." Jeff smiled. "More food for me!"

"Idiot!" Gina aimed a cushion at Jeff's grinning face.

*****

"Well, I tell you ladies, it's the first time I have had a Russian gentleman to stay, and very polite he is too, a gentleman of quality I can tell you." Mary McTavish raised her cup of tea to her lips as she spoke, her pinky finger standing proudly as she sipped. "Only booked in for a couple of nights to begin with, but was so satisfied with the service he extended his stay to a full week!" She glanced round to her listeners hoping to catch a glimmer of jealousy in their eyes.

The market day meeting with her fellow landladies for tea and scones and, more importantly, plenty of gossip, was the highlight of the week for all three women seated round the corner table. An excuse to wear their good clothes and take a trip into town, find out and discuss in length, the latest scandal, if at all there was any, and then spend the rest of the day shopping. It made a nice break from the day-to-day sameness of the working week.

"Of course, he has been very reticent about his business." Mrs McTavish lowered her tone conspiratorially while making a point of giving her fork a close examination and a brisk polish on the white linen serviette before taking a chance on plunging it into her slice of chocolate cake. "But he can't fool me. Old money I would say. Probably descendants of the old royal family. There are a number of them left you know, descendants of the old Tsar that is, and breeding always tells I can assure you. My gentleman has blue blood running through his veins, I have no doubt of that at all!"

One-upmanship, of who entertained whom in their establishments, was a game that all three fellow landladies played at each weekly meeting in the small and cosy tea rooms. She glanced around to her listening companions. A guest extending his stay was always a good point to rub in. But a guest of high quality was definitely a coup.   "Where did you say your foreign gentleman was from again, Maggie?"

Maggie Campbell forced a smile as she reached for another scone. "I do believe himself said Albania," she answered casually, wishing she had made more of an effort to discover more about her visitor's business. "But it may have been somewhere else. A very quiet gentleman, not one to brag about his origins, but of course I never pry - even though he has been my guest for over six weeks now!" She felt a little more triumphant at this final remark as she spread butter onto the warm scone and reached for the dish of strawberry jam. Russia indeed! She was not quite sure where Russia was in relation to Albania but would make it her business to ask her own gentleman at the earliest opportunity. She would have to be quick though, he had mentioned leaving for England within the next few days and, although scrupulously polite, her guest was hardly a fountain of information. "Are you sure he said Russia, Mary?" Maggie enquired sweetly. "You know what it's like with all these strange accents – they all sort of sound the same when you are not used to hearing them. After all, my dear, you don't have many visitors from abroad at your place do you, in fact you don't have many visitors at all really do you, Dear, but then of course maybe you want to slow down a bit – we are none of us getting any younger."

Mary McTavish refused to rise to the bait. "Nothing to do with needing to slow down Maggie Campbell, I am simply in the lucky position to pick and choose when I want visitors to stay and when I want to relax. I am certainly not desperate to fill each room every night." She smiled sweetly.

"Ah, well not all of us have had the forethought to invest in good insurances for our husbands, have we Mary?" Maggie Campbell smiled sweetly across the table. "But thank the good lord that you did, my Dear. It must be a good feeling to be nice and secure in widowhood!"

"I don't think I have had any other foreigners other than the English all season," cut in Fiona Finlay, a sturdy woman of no nonsense Scottish stock and always the one to referee the fierce competition between the other two middle-aged ladies sitting at the gingham-covered table. "And this season has all the hallmarks of being a really busy one. My husband says he is booked up well in advance for his photography at the wedding halls so that means plenty of business for all of us."

"Can't really go wrong around here can we ladies?" Maggie Campbell decided the competition was not worth following up until she had checked out her Albanian gentleman for more details. "All the young lovers re-capturing the romance of runaway weddings and heading for Gretna Green, they all have to stay somewhere."

"And the fact that they miss the whole point of the runaway bit and bring a whole host of friends and relatives with them, it does us all the world of good." Added Mary McTavish.

"Well I enjoy it." Fiona Finlay continued. "I like seeing happy smiling faces. It's nice to wake up every morning knowing that there will be more happy people around your breakfast table, and I always make an effort for the couples and the families, and why not indeed?"

Mary McTavish sniffed. "Of course we all make the very best effort, don't you know. None of us are sharp with our visitors Fiona Finlay, as well you know."

"Och, I'm not suggesting for one minute you are, ladies!" Fiona was quick to smooth the conversation. "But there are some that treat them like cattle and we all know who they are.

The three women were suddenly united against all other landladies in the vicinity. They nodded knowingly, raised their cups of tea in unison and launched into their favourite subject – who's guest house was not kept to the highest standard and who was a little slack in failing to serve the best quality food and the largest of portions to their guests.

Eventually, Maggie Campbell drained the last drop from her cup and glanced at her watch. "Well, ladies, no time to sit here any longer. I have a full house and need to get to the butcher's before all the best cuts sell out."

Both her companions knew only too well that Maggie purchased her meat in packs from the local supermarket but made no remark. "I'm sure we all have things to do, ladies." Fiona Finlay pushed back her chair and slipped her dark red, woollen jacket over her shoulders. Same time next week, my dears? It has been lovely as always. So nice to be with friends!"

The three landladies said their goodbyes and went about their daily business. Maggie Campbell making a firm note to glean as much information as possible from her 'Albanian' gentleman.

*****

"Oh, Carol, that's wonderful news!" Gina squealed with delight, flinging her arms around her friend. "Oh, come here you!" She demanded, turning from Carol and embracing Tony. "Oh, I am just so delighted, that's the best news I have heard in ages. Isn't that a wonderful surprise, Jeff?"
Jeff grinned and threw a wink at Tony. "Yes, Darling, wonderful news. Congratulations you two!"
Gina missed the conspiratorial glance between the two men and focused her attention once more on the ring sparkling on Carol's finger.
"That is just so divine!" she continued, her eyes alight with excitement. "What a wonderful, thoughtful man you are Tony, and what a great choice of ring, would you look at the size of those rocks!"
Carol laughed. "Well, I take it you approve of the ring then?"
"Approve!" Gina stood back. "I am insanely jealous, that is certainly a thing of beauty, and I can hardly believe that a man chose so well, but not forgetting that our dear Tony is Italian, so romance is in his blood, of course." She shot Tony a wide smile.
Jeff got to his feet and walked over to the rosewood cabinet. "This calls for a celebration drink does it not?" He popped the cork from the bottle of Champagne that Carol and Tony had brought and handed round glasses.
"Oh, it's going to be hard discussing business tonight." Gina was floating on cloud nine. "It will be all far too mundane after all this."
"Well, I certainly think we need something a little mundane to calm you down, Darling, before we have to scrape you off the ceiling!" Jeff pointed out, pouring the sparkling liquid into the proffered glasses. "We can't have you getting over exited in your condition can, we?"
"Rubbish!" Gina retorted with a sniff. "A bit of excitement never hurt any baby and if this one can survive through a truck ride to Bulgaria and back then I am sure he – or she – can survive pretty much anything, don't you agree, Kiddo?"
"Sure do." Carol replied, sliding onto the sofa next to Tony. "This kid will be one pretty tough cookie I reckon. What with you two for parents, the kid's off to a great start."

"In Italy, all the mothers-to-be get on with life pretty much as before." Tony put in. He had seen Mamma Gina carry his eight siblings without breaking her stride. To him another child was part of daily life. "They drink wine and eat pretty much anything they please while getting on with anything they feel like getting on with."

"I agree." Gina stated firmly. "All this molly-coddling never does any good to improve the baby's health, and I doubt if leading a more sedentary life does anything to benefit the mother either. I do whatever makes me feel good."

"Well, as long as you are careful, Darling." Jeff put in. "If anything is good for my little mother here, then I want to make sure you do it, Darling, whatever it is."

"Gina looks after herself very well Jeff, don't you worry." Carol cut in. "I see the way she takes care of what she eats and she exercises too, so there is no need to worry on that score."

Gina sniffed. "Oh, don't be such an old fusspot, of course I am taking care. Why on earth would I not, as well you know Jeff Meredith!" She put down her glass and walked over to the sheaf of papers lying on the side table. "That is why I have only had a sip of champagne and have no intention of quaffing back the whole glass – that you poured out for me, may I remind you husband dear!"

In the excitement of the moment, Jeff had momentarily forgotten that Gina was not drinking alcohol. Suitably chastened he smiled and nodded. "Sorry, Darling, carried away by the moment, I stand corrected! Mein Fuhrer has spoken!"

Gina stuck out her tongue and settled herself on the sofa with the paperwork. "Carol and I have already gone through most of this, so it's only really up to you, Darling, to check it out and see how things are going." Gina sifted out a sheet of paper and passed it to Jeff. "As you can see on there, the waste paper contract is still good for the next five months, but after that we will have to negotiate to renew and as you can see here," she handed across another sheet. "The rates have dropped slightly for continental runs. Some of the ones I have sourced are not even viable, quite worrying really, but the UK rates seem to be a little healthier right now."

Jeff studied the figures that Gina had provided. "I know what you're saying Darling, but to be perfectly honest, as I said earlier, I can't see anything here to cause too much worry." He took a sip of his brandy and settled back against the soft cushions. "This has always been the way with haulage. Up one minute down the next. It's just a case of keeping one step ahead and not getting too complacent about things, don't you agree Carol?"

"To be honest, Jeff, with this side of things I bow to your judgement. You have been in the game far longer than I, so personally, I am willing to follow your lead on rates and runs and the like. I am learning, but you have years on me where this side is concerned."

"Don't forget the contract you have with Poppa for the olive runs. That will be a permanent thing." Tony put in quickly.

Jeff laughed. "Well marrying into the family is one sure way of securing a contract Mrs Landers."

Carol stuck out her tongue. "That was not top of the list of plus's when I said yes to Tony, but now you come to mention it.............." She gave Tony a playful dig in the ribs.

"I had not thought of that." Tony pretended to look worried. "And I thought I was being clever and securing my permanent position as driver by marrying the boss."

"Well, don't you go thinking that this means a raise in pay, cheeky!" Carol quipped back quickly. "We can't have any nepotism in Transcon Haulage you know!"

"Seriously though, I think some more UK runs won't do any harm looking at the financial climate right now." Jeff pointed out. "And to be honest, I don't mind tramping across country over here at all. After my little extended stay in Bulgaria last year, continental work has lost some of its charm as far as I am concerned."

"Cannot say that I blame you one moment for that." Tony agreed. "That was a frightening time all round. Of course I can keep up with the waste paper run to Italy and haul back the olives and oil from La Casaccia, that's a home run for me, so I can keep on as long as required on that score."

Carol flashed him a smile. "Of course, Darling, you can see your family on a regular basis and if I am not busy I can come too – it's ideal really. But of course I don't intend to sit about doing nothing. The UK runs I have been doing do pay well, so we can't afford to turn them down can we?"

"Absolutely not!" Jeff agreed adamantly, setting aside the paperwork. "The more UK work we can grab the better, that's the way I see it.

Now we are getting more countries from Europe joining the community the UK runs will be as lucrative if not better than Continental ones."

"So you think that is where we should be looking to for the future?" Gina enquired.

"I think we keep our ear to the ground and go where the money is – wherever that may be." Jeff had been in the haulage business for too many years to believe that anybody could plan ahead so far. Go with the flow was his motto and in this case it seemed to hold sway.

"Makes sense to me." Carol agreed.

"This one is a good littler earner, if we can get it on a regular basis." Jeff stabbed his finger at one of the sheets of paper. "Nice one for you Carol, Derbyshire is home ground for you isn't it?"

"Yes, it is. The first one is booked in for next week."

"That's right, the old Transcon will do that no problems." Jeff remarked confidently.

"Yes, Derbyshire, that's handy isn't it?" Gina cut in.

"We can stay over can't we?" Carol added with a smile.

"Be great to see them all again too."

"Leave nice and early so we will be able to get there early, have plenty of time to chat."

"We can surprise them."

"And take that lovely little outfit I bought for the baby."

"Stay for the night, drop and reload the next day. That will be good won't it?"

"Brilliant. Just what I had in mind. More like a holiday than work."

"Is this some type of code or can anybody join in?" Jeff queried, having little idea what Carol and Gina where talking about.

Carol laughed. "Well, the job is very close to my old home, you know, where Andy and Anna live now, so of course we can go the day before and stay with them for a nice visit."

"We?" Jeff looked over to Gina. "You're thinking of going too Darling?" His tone of voice making it clear that he did not think it was the best idea in the world for Gina to be riding in a truck.

Gina was having none of it. "Yes, we!" She said firmly, her tone brooking no argument. "Is that a problem?" Her defiant glance told Jeff that if it was a problem, then it was his alone.

"Er, no Darling of course not." Jeff decided that discretion was the better part of valour for the moment and was not about to risk getting on the wrong side of his wife over the matter, although he was not entirely sure if a pregnant lady should be riding around in trucks. "I am sure the break will do you good and you will enjoy the trip." Personally he would much have preferred to know his precious wife was safe in her own home doing her breathing exercises and following the 'Good Mothers Guide' book or whatever pregnant ladies were supposed to do. But Jeff knew his wife too well and knew that nothing he could say would make any difference once Gina had her mind set on doing something.

"So what are you two planning to do once you are legally wed?" Jeff quickly changed the subject. "Have you made any firm plans as to where you will be living and that sort of thing? Will you be based here or Italy?" It was the first time he had considered the question.

"We talked about that at length today." Carol set down her brandy glass. "I have to admit, I did spend a bit of a sleepless night getting into a panic about all sorts of things and inventing no end of complications but in the light of day it was all so simple to resolve."

"Yes, she spent nearly all night pacing the house," said Tony. "For a while I thought she had regretted saying yes to me. "He glanced over to Carol, his diamond grey eyes looking into hers. "But we talked about it for most of the day and decided that we will carry on pretty much as we are right now."

"I think most of my worries were unfounded." Carol's fears of the previous night had melted away.

"Basically, our home will be Carol's house." Tony continued. "I will carry on working the Italian runs, so no change really. I had no intention of trying to uproot Carol and drag her off to Italy to make pasta and produce multitudes of bambinos! I also have no intention of interfering in Transcon Haulage. I have enough on my plate being Poppa's eldest son and my business interest in the olive groves, so all will be pretty much the same as ever after we are married."

"Good grief!" Gina's eyes widened in amazement. "You mean you were mulling all this over in the night? Honestly, Kiddo you can be an idiot sometimes. Talk about inventing problems!"

Carol raised her eyes. "Yes, I know. Things always seem worse in the depth of the night though. Must be some primeval brain-cell thing or some such scientific explanation." She brushed away her panic attacks of the previous night.

"It's amazing how simple life can be if you don't make it complicated." Gina noted. "Oh, and have you told Katy yet?"

Carol laughed. "Have I told Katy? Of course I have. I phoned her before we came here. My ears are still ringing with her squeals of delight! She tells me she is coming down soon, so brace yourself for a visit!"

"Oh, it is all so exciting." Gina wriggled with glee. "And when is all this to be? Have you set a date yet?"

"Well, no, we haven't actually." Carol admitted. "We haven't even thought that far ahead, have we Darling. What do you think?"

Tony shrugged. "Whatever you like Cara Mia. My fate is in your hands, but I would like it to be soon of course."

"Typical man!" Gina cut in. "Leave all the details for the women to deal with. You just sit back, let us do all the arrangements, then turn up at the church looking cool, calm and collected, as if no effort had been made in any way!"

"That will do nicely!" Tony flashed an impudent grin at Gina and Carol. "I am sure that no suggestion I could provide would be suitable, so I will just do as I am told, wear what I am told to wear and turn up on time!"

Carol cast her eyes to the heavens. "I expected nothing else, did you Gina?"

"But where will you do the deed? Over here or in Italy?" Gina had visions of a huge family affair in La Casaccia. Lanterns in the trees and the whole village invited, the tables groaning with food and wine.

"Hmm. Not sure just yet." Carol hedged the idea. "I think I need a few days to let the engagement sink in before making any firm plans." The last thing Carol wanted right now was a huge affair to have to deal with. Something simple and understated was much more to her liking but she and Tony had to talk about it before any hard and fast plans were set into action.

Gina took the hint. "Well, whatever you decide I am sure it will be lovely. Right now just enjoy the moment. Life flashes by so fast it seems a shame to keep looking forward to things instead of enjoying what is here right now."

"Very wise Darling." Jeff agreed. "So many people spend their whole lives saying next year this and next year that, and they are simply missing the good things that are happening, or could be happening, right now, today."

"My goodness, Jeff you are turning into a philosopher." Carol teased, but she knew exactly what he meant. Right now she was happy and content. She had the man she loved. A business that was growing well and friends she could rely on.

Whatever happened in the future she would treasure this moment in time and look back with fond memories. She would not wish it away by hurrying life along. She would live for the moment. After all, what more could anybody ask for.

CHAPTER TEN

Markov slowed the car to a crawl as he negotiated the sharp bend in the hilly country lane. Overhanging trees shrouded his view of the road, although oncoming traffic had not been much of a problem so far. The quiet single carriageway roads were a pleasure to use after the hustle and bustle of the city and under any other circumstances Markov may have even found himself enjoying his country drive.

He had not attempted to contact Carter. There was no need, he had nothing to report and as neither man were the type to indulge in small talk, a call would be unnecessary.

The lasts few days had been spent playing the part of the tourist. He had walked the length and breadth of the small town, studying the buildings, strolling in the colourful town park and gazing down on the town, admiring the view. He had taken tea and cakes in various welcoming cafes and spoken to any interested party that had taken the time to speak to him. He had laid all the ground work that he possibly could to make himself visible without being obvious.

Driving further afield seemed the obvious choice now, visiting the many small villages scattered around the area, nestling between the gently rolling hills and making sure he had been noticed wandering around church yards, sitting in snug little cafe's and browsing the local shops.

Markov braked as a white Rolls Royce, draped in brightly coloured ribbons, swept majestically around the bend, slowing as it passed before continuing on its way down the hill along the winding country lane. The rear seat of the car held a vision in white froth, a bride to be, being chauffeured on her way to her wedding.

Markov had taken note that an unprecedented number of brides had been observed in this particular area and had discovered that he was within walking distance of the most famous village in Scotland. Famous for its anvil weddings and runaway lovers many years ago, but now a popular tourist attraction for both visitors to the area and those romantic souls who wished to exchange their life-long promises to each other with all the romance of yesteryear.

At his first sight of so many impending weddings, Markov's brain had been jolted back to remember his own nuptials. The huge stone church, resplendent with onion globes, snow clinging to the tall, ornate windows as he and his beautiful bride made their way by horse drawn carriage to the door to exchange vows in front of the Russian priest, imposing in robes of gold and white, his face partly obscured by the traditional beard. For the first time in many years he had allowed himself to picture his beloved Valentina's face, her cheeks flushed from the icy chill as she threw back the fur trimmed hood of her full length cape and gazed up into his eyes as they exchanged their vows.

He could clearly remember the smell of the incense, hear the soft chanting and the flickering of a thousand candles and once more picture the sight of his lovely bride standing eagerly by his side. Was that really he who had walked down that long aisle so many years ago. Was he the same man that had promised to protect and cherish that beautiful girl who he had taken for his wife, or was he the man who had failed her so badly. Once more his heart twisted at the memory.

Curiosity had taken him to the blacksmiths forge at Gretna Green. He had spent an hour browsing the old building, now a tourist trap of painted anvils, marriage rooms and gift shops. So very far removed from his own wedding. A marriage which seemed to have taken place in another lifetime.

The sharp throb of the cellphone in Markov's pocket cut into his musings. He pulled the car over to the side of the road, driving the nearside wheels up onto the grassy bank before cutting the engine and pulling the phone from his pocket.

"Yes?"

Where are you Zhrav? Alone?" Carter's hacking cough barked into the phone.

"In the car on a country lane just outside a small village." Markov replied. "Alone."

"Right." Carter coughed again, his breath catching in his chest as he spoke. Markov could hear him gasping to get his breath back. "I've made arrangements for a cottage. I take it you have made the most of the few days in the hotel and put yourself about?"

"Of course – as much as needed."

"Hmm. The cottage, well farmhouse really, is pretty out of the way. Do you need to write down the address?"

"No. Just tell me where it is"

Carter reeled off the address and gave instructions on how to get there. "The farmhouse is rented in the name of Victor Drago."

Markov took a deep breath. Victor Drago. One of the killers alias's. A name that he himself had given the man, many lifetimes ago when Markov had been the man's superior and giving the trained killer the names and locations of 'inconvenient' people that needed to disappear. Sending him out on countless 'errands' in the name of his government. Commanding him to deal with any irritations that rippled the smoothly running surface of his department. Victor Drago. One of the many names used by the steel-eyed, ice cold operator in the course of his 'duties'. Markov could not help but admire Carter in his extensive knowledge of what were always considered closely guarded secrets. He would not waste his breath in asking how Carter knew this name. He even found it slightly amusing and admired the fact that the old man still had the ability to play the game with such a deadpan attitude.

"Of course you continue using the name Marek." Carter continued. "I decided to use Drago for the lease to set whiskers twitching. If our friend wants to do a little research and look into who is renting what, then that name should leap off the page for him." He coughed hard into the receiver. "You stick with Stefan Marek though for now, that is who you are to the locals, so let's keep it that way for now."

"I follow your thinking old friend." Markov observed. "I will move to the new address tomorrow."

"As I said, it's pretty out of the way," Carter continued. "Ideal for anybody who wants privacy, if you understand what I mean. Only a small farmhouse, but standing in large grounds, so very private. The arrangements have been done by only a couple of highly trusted people and if we wanted it to stay that way it would – but I will make sure it gets mentioned more widely within the department within the next few days. That should give you time to settle and find your way around, before the leak starts to drip." Carter made it sound like he was arranging a weekend break I the country.

"Thank you old friend." Markov felt surprisingly calm about the whole thing. He had accepted the situation he had been driven into and was now resigned to whatever fate had in store for him. "I am sure both you and I will be glad when this thing is over."

"It will kill two birds with one stone, if you don't mind the pun my friend." Carter tried to laugh but the cough took hold once more. "At least we will find where the leaks are coming from when this thing kicks off so that will be two things sorted at once."

Markov was silent for a moment. "It could go either way of course my friend." He stated quietly. "Only one of us will come out of this you know."

"You have the choice Zhrav." Carter put in, no coughing, his tone lower than usual. "You could cut and run – nothing is set in stone as yet. Nothing has been leaked as yet and far as 'he' is concerned, you may still be in London."

Markov gave a wry smile. Carter knew full well that Zhravko Markov had no intention of cutting and running. "You know the answer to that old friend. We don't run, we stand and fight – even to the end."

It was the only answer Carter had expected. "Go to the farmhouse tomorrow night and then wait. God knows for how long. Maybe a few days maybe a few weeks but he will find you. We will make sure of that and, if at all possible, I will give you some warning, but if I can't................." Carter left the sentence unfinished. He had been warned by the doctors that if he did not agree to hospitalisation his chances of recovery where slim to nil. But he had to see this through if it was humanly possible. "I am going to text you another number. If you get no reply from my number at any time use this one – but only if you can't get me, understand?"

"Yes, my friend – I do." Sadly Markov realised that Carter's days on this earth where numbered and it saddened him. "Thank you. God speed to you." He clicked of the phone and sat silent for a moment. So it was all beginning to happen. It was the beginning of the end – one way or another.

*****

The first light of dawn was just beginning to creep across the sky as the two friends gathered their coats and overnight bags and made their way from the warmth of Carol's kitchen into the sharp morning air.

"I am looking forward to this." said Gina with a smile. "It's been ages since we went out in the truck together hasn't it?" Her booted feet crunched on the gravel as they walked over to the 'Fighting Spirit', standing alongside the ivy covered wall.

"Since the Bulgaria saga." Carol reminded her wryly. "But I don't think we could count that as a pleasure trip could we – for either of us!"

"No, not exactly." Gina agreed, waiting for Carol to unlock the cab door and fling hers and Gina's bags up onto the bunk. "But we did manage a giggle on the way despite the circumstances."

Carol climbed up into the Transcon's tall cab and leaned over to unlock the passenger door. "Well, you have to make the most of the moment, I suppose." She observed as Gina clambered into the passenger seat and slammed the door. "But at least this trip will be happier, and shorter too!"

Gina smoothed any imaginary creases from her dark grey trousers and pulled her warm woollen coat more tightly around her body. "Just as well it won't be a long haul." She remarked. "Jeff was having kittens at the thought of me coming with you anyway. Honestly, you would think I was terminally ill rather than simply pregnant!"

"Well, that's men for you. They haven't a clue have they?" The girls laughed at the shared intimacy of the remark as Carol hit the starter button, the reliable Cummins engine immediately roaring into life. The girls sat there for a few moments while the low air warning buzzer droned monotonously and waited for the engine to settle itself into the familiar, gentle throbbing rhythm.

Speaking of kittens," said Carol. "Spyder is happy to be on Phoebe feeding duties as well as looking after my lot, by the way. I asked him yesterday and he will call in tonight on his way home."

"Oh, bless him. I knew he would do it. He's a diamond isn't he?" Gina replied. "You were lucky to find that one Kiddo. I wonder what he is like with babies?"

Carol laughed. "Well he has the new baby of his own as well as the two boys, so I suppose he could manage one more! Lucky for him though that Gill has offered to do the child minding, if and when you go back to work, or he could have found his employment contract being re-written yet again – not that he actually has one!"

Gina giggled. "Yes, Gill is wonderful with kiddies isn't she – I can't think where she gets all her patience from." She replied. Gill had been a staunch friend since Carol had moved to London and was devoted not only to her own children but to children in general. "But of course my little one will certainly not be tiny when I go back to work – if I ever DO decide to go back. I want to enjoy every moment that I can while he - or she - is little. I have promised myself a year off work at the very least."

Carol knew that Gina had no intention of abandoning her baby, even to the most reliable carer, unless it was absolutely necessary. "Alternatively I suppose we could always get a kiddie seat fitted in the cab for the odd jaunt away. Nothing is a problem is it?"

"Absolutely." Gina giggled. "Maybe we could invent a new item, 'Truck Seats for Truck Tots'. It would be great for the working mum!

"Mind you – that's flaming typical!" Carol remarked, half serious half amused. "A woman goes trucking and has to take the kids along. Men take it up and leave 'em behind – until they get older and are more fun of course."

"Well that's the difference between men and women." Gina observed. "We just get on with it regardless of what we have to do. Life would be pretty boring if we gave in to the slightest problem. And anyway....." Gina giggled wickedly. "Can you imagine leaving the kids at home with the other half and you having to answer the phone every five minutes because he has lost the kids favourite toy or they won't eat what he's cooked and where is the first aid kit! Easier to haul the brats along I reckon."

Carol joined in the laughter. "Yep, that would be right. Especially for you Kiddo – You can be one tough cookie when you want to be!" Even though she knew her friend well, Gina's indomitable character often took her by surprise. Carol remembered the arduous journey to Bulgaria in the grip of winter and Gina's solid determination to secure her husband's release from the filthy conditions of the prison. Even though neither of them had any doubt of Jeff's innocence, Carol was sure that Gina would have stood by her husband even if she had thought him to be guilty.

The buzzer began to splutter, then petered out. Carol eased the gear-stick forward and swung the Transcon around, heading for the gate. "Won't be much traffic on the road as yet." She observed. "With a bit of luck we should clear the worse places before the rush starts."

"I like an early start." Gina agreed, pulling the map from the overhead locker. "Where exactly is the drop place?"

"Just outside Buxton – there!" Carol glanced over and pointed at a spot on the map. "It's only a small wood-yard, or so I have been told, so we will probably be the only ones there, if so it will be a quick unload, not like the wait I had yesterday in Tilbury loading all this timber on board. I was there for ages hanging around."

"Well hopefully they will be quick and we can get straight on to Andy and Anna's.

"I can't wait to see the baby." Gina announced happily. "Three months is a lovely age."

"They are all lovely ages." Carol replied. "I enjoyed Katy at every stage she was at and still do." she dropped a gear as she turned a sharp bend leading into the town centre. The shops were still shuttered and unlit, the streets clear of pedestrians and very few vehicles as they made their way through the centre and onto the wider roads leading to the motorway. The old truck was pulling well as always and Carol had full confidence that they would get there in good time providing there were no hold ups on the motorways.

"Have you thought anything about the wedding?" Gina asked.

"Like what exactly." Carol pressed the accelerator and knocked the engine into top gear.

"Oh, don't give me that 'like what' business!" Gina was not to be deterred. "Like what you will be wearing and what sort of flowers you will be having and if there will be bridesmaids and who will be giving you away and....."

"Hey you, slow down! We have only just agreed the deed, we haven't even discussed a date yet or decided where."

"Well, start thinking!" Gina said firmly. "Don't be letting the grass grow, I hope you aren't thinking of one of these long drawn out engagements. You know five years down the line and still saving up or some such rubbish."

"Well, no, not really. I just honestly hadn't thought any further than – err, well right now to be honest. But now you come to mention it, I don't suppose there is any point in hanging around." Carol eased the truck down as she approached the big roundabout displaying the signs for the M25 and turned off onto the slip road. Thankfully the notorious road was running freely with little traffic. "But it is a bit of a daunting prospect. I do like my independence."

"Are you having second thoughts?" Gina's voice had a worried ring.

The laden truck gathered speed down the steep incline as they pulled onto the motorway. Carol checked behind her and joined the flow of traffic, sitting back and relaxing as she watched the wide lanes stretching ahead.

"No - not second thoughts. I love Tony and want to be married to him but....."

"But what!" Gina insisted. "Listen Kiddo, if you have any doubts at all then don't do it!"

"I haven't any doubts. It's just, well, a huge change of life. I have been single for so flaming long I have grown pretty selfish I suppose. What I want to do, I do, and what I want to have, I have." Carol managed to put her feeling into words.

"And do you think that Tony will stop you from doing what you want to do and expect you to change?"

"No, not at all. Tony is not like that. He is the most gentle soul I know. I know we will be happy together."

"Well there you are then, you've just answered your own query." Gina stated with a note of finality.

"Yes you are right. And no, I am not having second thoughts – it's just that my head is still struggling to take it all in. I sill can't believe how lucky I am right now that things are going so well in my life. I just am not used to things running smoothly and a little voice in the back of my head keeps telling me not to drop my guard down and that something awful could happen at any moment."

"Oh, good grief! And something awful may NOT happen at any moment – or in fact at all. Maybe you have had your share of bad luck in the past and things will be wonderful from now on. For ever and ever even! Don't be so pessimistic Kiddo. Life is for living and you can often spoil what is a happy time by worrying about what might be or what might happen. Nobody knows what the future will bring so just live for the moment and enjoy it for heaven's sake!"

Carol felt suitably chastened. What Gina said made absolute sense. Why on earth should she spoil this happy time by worrying about things that may happen or in fact may never happen. "Must be something to do with birth signs or horoscopes or something." Carol remarked. "According to my Chinese sign, or so I was told, I was born in the year of the dog which means I was born to worry. So far that seems to be correct!" Carol laughed, making a determined effort to heed her friends words and simply enjoy this happy time in her life.

"Hmph! Rubbish!" Gina huffed. "I was told that I was born under a sign of the rooster so that made me a really strong person and a leader and all that. Well I am not strong at all or would ever be any good as a leader. So you can't believe any of that!"

Carol raised an eyebrow but decided against passing any remark. Maybe there was more to these Chinese signs than she had first considered.

"So, most importantly, what are you thinking of wearing?" Gina changed the subject to the more important things that needed discussing right now. The Dress. Gina, of course had lots of ideas, but did not want to impress her own thoughts onto her friend.

"Well, I had considered sugar pink tulle with lots of net with puffed sleeves and of sequins, full length of course, with a huge bow at the back with a tall headdress of pink flowers and feathers." Carol mused.

"Err….." Gina shifted in her seat. "Well, maybe you should try different shades of pink. You have to be careful with Auburn hair you know." she said carefully.

Carol spluttered with laughter. "Ha! Gotcha! Can you really see me in sugar pink with puffy sleeves?" She glanced at her friend's expression. "I would look like a blamanche in full sail with a bonfire on my head!"

Gina looked thoroughly relieved. "Thank goodness for that!" She sighed. "For one awful moment….."

Carol laughed. "Course not. But I hadn't really thought about it to be honest. I was wondering what Tony was thinking about where he fancied getting married rather than what to wear. To be perfectly honest I don't fancy a huge Italian do and registry offices are so – well, bland!"

"We will have to give it some thought. Just you and I then when he gets back we will have some sort of scenario that we can run by him."

"Yes, we will, but not to forget that it is his day too so we will have to agree on it. Only fair isn't it."

Gina nodded. "But we can still get some books and look at dresses can't we?" she added hopefully.

"Of course we can." Carol agreed. No way was Gina not going to get involved with the fashion side of the occasion. But that was fine by Carol. She knew her friends taste was second to none and that she could rely on her for good advice.

*****

"Yee-ha! That's the best new I've had for ages!" Andy's yell of delight almost deafened Carol and Gina as they settled themselves onto the comfortable sofa in what had once been Carol's living room in the big stone built house on the outskirts of the small Derbyshire village that Carol had grown up in. "Anna – Caz's getting herself hitched!" Andy yelled again, this time to his wife who was in the kitchen making coffee.

"Calm down And." Carol begged. "I won't be able to hear the wedding march if you render me stone deaf!"

"Sorry Caz, but it's just such great news girl. I am so happy for you and hope you and Tony will be as happy as Anna and I are."

"I am sure we will be." Carol replied. "And I know you and Anna are happy, everyone can see that." Andy had been Carol's dearest friend for many years. He had been the closest thing to a big brother that Carol had ever had and had always been there to help with any problems when she was living alone, struggling to bring up her baby daughter. Both Andy and Anna still adored Katy and welcomed her regular and impromptu visits with open arms.

"Oh, we are fine, as always and so is your god-daughter, she is a real treasure!" Andy could hardly keep the open pride out of his voice. "Sleeps right through the night now and looks so much like her mother." He glanced down with pride at the tiny bundle as he picked the waking baby out of her lace covered basket and placed her gently into Gina's waiting arms.

"Anna was always disgustingly pretty when we were at school together." Carol put in, leaning over to admire her god-daughter. "I always looked like a ragamuffin up against her. I should hate her really – so pretty and a talented artist too!"

Andy laughed. "She still is a cracker, even after a day of running about after little Carol-Anna here. But I do my bit to help so she can keep up with her paintings. I am *very* new man you know!"

"You always were, Honey," Carol reminded him warmly. "You were always there to help me look after Katy and look after me too, as I remember. You all but rebuilt the house for me when it needed it."

"But I've reaped the benefits of my labours haven't I?" Andy laughed, gesturing around the cosy living room. "Seeing as that it's our home now it was lucky I didn't cut corners."

"This is a lovely family home Andy." Gina looked around the homely living room with admiration. "So full of character." She returned her attention to the baby. Little Carol-Anna was still wide awake, but lay contentedly staring about the room.

"It was full of rot and damp walls when Carol took it on all those years ago." Said Andy wryly. "But we knocked it into shape between us didn't we girl?"

"We sure did." Carol replied. "Although Andy had very little choice, I think I used to bully him really."

Andy laughed "That's true actually. She was a complete demon and a slave driver too."

Carol stuck out her tongue. "What else would you have been doing eh? Hanging around street corners with your mates and getting up to no good!"

"Honestly you two." Anna's gentle voice had an edge of amusement. "These two are more like brother and sister than some real brothers and sisters that I know!" Anna's long velvet skirt swished around her ankles as she swept into the room, carrying a large tray laden with coffee cups and a heaped plate of biscuits. She was tall and slim, her long dark hair tied back in a beaded scarf. A delicate silver chain with a small jewelled cross hung from her neck, complimenting her porcelain complexion. Looking every inch the bohemian artist that she had always been, her gentle nature shining through her soft brown eyes.

"I take it Katy is pleased with the news?" She enquired, setting down the tray of tea and biscuits on the rough wooden coffee table and gently taking Carol's hand to admire the ring.

"Oh, yes she is delighted, but she has always liked Tony so that makes life easier." Carol assured her.

"We know she likes him. Likes him a lot." Andy assured her. "Last time she came here to stay she was full of praise about him and really happy that you two were an item. I think she was secretly hoping that it would be a permanent arrangement." Katy had always confided her hopes and dreams in Andy.

"Funny how life pans out isn't it." Carol mused, staring about the familiar room in the old house where she had lived for so long and was now the well loved home of her dearest friends.

"But we would not want to change a thing would we?" Gina asked.

"No. We certainly would not." Carol agreed. Right now she could not think of one thing that she would be willing to change.

*****

CHAPTER ELEVEN

Spending the evening at Andy and Anna's was thoroughly enjoyable as always. Being Carol's oldest friends and living in the house that she herself had spent so many happy years, every time she visited them it felt very much like she had come home again. Gina was simply delighted to hold the baby and was happy to spend the whole evening with the child tucked safely in the crook of her arm.

The four friends sat in the spacious living room, curled up in the old, overstuffed sofas surrounded by Anna's handmade cushions and Bohemian crafts. The walls were hung with Anna's own paintings and hand crafted wall hangings and the large open fire gave the room a friendly welcoming atmosphere and, as always, prompted Carol to reminisce about her life.

Katy had been only a toddler when they had moved into this house. Katy's father had left after only a few months, running off with the local barmaid. At the time Carol had been hurt and angry but now she could laugh about it.

"Good job Danny ran off with that barmaid wasn't it Caz?" Andy laughingly remarked, his arm around Anna as they sat close together on the squashy sofa. "Made a vacancy down at the pub for you to get the job and earn a few bob. Really considerate of the pair of them!"

"Well, I sure needed a few bob at that time!" Carol replied wryly. "This place was a complete dump. Empty for years and damp right through – and do you remember that flaming leak in the roof!"

"Remember it!" Andy threw his arms skyward. "I tell you Gina, I spent more time on that roof shuffling slates than I did in here – and slate shuffling in a Derbyshire thunderstorm aint no fun I can tell you!" Andy did a suitable impression of hanging onto a roof in a high wind making the girls collapse with laughter.

"It strikes me that Carol makes a lifetime career out of moving into derelict properties." Gina observed. "You didn't see the state that her present house was in when she bought it – after only seeing as far as the hallway before she put in a bid for it I might add!"

"Typical Caz." Andy observed, stretching his long legs out towards the hearthrug and wriggling his bare toes in front of the crackling log fire. "Gets a notion into her head and jumps in both feet. Luckily she usually manages to paddle out before she is swept under."

"Oh, she has worked miracles with the place." Gina carried on enthusiastically. "We have had hours of fun doing the place up and of course Spyder is a real treasure. He can turn his hand to almost anything."

"It does not surprise me for one moment that Caz found herself another willing slave!" Andy laughed.

"Er, excuse me! I have done the odd bit myself you know!" Carol cut in. "I don't think Spyder would be any good on the sewing machine, making curtains and cushions and stuff!"

"Carol has always been gifted with being able to do that sort of thing." Anna put in, sitting comfortably, curled up close to Andy. "We will definitely come over in the summer and spend some time there. I am dying to see the place and what you have done with it. Carol sure has her own great sense of style."

"But never able to put onto canvas the wonderful paintings that you do Anna." Carol had always admired the beautiful watercolours and oil paintings that Anna was able to create, seemingly without effort. The fruits of her labours covered almost every piece of wall in the house. Her time at art college had certainly not been wasted.

"Anna's getting quite well known now." Andy stated proudly. "She has been offered many commissions and has had more than one exhibition of her own work and sold quite a lot too." He spoke with ill concealed pride of his wife's talents.

With typical artist's modesty, Anna turned the conversation away from herself and her achievements. "So when are you thinking of getting married Carol?" She asked. "Will it be over here or in Italy?"

Carol pulled a face. "Well to be perfectly honest. I don't know what to do. Personally I don't want a big fancy affair. I would much prefer a small intimate occasion that was just Tony and I and a couple of close friends. I know that weddings in Italy, especially those in Tony's family, are huge exciting occasions with half the surrounding population involved, but somehow it feels that the bride and groom are almost secondary to all the hustle and bustle and all the family and food and presents and things. They just seem to get swept along in the crush and to be honest, that is the last thing I want."

"Hmm, sounds like you may have a problem on your hands there Caz."
Andy observed. "I would suppose that Tony's lot are expecting the full
monty, violins and all."

"To be perfectly truthful we did not even discuss it." Surprisingly during the
last few days they had been so swept away with the happiness of the
engagement the wedding had not even been mentioned. "But I think we
must have a real good talk about it. I will ask him what he expects and what
he wants to do. After all it will be his day as well as mine."

"Why not just dive straight in and tell him what you would like and see what
he says." Said Gina. "No point in beating about the bush. "You never
know, maybe Tony would like a quiet affair too and maybe he would only
go along with a big occasion because he may think that is what you want.
This is really the sort of thing you have to discuss and agree together. It is
the start of a partnership in life after all so no point in not setting off on the
right foot is there?"

"Very profound Gina. Always best to be up front." Andy agreed. "But I
reckon Tony will be happy to go along with whatever you decide Carol.
Men are like that. Pretty lazy really!" He grinned.

"You could always run off to Gretna Green" said Anna, ignoring Andy's last
remark.

"Oh, yes, right. Run away. Elope to Gretna like they used to. Good idea!"
Carol laughed.

"No, seriously. You can get married there. We went to a wedding there last
year, didn't we Andy and it was really lovely. Very intimate and nicely
done."

"Really!" Gina was surprised. "I didn't know they did them there anymore."

"Well they do." Anna confirmed. "You can get details off the internet can't
you Andy?"

Andy got to his feet. "You sure can." He stated, striding over to the corner
of the room and switching on his computer. "Just wait a moment while it
comes to the boil and we will have a look-see."

"It's amazing what you can find on the internet these days." Carol
remarked. "It's not something that I spend any time on myself but, of
course, we had to get one for the business just to keep up with the times I
suppose. But that's Gina's department."

Gina laughed. "Yes, I do all the computer based stuff. Keeping the
accounts and things, but I have also found it handy for browsing around for
back loads for the trucks and it does give you instant communication instead

of all this telephoning and letter writing and posting and waiting for replies. Amazing really."

"Ah, but if it goes wrong then she has to call on her young neighbour to put it right, isn't that so Gina?" Carol laughed. "If there is one thing I do know about computers, is that if we old ones have problems then call in a twelve year old and they can usually sort it out within seconds!"

"Yes, that's true." Gina agreed. "I think that poor little Archie from next door spent more time in my house sorting out the problems I had than he did in his own when I first got the thing. Kids just know about these things don't they. Sign of the times I suppose."

"Our one is a bit elderly and not the fastest computer in the world." Anna remarked. "Andy keeps saying it needs a new elastic band!"

"Actually I think this one is steam powered it is so old, but it still works, so it will have to do." Andy replied, stabbing at his mouse.

"Ah, here we go." He typed in what he wanted and waited. "There we are, downloadable forms and everything."

Carol walked over to the computer and studied the site that Andy had selected. "It looks really nice." She said with surprise. "Not at all commercial and very quaint – I love it – what do you think Gina?

"Well, it isn't really important what I think is it?" Gina pointed out, carefully getting up and walking over to the computer still holding the precious baby. "It's your wedding so it should be your choice."

"But you know I value your opinion and two, or in this case four, heads are better than one." Carol replied clicking onto another page of the site and admiring the pictures of the pretty venue.

"It is a lovely place, very intimate and friendly. It is not in Gretna Green itself - that seemed a little commercial to us, didn't it Anna?" Andy remarked. "But this place is just outside the village and personally I felt it could not have been nicer. We both agreed that we would have been happy to get married there ourselves – if we had not already tied the knot!"

"It certainly looks wonderful – and so romantic." Said Gina.

Carol laughed "Yes, it does and I think you have sold me on it. Shall we mail them for details? It won't do any harm to enquire will it?"

"No, not at all." Andy agreed. "Nothing set in stone with a few enquiries, so why not?"

"Why not indeed!" Carol agreed as Andy sent off for further details, downloaded some forms and printed them off. Although she had said that she was only making tentative enquiries, deep down she had a feeling she had found the perfect venue. She only hoped that Tony would agree with her choice. "They will send a brochure." Andy announced, clicking the mouse to print off the forms.

"There are all the details here to send off to the registrar and everything and according to the 'Frequently Asked Questions' bit it seems you can get it organised within six weeks if you want to, venue vacancies permitting of course." Said Carol, peering at the screen.

"Six weeks!" Gina's eyes widened with amazement. "Six weeks, I had no idea you were thinking of doing it that quickly!"

"Well, no I wasn't really." Carol admitted. "I just remarked that you could if you wanted to, that's all."

"But if you do really want a quiet no-fuss affair then the quicker you get it organised the better really." Anna pointed out, her gentle undertones the epitome of calm and reason. "If you think the Italian side of the family will want a huge fuss, then simply organise a small intimate wedding over here, enjoy it with your closest family and friends then ask them to go ahead with a huge party and all the trimmings later in the year and have a blessing over there too. Don't forget that with you being divorced Carol, there is definitely the point that there may be problems with a church wedding in Italy. Many churches in England won't do the deed with divorced people and Italy is much more so I would think, so it would have to be a registry office ceremony anyway."

"Anna's right of course." Andy put in. "They are even more strict over there than they are over here about things like that, but our friends who got married at Gretna were allowed a chapel wedding with a proper traditional service even though they had been married before. So I am sure that would go down well with Tony's Mamma. Don't forget that with her upbringing she would only feel you were properly married if the deed was done with full benefit of clergy." Andy pointed out with a laugh. "So maybe my clever wife has come up with the obvious answer once again." He smiled proudly at Anna. His softly spoken wife always managed to come up with exactly the right thing at exactly the right time.

"Anna always was the sensible one, even at school." Carol agreed, with a warm smile for her old school friend. "When the rest of us were dashing about in circles over some huge teenage crisis, Anna would float above it all with an ethereal air then find a few choice words to solve any problems that we had probably only created for ourselves."

"I did not 'float' you ass!" Anna laughed flushing slightly with embarrassment. "You lot were always so busy hurling yourselves from one crisis plan to another it was just so simple to stand back and see the clearer picture."

"Well, there you are then. You saw the clear picture that we all missed. We would have been lost without you and your calming ways."

"No wonder you turned into such a wonderful artist, Anna." Gina observed. "You have inner sight without a doubt."

"She also has excellent taste." Andy cut in, gathering up empty tea cups and heading for the kitchen. "She took one look at me and knew I was perfect husband material!"

Anna smiled after her disappearing husband. "He is a good man." She admitted. "The first time I met him he was up a set of ladders in the back bedroom here, fixing a leak in your ceiling, Carol, and even though the job was fiddly he still had the patience to carefully keep on explaining everything to little Katy as she stood at the foot of the ladder watching him. I think that's when I fell for him, right there, at the foot of the ladder."

"Yes, I know." Carol replied, thinking back to the day Anna came to stay. "I saw it in your eyes right away and Andy was about two full seconds behind you! I thought 'Oh here we go – watch out for violins and the smell of roses!"

"Of course at first I thought he was Carol's new boyfriend" Anna admitted shyly.

"Yuk! Horrid thought!" Carol and Andy both pulled 'want to be sick' faces and giggled. "But I soon put her straight on that one." Carol laughed. "Told her straight away that Andy was the brother I never had and I would be delighted if she snared him. It would be like having your best friend for a sister in law"

"Love at first sight then." said Gina. "How romantic - and you now live here in the house where it all happened."

"And now we are planning another wedding. I think this house must be charmed." Anna remarked, glancing at her watch and walking over to gather her now sleeping baby from Gina's arms to take her to her cot for the night.

Gina sat back and smoothed her clothes after holding the warm sleeping baby. "Oh that was a lovely cuddle." She smiled wriggling life back into her arm. "But they sure do get heavy when they sleep don't they?"

"Heavy when they sleep – noisy when they are awake. You have got it all to come, Gina!" Anna laughed as she swept from the room and headed for the stairs.

"Do you think that you will get married very soon then?" Andy's disembodied voice called from the kitchen.

"Hmm, don't know really." Carol answered, raising her voice to be heard out in the kitchen. "I will have to see what Tony wants to do of course, it's his wedding day too, but having made the decision to do it I can't see any point in all this waiting and planning. I know some people are engaged for two or three years while they spend every waking moment planning the wedding. Every detail like a military manoeuvre. Not to mention the expense they go to. Some couples spend thousands on that one day. Ludicrous!" Carol's sensible approach to life was not going to desert her even for her wedding.

"Andy and I didn't spend a fortune." Anna remarked coming back into the room. "And it was a really lovely day wasn't it?"

"Oh, it certainly was!" Carol replied enthusiastically. "Anna wore the most beautiful antique lace dress that had been hanging in her Gran's wardrobe forever. It cleaned up wonderfully well and she had fresh flowers in her hair."

"Neither Andy nor I wanted a huge Fuss." Anna explained curling up in her chair. "We just wanted the day to be about us exchanging our promises. Not a huge show for the world to see. His family and mine and a few friends to witness our vows – that was all."

"Then afterwards we all came back here for the cake and a buffet in the garden." Carol added. "Do you remember how we spent all morning looking at the sky and wondering will it rain or won't it rain – so will it be inside or outside for the party!"

"In the end we did all the food and left it in the kitchen while the weather made its mind up. When we came out of church the sun was streaming down so we all dashed back here and hauled out tables and chairs and plates of food into the garden – Everyone got involved and it was such fun. A really happy day!" Anna smiled at the memory.

"Night-time treat – hot chocolate all round." Andy returned with a tray of steaming mugs.

"Yes it was a happy day." Carol replied taking a large mug of deliciously thick hot chocolate from Andy. "That is the sort of thing I was hoping for on our wedding day. Just a lovely easy day to be enjoyed, no stress or worries, and lovely memories to look back on in years to come.

"Then we will have to think of how to do it exactly that way. Small and intimate but memorable." Gina mused as the warmth of the chocolate slid down to her tummy. "Nothing over the top but something meaningful with lovely wording in the vows."

"Yes that's exactly it." Carol replied curling her feet underneath her and hugging her mug with both hands. "The more I think about it the more I think this place will be just right for the way Tony and I feel about each other. And also the more I think about it the more I believe Tony will love it too. Next time he is home the brochures will have arrived and we can go through it together!"

"Carol, can I make your cake?" Anna asked quietly. "Unless you have something particular in mind that is that would be beyond me."

"Oh, Anna!" Carols eyes sparkled. "How wonderful, what a lovely idea, I would love that. Oh yes please! And I will leave the design absolutely to you – your taste is impeccable so I know it will be wonderful."

Anna smiled. "Then that will be my wedding present to you. I will make it for you. Andy and I will bring it along to the venue for you – if you want us to that is." She added quickly.

Carol's eyes widened. "It would not be the same without you. When I said close intimate friends I meant it." She leaned over spontaneously and hugged Anna with her free arm trying not to spill the remains of her hot chocolate that sloshed worryingly about in the mug. "In fact I am pretty sure that Katy will be spending a few days here at 'home' with you and Andy so no doubt you will all arrive together."

"Knowing Katy she probably will." Anna replied. "She is always more than welcome here as you know and it will be lovely for us all to travel there together. Katy will be over the moon about the whole thing. Probably want to give you away too."

"I am sure she will. How lovely and unconventional it will be but special all the same." Carol laughed. It all sounded almost too perfect.

"And I will take you dress hunting!" Gina decided. She could hardly wait to start searching for the perfect gown for Carol's big day.

"Well let's not get too excited straight away." Carol warned. "When we get home we can look into the venue and see if it's do-able and then find a nice frock and go from there eh?"

"Frock!" Gina snorted. "Honestly Carol you can be a nightmare at times."

Carol laughed. Sometimes it was just far too easy to set Gina off.

*****

The safe house that Carter had arranged for Markov to spend the next weeks, or maybe even months, in waiting was well off the beaten track. Once an old farmhouse, but now updated and renovated, to suit the discerning summer visitor to the area. The farmhouse was approached by a long gravel drive leading from the road and was surrounded by a large area of garden, much of it shaded with tall established trees. Many holiday makers would have found the seclusion of the setting a delightful rural haven from the hustle and bustle of city life and would no doubt have enjoyed the peace and isolation. For Markov's purpose it was ideal. No immediate neighbours to show any interest in who was in residence or what took place there. No passers-by to notice anybody coming or going from the property and certainly nobody within earshot of any sounds that may emit from within the thick stone walls of the old building or its surrounding grounds.

Detached from the farmhouse were two stone outbuildings with heavy wooden doors. One housed a stock of logs, the other was presumably once a garage, and was large enough for at least two cars.

Markov did not bother to hide his vehicle inside the outbuilding. He parked a few feet away from the front door, leaving the car where it could be glimpsed from the road. The driveway was long but straight so any interested by-passer glancing down the drive could see the rear of the vehicle parked alongside the tall hedge marking the property's border from the adjoining fields. He stood back and surveyed the immediate layout. The only obvious way to the farmhouse was from the road, directly up the drive, and approaching the gable end of the building. There was no downstairs window on that end to be able to see down the length of the drive. The farmhouse lay sideways with two square windows one side of the front door and further large picture window on the other. All windows overlooking the driveway. An inconvenience, Markov decided, but noticed that there was a small side facing window upstairs that looked down the full length of the drive and possibly, if the hedgerow was not too high, over to the road beyond.

Markov stood back for a short time and studied the solid stone building but made no move to go inside. He strode past the farmhouse and into the garden beyond. The high hedges surrounding the property offered complete privacy to those in residence. Markov checked the boundaries out more closely. Running through the thick hedges was a double string of barbed wire. Obviously to deter an invasion of the local sheep, but would also suit his own purpose well. It would not be easy to break through the hedges to approach the main building from either the back or the side. The obvious, and seemingly only route, was directly up the driveway. The wooded area right at the end of the large garden was particularly dense. Young saplings struggled for prominence amongst older, long established oaks, ash and hazel. Many fallen branches lay in a tangle, partly overgrown by bramble and ivy. The smell of rotting wood, damp and decay hung heavily in the air. Markov bent and pulled a thick, twisted piece of wood from by his feet. Carefully he studied the piece, turning it over in his hands as though each curve and knot needed detailed examination. The smell of the wooded copse, the breeze drifting through the leaves and the tall trees standing proudly amidst their fallen companions had stirred his memories.

Still holding the intricately twisted piece of wood, Markov turned on his heel and strode back to the house, opening the door and stepping inside. He found himself in a large square entrance hall, stone floored with exposed brickwork on the walls. Obviously the renovators idea of keeping the farmhouse in sympathy with its past. A large sweeping staircase led to the upper floor with a bathroom tucked neatly underneath. On the right was a huge living room, echoing the exposed brickwork of the hall way with a full height stone chimney in which grandly stood a wood burning stove, obviously the reason for the store of wood in the outhouse. A roll top desk, two overstuffed sofas and an imposing oak dining table at the far end completed the furnishing.

Two wide picture windows were placed each other, offering an overall view of both the woodland side of the garden and the driveway on the other. Markov noted that this wide view could be a double-edged sword. Yes, he could see outside with hardly any limitations, but also it offered any prowler a good view of anyone in residence. Although the room was obviously the piece de resistance of the farmhouse, Markov felt reluctant to make much use of it.

He walked back across the hallway and into a smaller room, darker to the point of being gloomy, with only one square window overlooking the driveway. Sparsely furnished and cold with the continuation of exposed brick, the room was far from inviting, but to Markov, felt secure. Passing though the second doorway Markov found himself in a spacious stone flagged kitchen. An Aga cooker stood in pride of place along one wall with a row of oak cupboards along the other and, for culinary backup for the less adventurous, an electric cooker tucked unobtrusively in a corner. A large scrubbed pine table with six mismatched chairs took precedence over the centre of the room.

The room was surprisingly cheerful with sunlight flooding in through the window, which once again afforded a view onto the driveway. Markov noted that the house only had the two doors and both faced the driveway. The only way anyone could possibly enter the house from the rear would be through the large rear window in the living room but that was solidly double glazed with adequate locks on the handles. The ground floor certainly felt secure enough.

Casually dumping his piece of wood on the table, Markov committed the layout to memory before retracing his steps to the hallway and striding up the stairs. There was one large bedroom, to the right of the small landing boasting an oversized four-poster bed and comfortable pile carpet with two adjoining rooms on the left, each simply furnished with the minimum of fuss. Markov was not particularly interested in the décor. The farmhouse was private, secluded and had a solid door. It would suit his purpose well. His only concern with the designer's idea of modernisation was the complete lack of window cover. Not one of the windows boasted blinds or drapes. Presumably the decorator had noticed that as no window, either upstairs or down in the solid stone building, were overlooked in any way, that the addition of window coverings were unnecessary. The newly fitted windows boasted multiple squares of glass allowing views over the garden, woodland and glimpses of farmland beyond. Again Markov decided that he would have to turn this exposure to his own advantage, if, and when the time came. He decided to disregard the sumptuous master bedroom with huge windows, in favour of the furthest small bedroom, the only one with a window facing the entrance to the drive and a limited view of the road entrance. Not ideal, but nothing in life had ever been that, he was used to having to make adjustments and compromises to his situation.

He walked back down stairs and out to the car, hauling out his travel bag and two plastic carrier bags of provisions before locking the vehicle and leaving it where it stood, slightly on view from the road, and carrying his burdens into the kitchen. Markov flung the upper portion of the stable-type door open, allowing the spring air to fill the large room, the smell of heather and woodland pleased him as he unpacked his supplies, stored them into the empty cupboards and put the kettle on to boil for coffee. He had no idea how long he would be in residence in this lonely place but was prepared to wait. Wait for as long as it took for his counterpart to track him down. Only when they had met face to face would the outcome of the exercise be decided. Much hung on this outcome. Not only the life of Markov himself but probably the lives of Oliver Carter, his family and also the drivers who had brought him into England.

The big man felt suddenly weary. He slumped onto a chair and leaned his arms on the table, picking up his twisted branch and turning it idly in his hands. He was no longer a young man and the weight that he was carrying on his shoulders had suddenly became a huge burden. He wanted peace. Wanted a quiet uncomplicated life. Simple and undemanding. He had no wish to be rich or powerful. Too many years of responsibility had erased any wish for power from his psyche. All he wanted now was the freedom to live his life without constantly being on his guard, constantly looking over his shoulder. He wanted to be able to sleep in his bed without every nerve being on the alert for the slightest sign of danger. Would he ever be blessed with this simple luxury, he wondered.

The kettle whistled as steam began to pour from the spout. Everything reached a climax in life, he thought ironically as he made himself a strong coffee and lit a cigarette, leaning over the stable door and gazing out without really seeing. Everything would come to a natural end in this life. But how this end was accomplished made a lot of difference. This he knew well.

*****

CHAPTER TWELVE

"Hey Kiddo I have seen the most perfect dress – or actually a choice of dresses. You just HAVE to come and look!" Gina's voice sailed down the telephone full of enthusiasm.

Carol sighed. "Oh, Gina, I am sick of looking. There is nothing out there that grabs me, it's either far too young and frilly or old and frumpy or 'mother-of-the-bride' sort of thing in peach with matching handbag and hat!"

"Well this lot sure are not." Gina announced firmly. "You just wait and see. I tell you they are definitely different and I would swear that you will love at least one of them – trust me!"

Carol glanced at her watch. Mid afternoon, not her favourite time for venturing out to the shops with all the crowds and screaming children being dragged unwillingly around by irate mothers. She had looked at so many dresses she was sick and tired of looking and had actually started to get to the stage where she wondered if she had been right at agreeing to a wedding at such short notice in the first place. The whole thing was starting to get rather depressing and had lost its sparkle somewhat. Oh well, if she had to look one more time then so be it. "Well where is this wonderful magic shop then?" She ventured, feeling that the battle was already lost.

"Well it's actually by the market." Gina replied tentatively. "But they are not cheap and tacky, believe me!" she rushed on. "If you want to go right now I will pick you up and we can go straight there and then straight back – no messing about and staring in other shop windows."

Carol knew she was on a losing battle with Gina. "Well, okay you got me. Straight there and back mind. I am worn out right now after that early morning run to Norwich and to be honest Kiddo I am fast losing heart with all this looking and finding nothing." Carol hauled herself out of the comfy chair and pushed Bruno to one side to search for her shoes.

"I think this will be worth it." Gina persevered. Get yourself ready and I will pick you up in ten minutes. Okay?"

Carol agreed and reluctantly took herself off up the stairs to run a brush through her hair and apply a dab of lipstick before Gina arrived. The search for a suitable dress was beginning to get on her nerves. In fact she was fast approaching the stage where she just might take her walk up the aisle in either jeans and trainers or her old - very old - faithful little black dress! Tony would not care. As long as the wedding took place he would be happy to slip the ring onto her finger regardless of what she was wearing. Although a little voice in the back of her head told her that she really did want to look as wonderful as possible. This was to be the one and only wedding for her and she knew she wanted it to be a happy day to remember for the rest of her life.

Tony had been delighted with her suggestion. He had carefully explained to Mamma Gina that he and Carol wanted a very quiet church service with no fuss but would love a huge family party a few weeks later to celebrate with all the family. Thankfully Mamma had been in full agreement. Secretly it had been worrying her that her eldest son might actually have one of those civil weddings that, in her eyes, was far from a proper marriage. To Mamma Gina a church was vital to make a marriage sacred, so she was thoroughly relieved to hear that Carol had found a way to be married properly. Mamma was happy with the arrangement - despite the fact that it was so far away. But a huge family party with singing and dancing and music and of course tables groaning with food, would be a perfect way to celebrate later on. Mamma was planning the menu already.

The paperwork for The Mill at Gretna was on Carol's dressing table. It looked wonderful. An intimate venue with a tiny chapel and stone built chalets all set around a quaint cobbled courtyard. It was like something out of a fairytale and only six short weeks away. Carol could hardly believe it. There was also a small bar with an intimate function room that had been booked for a celebratory meal after the wedding. Gina and Anna had conspired and taken the booking out of Carol's hands. She did not know for sure but guessed that they had arranged one or two special surprises for her and Tony's special day but kept up the pretence that she suspected nothing. All was arranged and all in place except for one thing. Her dress! The sound of Gina's car horn broke through her reverie. Oh well, thought Carol as she grabbed her bag and headed down the stairs. Last chance to find the gown of the year I suppose. But she held out little hope.

*****

The drive through the afternoon traffic was slow and arduous and frankly Carol could well have done without it, especially after a long day at work. Gina chattered happily along the way, full of enthusiasm about the dresses she had discovered.

Carol tried not to sound ungrateful but would much rather have been sitting at home with her feet up instead of contemplating the battle of making her way through the crowded market road with shoppers pushing past in all directions.

The girls managed to find a parking spot in a side street a short walk away from the market, Gina quickly seizing the opportunity as another car pulled out and disregarding the dark looks she was given by another driver who had been cruising along searching for a suitable spot.

"Not a hope in hell of getting parked up anywhere nearer this time of day." Gina remarked cheerfully locking the car and leading the way forward, ready to throw herself into the throng of shoppers. Carol followed behind, right now sadly lacking in enthusiasm and wishing she was at home soaking in the bath tub.

The shop looked rather un-inviting as they approached and the smell of curry from the Caribbean café next door did nothing to endear it to Carol's unenthusiastic mood right now but she dutifully followed Gina inside.

"Well – err *wow*!" Carol was taken aback at the long run of dresses on the back wall of the small shop, the like of which she had not come across in her futile search. "Gina, I must admit that I never expected anything like this!"

"I think they are either ballroom dance dresses or 'prom' dresses." Gina remarked with glee, hauling out a beautiful blue silken gown with a jewel encrusted bodice. "But who cares what their original destiny was - they are wonderful aren't they? - and just look at the price. Absolute peanuts. They are all but giving them away!" Her eyes were sparkling with delight.

Carol didn't answer. She had disappeared into the morass of swirling material and was standing on tiptoe to reach one of the hangers. With a gasp of breath she managed to unhook the chosen one and fall back out of the fray with her prize in her hand. "Now then – what do you think of this!" The gown was stunning. Brilliant red organza, falling in a multitude of shimmering flounces over a satin underskirt, the strapless bodice encrusted with gold beads. Gina turned to see Carols face alight with anticipation. "Well snap!" Gina laughed holding up the identical dress in royal blue. "Same style different colour!"

"Hmm. Carol held the two dresses together. I just adore this colour but RED with my hair. Maybe not!"

"Try them on - both of them, it costs nothing to have a try on so you might as well. I love them both and there are lots of others here that are definitely different. They all make a statement."

The girls gave up trying to fit into the rather pokey changing room together with both gowns and Gina's bump and sent for help in the shape of a tiny mini skirted shop assistant. "Well, at least she will fit into the changing room!" Gina whispered wickedly as the stick insect teenager led the way towards the row of cubicles.

Carol gave a twirl in the stunning royal blue. "Very nice." Gina remarked leaning back to get a better view. "Needs a little adjustment on the hem length but that's nothing. The bodice fits beautifully and as for the layers – they don't look over the top at all, in fact they look very Southern Belle and very you. Try the red one – you know you want to!"

Carol grinned mischievously and nipped back into the cubicle, the young assistant helping her with the zip as she shed the blue dress and stepped into the red one. "Wow! Well, that's all I can say. Wow, and Wow again!" Gina's eyes popped as Carol stepped out of the cubicle in the stunning red dress.

"I never would have thought that red would look so good on a lady with your colour hair!" The young assistant chimed in, as Carol stepped forward to twirl in front of the full length mirror, grasping her hair and piling it on top of her head as she spun. "But it does and you look amazing! Come and look Rita" The young girl called to another twig like assistant. "Come and see how gorgeous this lady looks in this dress!"

Carol suddenly found herself surrounded by admirers cooing over how lovely she looked in the stunning red dress. "Oh I love it!" She cried, her face alight with happiness as she turned, the golden beads on the bodice catching the light and shimmering like real jewels.

"I think it's the gold beading on the bodice that does the trick!" Gina remarked. "It breaks up the red, and I have to agree. It's absolutely stunning. You look a million dollars Kiddo!!"

"This is definitely the one!" Carol said with conviction. "I have never seen a dress like it and could not have even imagined it. It's wonderful, and I feel wonderful wearing it!" Carol enthused on. "I can see it with silver jewellery and silver shoes. I know just which shoes too. That lovely Indian shop just around the corner has some wonderful silver shoes that just drip with beads. I have to have them – in fact we can get them right now. Oh, Gina thank you, thank you for finding this shop. I had almost given up hope!" All her weariness forgotten, Carol's joy bubbled from her in waves.

Gina laughed as Carol continued to turn this way and that in front of the mirror. "Well, thank goodness for that is all I can say. I thought I was going to have to watch you walk down the aisle with your boots and jeans on at one point!"

"You were not far wrong there." Carol reluctantly made her way back into the cubicle to divest herself of her dream gown. "It had almost arrived at that until you found this shop, so that's all the problems solved!"

"Well, not all of them." Gina reminded her as Carol emerged from the cubicle and the young assistant made off towards the counter to wrap the dress. "We have to think about your flowers of course."

"With a dress like that the flowers will also have to be a statement. Pure white lilies in a long trailing spray. Stunning from head to foot. So while we are here we will get the shoes and also the silk flowers for the bouquet and we can make them up tonight. Oh, Gina I am suddenly so excited I can hardly wait!" Carol was ready for anything now.

Gina laughed. She was so happy to see her friend's enthusiasm sparkling in her eyes and it now looked like everything was well on track for the most wonderful wedding ever.

*****

Markov was not a young man. No longer was he match fit and honed to physical perfection. No one was more aware of this than Markov himself. The bearded giant stared into the bathroom mirror, partly obscured by steam from his shower. How long he had before his nemesis arrived there was no way of knowing, but he was using his time well. Each day he had taken an axe and gone into the wooded area behind the house, swinging the axe with supreme effort and hewing thick branches from the lower portions of the stronger trees and binding a strong rope around them before dragging them back to the outhouse where he chopped them into suitable logs for the fire.

He had disregarded the store of ready cut wood in favour of cutting his own. He had started with fallen branches and twigs, building up his muscles and strength by hauling them from the tangled undergrowth and clearing them of clinging brambles before tackling the stronger, thicker branches. At first he had found himself out of breath, his muscles aching with a burning pain that permeated throughout his body. Despite soaking his body in hot showers after each day of toil, he had awoken stiff and aching, his muscles screaming for mercy as he forced them into action once again. But as the days wore into weeks he was finding the work easier. He no longer had to stop at regular intervals to catch his breath and although he still broke out into a sweat as he worked, he found less difficulty in the work and was able to keep the axe swinging for hours on end.

He had also made a point of striding out daily. He had discovered a public footpath that began yards from the entrance to his driveway. A quiet path that took him in a semi-circle, out towards the headland then turning towards the village, cutting through fields and woodland and undulating in gradient. Once again the first walks were tiring, but now he found that he could take a walk before breakfast and another in the evening, even managing to jog some of the way and still be able to breathe at the end.

His evenings were spent in solitude. The first few nights in the farmhouse had been spent working on his salvaged piece of wood. He had peeled away the cracked bark to expose the fine grain of the wood, then carefully shaped and smoothed the intricately twisted piece into an object of beauty. As he worked on his sculpture his memory had floated back in time. He imagined himself as a small boy, sitting by his father's side as the older man taught him about the different trees of the forest. Taught him what wood was best for which purpose, instilling in the growing boy a deep and abiding respect for nature's bounty. The tall fir trees that had grown in abundance around his childhood village had provided fuel and furniture for all the people of the area, each man being proud of his skill with the carving tools that every villager used to make their homes well furnished from the surrounding forests. Markov had since found other interesting pieces of root and branch that he had brought back into the house to work on and by now had built up somewhat of a collection of finely polished and shaped pieces. Working with the familiar material had given him a sense of comfort. A feeling of ease and contentment as he whittled, honed and polished his pieces of wood, sitting quietly in the evenings as though all was well with the world.

He wiped a hand over the mirror to see more clearly. Stripped to the waist with only a towel wrapped around his hips he studied his reflection. The soft body was slowly giving way to a more solid and defined shape. His biceps had grown over the weeks and he could see the beginnings of a six pack starting to take shape in his abdomen. Raising his eyes he decided that the time had come to do something about the rest of his appearance. For too long he had hidden behind the thick, full growth of beard and wild hair. Here in Scotland he had not looked out of place, he had been surprised to notice. Many of the men strode around the small towns and villages, wearing their kilts with the ease of years and sporting a full set of whiskers which appeared to be the norm.

Markov had blended in well for the short time he had been resident in the area but now felt that a change was needed. He reached into the bathroom cupboard for scissors and a razor. Starting with his mass of unruly hair he began to chop, trimming the thickness around the back of his neck and making what best he could of the job of barber. The floor was littered with hair cuttings before he was satisfied that he had done enough. Although nothing similar to what could be classed as short back and sides, the finished result was what he had been hoping for. Still a thick mass of dark waves but neater and far less bohemian than before. The next part of his plan did not include him being seen around the area like a Rasputin look-alike. It had to appear, to his enemy at least, that he was attempting to conceal his identity.

Without further thought he started to trim the main body of his beard to as close to his chin as he dare without drawing blood. He carefully snipped until only a short, uneven stubble was left. Searching further into the cupboard he found the aerosol of shaving cream he had purchased for this moment and lathered up liberally, before taking the razor and scraping the remains of the hair from his face. When he was satisfied that no more stray hairs were stubbornly protruding from his chin he rinsed with copious amounts of water then stood back to survey the finished result.

It was disappointing to say the least. The skin on the lower part of his face had spent so many years covered by the dense undergrowth of beard it has lost all colour. Contrasting starkly with the weather-beaten upper half, the lower half of his face looked pallid and sickly, standing out as obviously newly shorn. It was not unexpected. Markov had been prepared for this and had used his initiative on his shopping expedition. Instant tan in a bottle. He had been treated to a puzzled look from the young shop assistant in the chemist where he had purchased his toiletries but had ignored her. In the past, there had been many times in his line of work where unorthodox steps had needed to be taken. He glanced at the instructions before smoothing the lotion over his exposed skin: it stung at first but he ignored the slight burning. It would no doubt take more than one application to reach the required results but he had time – which was the one thing he had plenty of. He also had the weather on his side. Wind and spring sunshine, coupled with the amount of time he spent outdoors would surely complete the job. Markov dropped the towel over the side of the bath and walked naked up the stairs and through to the small bedroom with the side window. He automatically stood well back from the frame and peered through. As usual, no sign of life. The odd car swooshed by on the small road but none had slowed or shown any interest in the secluded farmhouse. Any less experienced man would have been lulled into a sense of security, but Markov's wits grew more sharp by the day. He stood for a few moments staring out of the window, watching, listening and checking for any tiny sign that the gravel driveway had welcomed any visitors. The gate at the end of the driveway was neither closed tight or fully open.

He studied it for a moment to check that nobody had moved it from the position he had carefully placed it. Satisfied, he pulled a pair of cord trousers from the cupboard along with a thick woollen lumberjack shirt and dressed, pulling on his boots, and reaching for the quilted jacket he had purchased from the 'Highland Walking and Climbing Shop' in the nearby town. He would take his morning walk, then drive into town to replenish his supplies. He had no idea how long he would have to wait for his hunter to arrive, but wait he would – but not without a plentiful supply of coffee and cigarettes.

*****

CHAPTER THIRTEEN

Chaos reigned. Not that this was unusual when Katy arrived. Her sparkling personality and effervescent zest for life seemed to fill each room that she visited.

Carol had come home from her supermarket expedition and found her old mini parked in the yard next to Spyder's vividly painted pick-up truck. Katy had been delighted when Spyder had made the well loved old vehicle road worthy again and Carol had given it to her after she had passed her test.

Walking into the hallway Carol had negotiated around the bulging back-pack that had been dropped haphazardly in the hallway and followed the sound of laughter into the kitchen.

"Look who's here!" Spyder swung an arm dramatically, though rather unnecessarily toward Katy who was peering hopefully into the rather bare kitchen cupboards.

"Mum!" Katy leapt across and flung her arms about Carol. "Surprise! Aren't you just *thrilled* to see me?"

Carol held Katy at arm's length so that she could get a good look at her adored daughter. "Of course I am darling, and you look wonderful, a picture of healthy living!" Katy was indeed an advert for a healthy lifestyle. Dressed in lightweight walking shoes and combat trousers, a plain linen blouse tucked into the slim waist and a lightweight fleece slung casually over her shoulders, Carol had to admit that her daughter had developed into one of those people who could look effortlessly elegant despite her casual dress. She hugged Katy back close. "I am always happy to see you Sweet Pea, as you well know!" Carol and Katy eventually disentangled themselves from each other as Spyder filled the kettle to make tea.

"Is there anything to eat?" Katy enquired hopefully opening yet another cupboard door. "I'm starving!" Katy always arrived starving!

"Well if you ever bothered to give me some warning about your impending arrival then I just might be able to get something to eat in stock before you arrive." Carol admonished, fishing mugs out of the top cupboard as the kettle came to the boil. "But as luck would have it, I have just got back from shopping so if you would like to help me unload the Chevy I think we may be able to rustle up a crumb or two for your poor little empty tummy!"

"Oh, we'll do it!" Katy made for the door. "Come on Spyder, give me a hand and Mum can make the tea!" Spyder shrugged with a happy grin and followed Katy out of the door like an obedient puppy. Carol smiled. It seemed that nobody that had ever met Katy had not fallen under her spell and it seemed that the whole world loved her as much as she did herself. But Katy was a lovely girl, Carol thought proudly. She was open and friendly and full of life and eager to help anybody who needed it. Carol was thoroughly proud of her daughter and secretly gave herself a small pat on the back for being her mother.

*****

"Oh lovely, Feta cheese!" Katy slid the soft white cheese out of the packet and cut some into squares and threw them on top of the bowl of salad. "Stuffed olives as well?" She enquired.

"Yes please." Carol answered. "Pile it on. You can never have too much in a good mixed salad can you?" She laid out thickly sliced ham onto a platter and plonked it in the middle of the table next to a plate of thickly cut fresh bread and a large fruit cake.

"I had better not make a pig of myself right now." Spyder remarked rather mournfully. "Suzie has threatened me with one of her spaghetti Bolognaise's when I get home and if I don't eat at least three buckets full she will think I have gone off her cooking!"

"Suzie spoils you rotten as we all know, but you'll work it off this afternoon anyway." Katy remarked quickly. "You said you would check my car over so that will burn up a few calories I am sure."

Spyder laughed. "Well said miss, so if I go pop later I will blame you." He helped himself to a slice of bread and ham and piled the fresh salad on the side.

"Gill said she would bring the boys around later." Katy remarked. "I gave her a quick ring when I got here. I am dying to see how the boys have grown." Gill had been Carols neighbour when she had first moved up to London and had been a good friend to her and Katy when they were first settling into the strange area. Katy loved Gills small boys and rarely visited without a small gift for them. "I suppose little David still thinks that Thomas O'Malley is his kitten?" Katy giggled.

"Oh yes." Carol replied. "Without a doubt. Whenever I bump into them he asked if his cat is well and am I looking after him properly. He also says when they move into a house with a garden then Thomas will be able to move in with them."

"Well, as they are not moving yet it is not a problem." Katy remarked through a mouthful of thick bread, dipped in fresh olive oil.

"To be honest I cannot see Gill and Frank moving anywhere for a long, long time." Carol replied. "She did mention some time last year that it maybe a good idea to get somewhere with more room and a garden but they seem perfectly happy living in that little rented flat above the shops. Personally, it would drive me insane, but Gill seems to take it all in her stride and just take life as it comes. I know when I lived next door to them I only ever felt that it was a stepping stone to better things."

"Yes, I know you did Mum." Katy took another piece of fresh crusty bread and dipped it into the pot of olive oil. "But everyone is different. You have always wanted better things and a better lifestyle and looked to improve your life all the time, while other people are happy with what they have and where they are. I don't know if that's right or wrong but just let's say some people have different ambitions than others. Not lower or higher – just different."

"I never really thought of myself as madly ambitious." Carol said thoughtfully. "I just always knew that I wanted something good in my life and had no intention of settling for second best. We can all have what we want if we push hard enough for it I suppose."

Oh I do so agree." Said Katy. "All I am saying is that we all have ambitions on different levels. There are no two of us exactly alike so why would we all want the same things. For example, to some people perfection is a small flat in an expensive high rise with a good view and a concierge downstairs. Others people long for a rambling farmhouse and lots of land, whereas others once again like a busy city centre. As long as we all get what we want nobody can complain."

"Well, I for one would like a place with a bigger garage." Spyder put in. But Suzie is happy with our nice little three bedroom semi and, as she keeps pointing out we do have one large garage and if I had more I would only go out and fill it with more cars so what's the point?"

Carol laughed. "Well there you are then. Your life is pretty perfect. Suzie has the house she is happy in with a nice garden for the children to play in and you have all the room in the world here to fiddle with your mechanics so peace on earth as they say."

"That is my point exactly." Katy added. "We are all happy with different things and if Gill is happy to live in that little flat with her family then why worry? If she was unhappy I could see a point in feeling sorry for her but she is not unhappy is she? In fact she never seems to worry about a thing. She does not even have to worry about having a kitten for little David. You have him here!" Katy giggled. "So there you are – I rest my case!"

Carol nodded in agreement. "I don't suppose Thomas would want to move house anyway now – he would miss Bruno and Digger far too much." Bruno pricked up his ears at the sound of his name as he lay under the table, the black and white Digger curled up between his paws.

"Yes they are certainly joined at the hip those two." Carol agreed. "It's lovely how animals make friends just like we do."

"Except that animals are probably a lot more loyal to their friends that some people are." Katy replied fervently. "Animals were too underestimated in my mind. They have a depth of feeling that some people just don't understand – and they should."

"I agree." Spyder put in. "You know where you are with animals. If they like you they will love you regardless of who you are, what you look like, or what you do. If they don't like you they will show it. No half measures. I have never met an animal yet that is two faced. But people..... Now there's another matter!"

"Oh, absolutely!" Carol could not agree more. "I have learned from bitter experience that some people just cannot be trusted however nice you think they are. Then again, there are some people who are really good when you need it and it's often the people you least expect to be. It's true what they say – you find out who your friends are only when you are in trouble!"

As everyone nodded in silent agreement a flurry of ginger and white fur flew through the back door and hurled itself onto the table amongst the plates.

"Get off!"

"Scram you dirty little beast!"

"Watch the paws on the bread – Yewwwww! What were we saying about animals being so flaming wonderful?" Carol leapt to her feet and scooped Thomas O'Malley under the belly and whisked him off the table, dropping him firmly onto the floor. "You bad cat! You know you are not allowed up on the table!" she admonished. Thomas totally ignored her and strolled over to the food bowl as Katy and Spyder collapsed with laughter.

"And that's another thing you can always rely on!" Spyder spluttered through a mouthful of hastily chewed bread and ham. "They will always show you up without fail when you least expect it!"

Carol sighed in agreement as she searched the table for stray cat hairs before any could be inadvertently swallowed. "Honestly! What a pest! Now if little David says he wants that flaming Thomas O'Malley to take home today, I just might be tempted to bag him up and send him over, like right now!!"

Katy giggled. "She always used to say that about Bruno when he was little – and me too for that matter! She used to threaten to sell me to the goblins. But I never believed her and anyway, it sounded fun living in goblin city." She grinned. "But everyone knows she is all talk. She loves us all really."

Carol pulled a face. "Only because I am a complete saint young lady!" She wiped down every spare bit of space on the table and made sure there were no traces of paw prints or cat hairs. "There were times when you and Bruno drove me mad – dashing into the house and trailing mud all over my newly cleaned floors then dashing back out to collect some more!"

"Hmm, saint she says." Katy twinkled at Spyder. "This coming from a woman who has announced her intention of walking down the aisle in the devils own colour!"

"Aha!" Carol grinned at her daughter. "I knew that was what this visit was about. You have come to give my wonderful dress your seal of approval."

Katy grinned sheepishly. "Well, erm yes, I do want to see it. Your description over the phone was – err ... well not clear." She finished diplomatically.

Carol stifled a giggle. She knew exactly what Katy was thinking. She had described the dress as best she could over the telephone, but in retrospect she had to admit even to herself that it did sound a bit outlandish when described in that way. Row upon row of red frills with a gold encrusted bodice. It did sound rather reminiscent of a pantomime dame – or worse still a drag queen.

"Well, okay then. As soon as you have finished stuffing your face and Gill gets here we will go and have a full dress rehearsal – you are not the only one that's dying to see it you know. Gill can't wait."

Spyder pushed away his empty plate. "Well, thanks for that Boss." He smiled. "I had better get back out there and check out Madams' car before those two little boys get here and want to 'help' me. If that happens it could take all day." he laughed.

Carol smiled. She appreciated Spyder's patience with visiting children and also appreciated the fact he would keep the boys occupied while she showed off her wedding dress to her friend and her daughter. But having three children of his own at home he was certainly not short of hands on experience with small boys.

Carol and Katy set about clearing the table and filling the kettle yet again to replenish their coffee mugs. "So this is really it now Mum." Katy remarked, running hot water into the sink and dropping in the plates. "No changing your mind now you have bought the dress!" She eyed her mother sideways as she spoke.

Carol smiled. "No way would I have changed my mind even if I was wearing a sack." She replied. "Yes, I am happy and yes, I have thought about it and yes, I am very sure I am doing the right thing!"

Katy raised her eyebrows in mock innocence. "Now did I query that for one moment. I am shocked and hurt that you would even think such a thing Mother!" Katy stuck her nose in the air and started to pile the clean dishes onto the draining board.

Carol laughed. "Well I know for sure that you think the world of Tony so that's one huge hurdle out of the way. I knew you were never keen on Nick."

"No wonder – he wasn't the nicest person on earth was he." Katy pulled a face as she remembered Carol's ex boyfriend. "But I knew it would not take you long to see through him and as I was living away at Uni it was hardly my business and anyway – if he had made you happy I would have made the effort to like him. But you are well out of that Mum and Tony is in a different league altogether – he is one of life's really nice people and I am so glad you and he are going to make it a permanent thing. Marriage even. Wow!" Katy searched in the drawer for a clean tea towel and started to dry, handing the plates to Carol to stack into the cupboard. "And Gretna Green too! My dear old down to earth mum has turned into a real romantic!"

Carol beamed widely. "Yes, it's going to be lovely isn't it? And the fact that you like Tony so much makes things perfect. – and you my darling have turned into one of life's 'nice' people yourself so I personally feel very blessed with my family and friends."

"Speaking of friends I can hear the chatter of happy voices." Kate leaned forward and peered round sideway through the window. "Yep, it's Gill, she heard that kettle come to the boil. I'll shout the boys and give Spyder half a chance to get stuck into the car."

A flurry of feet and paws heralded the entrance of Bruno with Gills two small boys in hot pursuit. The kitchen was suddenly filled with the sound of exited voices as little David demanded to see 'his' kitten and Frank junior started to search for Bruno's ball to play in the garden.

Katy took little David by the hand as they went in search of Thomas O'Malley and Frank Junior happily ran into the garden with Bruno.

Gill divested herself of her coat and plonked down at the table. "Well then, not long now is it?" she beamed happily helping herself to a biscuit as Carol poured the tea.

"Two and a half weeks, and counting." Carol replied with a smile. "I can't believe these last weeks have flown by so fast!" Indeed she could not. It only seemed like yesterday that she and Gina had been sitting in her old home with Andy and Anna printing off details of the wedding venue and now things were flying by so fast she felt her feet were not touching the floor.

"Any second thoughts Honey?" Gill asked seriously. "Not that I am trying to worry you or anything." She rattled on quickly "but I do think a lot of you, you know, and I do so want you to be happy – not just now but for the long term."

Carol smiled as she sat down at the table with the two steaming mugs of tea. "That is really lovely of you to say Gill but no - no second thoughts at all. I can honestly say I have never felt anything was so right. Right for me that is. I always feel so safe when I am with Tony and I don't ever worry that he does not feel the exact same way about me, because I can feel that he does. We just feel comfortable together."

"Well that's important." Gill replied. "Frank and I had been friends since school days and to be honest it never crossed my mind to be any more than friends for many years. Just like brother and sister really. In our teens we used to knock about together – going bowling or off to football matches together as well as parties and things. We even used to go camping together – sharing a tent in all weathers. We did have a laugh I have to say." Gill giggled at the memory. "I never thought of phoning a girl friend to go out and about with, it was always Frank I would call on. Same with him too. He used to have other friends, like the guys he played football with, but it always seemed like he and I were together most of the time. I hadn't thought anything about it really until one day his Dad said something about us never getting the chance to meet anybody to get serious with if we kept going about together. It dawned on us then that we didn't want to meet anybody else so we just got married!"

Carol had never heard that story before. "That's a really lovely tale Gill!" She said with a smile. "I never knew that you and Frank went back so far. Lovely really to marry your best friend. How perfect."

"And the nicest thing I suppose is that we are still best friends." Gill smiled. "I can't ever think of being married to anybody other than Frank – It just would not feel right!"

"I think that's really romantic" Carol said with feeling. To be married to your best friend. It sounded perfect and Tony was certainly a friend as well as a lover. Carol was sure of that.

"Oh Frank and I have our moments!" Gill replied with a grin reaching for another shortbread biscuit and dipping it into her tea. "But Gretna Green! Well that's a real bit of romance I must say. So come on – show me all the leaflets on the venue and then show me this dream gown. This is a real treat that I am just dying to see!"

*****

"Oh, Mum – it's lovely!" Katy was genuinely taken aback at the sight of her mother wearing the beautiful gown.

"Absolutely!" Gill agreed. "Give us a twirl then."

Carol twirled. The layers of the dress swished gently around her ankles as the brilliant gold beading caught the light from the window and reflected in the long mirror. Katy was admiring the choice of jewellery. The silver necklace and bracelet and the discreet tiara complimented the outfit to perfection and the silver shoes sparkled with droplets of pearls and diamantes as they peeked from underneath the dress.

The matching wedding rings that Carol and Tony had chosen where nestled safely into a velvet lined ring box. Both perfectly plain traditional wedding bands. Heavy and smooth with Tony's band being slightly heavier than Carols – otherwise a perfect pair.

Gill handed Carol the bouquet to hold. "Perfect!" She announced standing back and clasping her hands together as she drank in the sight of Carol in her full bridal splendour.

The bouquet of pure white lilies cascaded almost to the ground, interspersed with delicate green leaves and sprays of tiny seed pearls which looked striking against the scarlet of the dress. "Absolutely stunning my dear. A wonderful choice. What do you think Katy?" Gills voice was full of admiration.

"Yes, wonderful." Katy agreed. "I have to admit, when Mum described this dress over the phone I thought she had taken a funny turn – or was teasing me - but when I see it 'in the flesh' as it where I could not agree more. Its stunning and it suits mums personality down to the ground."

Carol laughed. "You really should have more faith in my dress sense you awful child!" She turned around so that Katy could unzip the dress. "And anyway, Gina was with me when we chose it so I doubt that she would have let me walk down the aisle looking anything less than just right."

Katy had to agree as she helped fold the dress back into the dust proof dress covers and hung it carefully over the back of the bedroom door so that it could hang without fear of creases.

"Tony is barred from this particular bedroom" Carol announced as she closed the door firmly. "I am making sure he has no idea whatsoever about my outfit. I want it to be a complete surprise on the day."

"Of course. It's part of the joy of the day seeing the look on the grooms face when the bride walks down the aisle to meet him at the alter." Said Gill as they trooped down the stairs. "Oh, do they have an aisle and an alter in Gretna Green?"

"Carol laughed. "Yes of course they have an aisle. The venue is really beautiful. Apparently the groom goes ahead as is normal then a piper in a kilt comes and escorts the bride to the chapel, piping her along the way and all the way down the aisle. It sounds lovely and at the end of the service they bang the anvil with a hammer. All traditional stuff."

"Well, as long as you don't forget the rings in all this excitement." Gill laughed.

Absolutely not!" Carol replied fervently. "That is Katy's department. She is giving me away and is also ring bearer and my general maid of all work for the day so if the rings are lost and we have to use pieces of tied string it will all be her fault!"

Katy sniffed. "My fault indeed!" The first I will see of the rings is when I get there with Andy and Anna on the day. So it is you, Mother darling, that has the responsibility of getting everything to the venue in one piece. All I am doing is helping Anna to take care of the cake on its travels, which – I have to announce – is looking like a work of art, but it's also a surprise so I am sworn to secrecy!"

Gill called to the boys and slipped on her coat. "Well, thank you for the preview Honey and so glad to see you looking so happy. I will be calling back in a few days as I have something I want to show you but right now I have get home. Frank is finishing early and he does like me there when he gets home – the big softie. If I am not in I get the sad puppy dog expression for hours after!"

Carol hugged her old friend then she and Katy saw her to the door, waving to the little boys as they scampered through the yard towards the road and the bus stop. "Phew, that was hectic!" Carol remarked not unkindly, the house feeling suddenly silent now the exuberant children had left. "Well, now the dress rehearsal is over and you are now satisfied a that I am not going to show you up at the wedding we can sit down and have a good old gossip." Carol was always eager to hear what her adventurous daughter had been up to. "I want to know all about what you have been up to and what you plan to do next." She

announced, leading the way back to the kitchen. A long gossip always meant a plentiful supply of tea and biscuits and today was going to be no exception.

"And I am going to show you my latest recipe too." Katy announced. "Tonight we are having cheese and onion bread and butter pudding for dinner, served up with roast potatoes."

"Cheese and onion Bread and butter pudding!" Carol raised an eyebrow. "That's different."

"Well being a starving student you get used to making cheap meals and this one is to die for believe me." Katy licked her lips. "You start off in the usual way with buttered bread triangles in a dish but instead of jam and sugar and raisins and things you put grated cheese and onion between the layers. When you pour on the egg and milk and cook in the oven it comes up just like a cheese soufflé – believe me its wonderful."

Karol had to admit it sounded nice. "Well in that case my darling, tonight the kitchen is all yours!"

*****

CHAPTER FOURTEEN

The morning was bright and fresh with a strong breeze blowing from the sea. The smell of ozone lifted Markov's spirits as he strode out strongly, marching along the gravel path on his morning route. The days were beginning to become monotonous. Markov knew that he must not let himself slip into a false sense of security. The killer was out there. By now he would know that Markov was in the area and be making his own enquiries to track him down. The monotony of each day must not be allowed to dull the edge of the big man's wits. He must be ready at any time. The moment would come, maybe today, maybe next month but come it would, Markov knew this well.

As he rounded the bend by the headland his attention was caught by the yapping of a dog. Markov stopped and listened. The yapping continued. It was not the deep bark of a farm dog, this animal sounded small, hardly one that would be used for sheep or guard duty. Immediately on his guard for any occurrence that was out of the ordinary, the back of Markov's neck tingled with anticipation. Every nerve ending was alive as adrenaline kicked in. In all the weeks of his stay he had not met another soul along this deserted path and certainly not heard or seen any dogs. He stood still and listened carefully. The yapping seemed close by but he could see no sign of the animal. Cautiously he stepped forward towards the rocky outcrop overlooking the sea. Behind a clump of bracken he spotted the beast. A small brindle dog, smaller than the average cat, was lying behind a clump of long leaves, whimpering and yapping and peering down over the rocks. Curiosity took over as Markov stepped nearer, only then did he notice a knitted scarf lying by the dog. Ignoring the animal he took another step forward then saw a woman slumped by the rocks on the steep incline below him.
As he approached the woman looked up. "Och hello man!" She sounded none the worse for wear despite her predicament. "Am I glad to see a human face. I seem to be in a bit of bother and if you would not mind lending a hand…..?"

Markov looked around him. Was this a trap. An elaborate ruse to catch him off guard? There did not seem any place that another person could be secreted directly nearby so Markov turned his attention back to the woman. "Madame, you are hurt?"

"Och, not really man." The woman was exceptionally cheerful considering her situation. "I just took a short tumble and ricked my ankle. Was just waiting for the pain to ease before scrambling back up again. But I would appreciate a little help as you are here man!" This lady was obviously not the sort to dwell on her disabilities.

Markov took one more look around before dropping to one knee and reaching his hand down the steep incline for the woman to grasp and hauling her up next to him on the path.

"Och thank you, man, that saved me a lot of hard work!" The woman leaned on Markov's arm as she pulled herself to her feet, wincing with pain as she tentatively tried to stand. She was small and plump with short brown hair that curled around what once had been a pretty girlish face. Now, although no longer a young woman, she still had bright eyes and a ready smile. "I don't often see another soul along this track." The woman chatted on, still holding onto Markov's arm and trying to regain her balance despite the small dog leaping around her feet. "That is part of the attraction of walking here." She continued, "But thank the good lord that you were here this day. It would have been very painful to clamber back over those rocks all by myself." She smiled warmly once more, leaning her head back in order to meet the tall man's gaze. "If I could trouble you to hand me one of those stout branches over there." She pointed to some fallen wood lying along the side of the path. "I will detain you no longer and make my way home."

"How far have you to travel?" Markov had no idea why he asked the question. He did not make a habit of involving himself in any other person's life and especially under the circumstances he was now living under his own words took him by surprise.

"Och, only around a mile and a half away, not at all far." The cheerful tones sounded as though it were simply a few yards. "I will soon be there and able to strap up this ankle and get on with things."

"That distance will seem longer with an injured ankle Madame." The words seem to come out of their own accord. "I must assist you, please, show me the way." Markov had no idea why he was getting involved with this woman. It was against all his instincts, but for some reason he wanted to do this small act of kindness. Maybe it was the friendly, open smile of his new acquaintance or maybe it was the normality of the situation. Being able to speak without being on his guard, in fact speaking at all after weeks of isolation. Being able to act normally and help a fellow human being without fear of the consequences. He glanced around once more. There did not seem to be any other person in sight, just the two of them, standing alone on the headland. He slipped an arm around the woman's middle – it could hardly be called a waist – and held her close as they turned in the direction she indicated.

The journey took some time. Rhona Kirkpatrick chatted cheerfully despite the obvious discomfort of her twisted ankle but asked little about Markov or his reasons for being in the vicinity. Eventually the pair turned off the public footpath onto a smaller track leading to an old stone cottage. The cottage was completely hidden from the main footpath by thick woodland and a tall overgrown hedge bordering a small cottage garden with a copious vegetable plot. Markov noted that the door was unlocked as he helped his companion into the cosy living room, the tiny dog bolting through and taking up residence on a well worn chair by the fireside.

"Thank you so much Mr Marek." Rhona announced gratefully sinking into her armchair. "I appreciate you going out of your way to help me and trust I have not put you to too much inconvenience." Markov had of course introduced himself by his recently adopted alias.

"No inconvenience Madame." Markov bowed slightly. "My time, for the moment is my own, so an extended walk is of no consequence. If you are sure you are completely recovered enough to be left I will bid you farewell."

What lovely manners you European gentleman have." Rhona smiled, lifting her injured leg onto a tapestry covered foot stool.

Markov hesitated, then turned to help her ease her foot out of the stout walking shoe. "You have met many European gentlemen Mrs Kirkpatrick?" The question was not as idle as it sounded.

"Och, no, Mr Marek. It was simply a general observation as I see it. I have never met any other man with such an attractive accent, in fact I rarely see anybody at all. I am what some folks would call a bit of a hermit, but it is simply that I prefer my own company than the company of those gossiping women who live in the villages. I like to be alone and get on with my own life." Markov noted that Rhona Kirkpatrick was obviously not one to be idle. All about the small room where strewn pieces of cloth in the process of being stitched together in intricate patterns. A large cardboard box stood by the hearth filled to the brim with spools of gaily coloured cotton threads, needles and scissors. An easel stood by the side of the window holding a half finished painting while other handicraft items spilled over the dresser.

"I can understand that well, Mrs Kirkpatrick." Markov placed the shoe by the chair and straightened up. He noticed that the low ceilings in the cottage were only just high enough to accommodate his not banging his head as he did so. "I too enjoy solitude, and now, if you are comfortable I will leave you to recover in peace."

Rhona Kirkpatrick thanked him once again, smiling warmly as she bade him good day. Markov ducked under the low door frame and left the cottage. Striding quickly forward he made his way back to the more familiar path and set off in the direction of his temporary home. Today had been a break in the monotony of his routine and Markov found that it had cheered his spirits somewhat. It had made him feel almost normal to speak to another human being without choosing every word. In fact he realised that he had said very little to the woman all the time he had been in her company. She had done most of the talking herself and had not pried into his own business at all. She told him her name and he in turn had told her his – or rather the name he had adopted – but other than that he had revealed nothing about himself and it appeared that his companion was not one to pry. She had not asked where he had come from or what he was doing in the area, or even where he was staying. It was a rare breed of woman that was not curious about her fellow beings. Markov stiffened slightly. Why had she asked him nothing? Was she a plant? Was she there to lure him into a false sense of security. He puzzled the thought as he turned off the footpath and walked the few yards along the road towards his driveway.

She had seemed a very self contained woman. Markov had no doubt that she would have managed to make her way home alone despite her injury and taken the events of the day in her stride. She certainly did not seem the type to wait for rescue: she would have taken charge of her own problems and dealt with them. Also she had not been overly curious about her rescuer – or gushingly grateful either, he noted. She had thanked him and waved him on his way. Other women would have asked for further help he was sure. A telephone call to a relative or friend or at least a doctor, or asked for a drink to be laid near to hand. Rhona Kirkpatrick had asked for none of this. Markov felt a small twinge of guilt that he had not offered, but taking time to do as much as he had done was something of a diversion from his usual mode of life, and had this been part of an elaborate plan to lure him into a trap then the woman's behaviour would surely be on par – or would it? If it were a trap then surely the woman would have asked more of him. Asked him to return the following day or maybe................

Markov could not think any further about it. Whichever way he looked at it, the situation could be either an elaborate plot to trap him or simply that a decent, middle aged and very tough and independent Scottish lady had fallen and he had helped her. Nothing more nothing less and nothing sinister about it. He would forget it for the moment. Maybe it was time to stop thinking the worse all the time, but he knew that right now he had to keep thinking that way. Had to keep on his guard at all times. However tempting it was to relax and live what could be called a normal life was not an option right now.

Out of habit he stopped at the gate and measured the exact position he had left it in on his way out. The last rung of the gate was exactly over the same stone. Just the way he had set it on his way out. Nobody had called on him that day.

He flung the gate wide and made for the farmhouse. He would make a cup of strong coffee, smoke a cigarette then drive into the town for his supplies. While he was there he would buy a detailed map of the immediate area. The type that shows all the side tracks, houses and cottages and mark their position. He would also spend some time in the local library searching the parish records. Rhona Kirkpatrick would surely be recorded there and so he would learn a little more about his recently met acquaintance. If there were no records of her existence then that too would tell him all he needed to know.

*****

"Of course something had to go wrong!" Carol sighed holding the phone under her chin as she ran the tap to rinse her coffee cup and lean forward to peer out of the window to make sure Bruno was not still trying to tunnel to Australia under the old privy shed. "But I suppose it could have been worse."

"A lot worse!" Gina's confident tone down the telephone line brooked no argument. "Falling from the catwalk of a trailer can cause real injury, Tony could have been badly hurt and then the wedding would have had to be postponed for - well lord knows how long. At least he is on his feet with nothing broken."

"Thank the good lord for that – Amen!" Carol replied fervently plonking herself down onto one of the kitchen chairs. "But it's not like Tony at all to be careless; he is usually the most careful person around trucks and machinery. This just had to be a fluke accident."

"Hmm - according to Jeff the olive oil must have spilled a bit when the barrel broke." Gina continued referring to a small and what was then an insignificant incident of a spilt barrel of olive oil. "If it leaked onto the catwalk it would have been pretty unnoticeable until poor Tony stepped onto it and lost his footing."

"Certainly a freak accident." Said Carol. "Who would have thought a small thing like a drop of olive oil on a mesh catwalk could have caused such a slip?"

"Jeff said if he had managed to grab the safety handle as his foot slipped that would have been the end of it but he missed it by a fraction and just went down, hitting his back on the metal as he fell."

"Ouch! I can't bear to even thing about it. It must have hurt like hell, he was white as a sheet when he got back here poor darling." Carol still cringed at the thought. "But it's been three days now so I think the worse is over, but he is still pretty stiff and of course getting bored out of his mind. Tony is not used to not doing something all the time."

"Well that's a blessing. If he is bored it proves he is on the mend." Gina agreed.

"Well, as we say it could have been worse" said Carol "But Tony is really upset that it could affect the wedding day. I told him not to be so silly and just sit about and rest. There is nothing worse than a bad back and he has torn the muscles all down one side so is walking a bit crab-like, but at least he is actually walking, although right now he has wandered out to the yard to chat to Spyder, but I am keeping an eye on him to make sure he isn't doing anything strenuous."

"Oh, don't worry – Spyder will make sure he doesn't do anything like that, he's a sensible lad. Of course this will change a few plans, but nothing we can't work around." Gina was being decisive. "We have three days before we have to drive down to Scotland and Jeff has come up with the best idea I think"

"Good! I am open to any and all suggestions right now" Carol replied heartily. "Whatever we can do to get there right now!"

"Well, although you have finished all the deliveries and parked the trucks up for the wedding week, Jeff suggested that you take the Flying Angel down to Scotland instead of going by car. That way you can do the driving and Tony can lay on the bunk for the journey and that way it will help his back. Bruno can go with you in the cab too and have much more room – seeing as you insist he be there at your wedding - and he could use the cab as a kennel while we are all there. More room for him than sleeping in the car even though it's only two nights, so no real probs is there?"

"Gina that's a brilliant idea. Tell Jeff he has won the top prize for solving problem of the week!" Carol laughed. "What a good idea. Of course that would be wonderful and would be so much better for poor Tony. Travelling any distance with a bad back is not good at the best of times but why suffer when we have a bed on wheels that he can use. Well done Jeff!" Carol repeated "I am impressed. And as Bruno has seen me through bad times and good both Tony and I agree that he should be part of the family on our big day. Even the venue have agreed to him being in the chapel, although they do have strict 'No Dogs' rule in the chalets so we had planned on him sleeping in the car, but the truck, as you say is a far better option. Yes that's a brilliant idea but I don't know what the people at the Mill will think about having a truck parked there."

"They don't mind at all Kiddo." said Gina. "I phoned them straight away and asked. I also told them that as you and Tony were two truckers getting married we all thought having the truck there instead of a Rolls Royce was far more in keeping and they were fine about it."

"Goodness you are on the ball today." Carol laughed. "You are my wedding organiser supremo – although hats off to Jeff for the truck idea in the first place!"

"Oh, my lovely husband has his moments!" Gina giggled. "I will tell him you are pleased and that will make him insufferable for at least a week but I think we can live with it don't you?"

"Most definitely!" Carol replied with conviction. "But when he has had his week of glory we will put him back in place!" The girls laughed. The worry of Tony's accident had put a damper on the wedding preparations but at least they had come up with what would pass as a half way suitable solution.

"I have also been on the phone to Anna and it seems the wedding cake is her masterpiece to date." Gina announced with delight.   She and Anna were spending many hours on the phone conspiring for Carol and Tony's big day.

"Well, I expected no less from Anna." Carol replied truthfully. "The girl is an artist in more ways than one and if the cake is anything like her paintings it will be beautiful." Carol had no niggling doubts that the cake would be anything less than perfect.

All the other plans were in place and so far working well. Carol had been determined to keep the fuss down to a minimum and had insisted that the wedding would be a happy simple affair. Even so it had been planned a little like a military operation as travelling to Scotland from London was not exactly around the corner.

Derek had laughingly offered them the use of one of his coaches to transport everyone to Gretna but, as Carol pointed out, as the wedding party would be so small and half of them setting off from halfway up the country to start with it hardly seemed worth it.

Carol and Tony and Jeff and Gina were to arrive at the venue the day before the wedding and had reserved a small chalet each at the Mill itself for two nights. As Carol had said, a little holiday with no rushing about will do them all good and staying right inside the venue where she could simply walk the few strides to the tiny chapel would be perfect and cut out any need for wedding cars and the like.

A further family chalet was booked for Katy to share with Andy and Anna and the baby for the night of the wedding. Katy would be travelling to Scotland on the day of the wedding with Andy and Anna and was already bursting with excitement and bombarding her mother with calls to check that all was organised and nothing had been forgotten.

The only other guests were Spyder and his wife Suzie who were also arriving on the day of the wedding and staying overnight in a small bed and breakfast cottage a few yards down the road as the chalets had all been taken. But as Spyder had pointed out, any place away from home would be a treat for himself and Suzie while his Mother took care of the children, so it seemed that everyone was looking forward to a thoroughly enjoyable day.

Carol whistled to Bruno who bounded into the kitchen, tongue lolling and paws covered with mud.   "You are a pain!" Carol admonished him and grabbed an old towel and wiped the worst of the mud from his paws before he managed to spread it around every spare inch of floor he could reach before making her way up the stairs to the empty spare bedroom that she was using to store her wedding finery.

Her wedding dress was hanging behind the door, carefully covered with two cheap plastic dress covers then once again with a heavier opaque zipped gown cover. She had no intention of letting Tony have the tiniest peek and spoil the surprise on the day. He had no idea what she would be wearing and she was sure the colour would be the last thing he expected.

Her silver shoes were packed into a tissue lined box and her bouquet slid carefully inside a black plastic bin liner. She checked once again that all was ready. Suitcase packed with everyday clothes and her jewellery box tucked down the side. A small make up bag and her brushes and combs and of course her shampoo. No professional make up artist for her on the day. Carol was quite happy to set her own hair and apply her usual amount of make up sparingly. She had no intention of changing from the 'real' her to walk down the aisle any more than she would her beloved Tony to look any different – although she was hoping and praying that he would at least be able to stand upright while they exchanged vows!

She checked her jewellery. A discreet silver tiara headband with tiny diamantes catching the light. A silver filigree bracelet and matching choker necklace with tiny diamond droplets. Very understated. She did wonder for a moment if it were all too understated but decided that at this late stage if it wasn't ready then it would have to be left out. The dress surely was statement enough. She checked once again that she had packed socks and underwear for Tony as well as his new Italian leather shoes and the perfectly tailored suit that his brother Marco had insisted on buying for him. The suit was certainly a triumph of Italian design as even the most inexperienced eye could see and Carol had been choked with pride at how handsome Tony had looked in it when he had modelled it for her approval.

"Weddings are certainly an occasion when women are in sole charge, I see Cara Mia!" He had teased her when she had insisted on him giving both herself and Gina full dress rehearsal. "We men have to be checked and approved by the ladies but heaven help us if we dare to glimpse the bridal gown a moment before the service!"

Bruno's barking and the ding-dong of the doorbell interrupted Carols though. She bounded down the stairs. "Gill! What a lovely surprise."

Bruno bounced up and down with delight as Carol's old friend bustled through the door, laden with shopping bags.

"I can't stay long Honey!" Gill dumped her bags in the hallway and followed Carol through to the kitchen. "Just been for a few bits to keep the brood fed until the big shop this weekend but wanted to call in and wish you the very best of luck my darling – I know you really deserve it and I know you will be happy!"

As Carol clicked the kettle on to boil Gill produced a small box from her pocket. "I remembered this and thought of you!" She announced. "If you don't like it then no problem but if you do then wear it with my love. Something borrowed and all that"

Carol took the box and looked inside. The most stunning bracelet lay inside nestled on a bed of velvet. A band of gleaming rubies set into old finely tooled silver caught the light as Carol held it up to admire.

"Oh, Gill its stunning!" Carol could not think of anything else to say. "Where on earth did this come from?"

"Oh, it's been lying in my little treasure box for years." Gill replied. It was my great grandmothers and yes, they are real rubies before you ask, so it's far too precious to wear out shopping or taking the kids to the park of course – but when I saw your dress I thought straight away that this would be the perfect time to dust off the cobwebs and give great-grannies bracelet an airing!" Carol was almost speechless. The bracelet was certainly stunning. That was the only word that Carol could think of to describe it, and what's more it seemed to be just the one thing that had been missing from her ensemble. She had the silver filigree bracelet for one wrist but this one would be perfect for the other and tie in with her gown as though they were meant to be.

"Oh, Gill - I don't know what to say!" Carol stammered the words. "I can't believe you will trust me with such a valuable item and one with such sentimental value too!"

Gill waved her hand dismissively. "Nonsense!" she sad briskly, whisking the lid off the biscuit tin and searching for her favourite coconut creams. "What use is it rotting away unseen in the bottom of my wardrobe? You take it for a run down the aisle and I will be happy to think of you wearing it. But, you make sure you bring back some photos for me won't you!" She waved a finger at Carol. "Frank and I would have loved to be there but you know how it is with Franks' work and the kids and all.'

Carol had always known that Gill's life was totally different to hers. Gill's life revolved round Frank and her two small boys and the whole family were perfectly happy living a simple and happy life. Carol sometimes even envied Gill her lack of ambition and her contentment with what she had. Carol had always striven for more and often wondered if those who were happy to settle for less where so much better off in the contentment stakes than she was herself. But now she was marrying Tony she realised what it was to be thoroughly contented with life and all at once it became clear to her how Gill herself felt about life. Spontaneously she gave her old friend a huge hug. "Gill my sweet, you are an inspiration and a good, good friend!" She blurted out, suddenly feeling that she really understood Gill properly for the first time since they had met.

"Well, good grief!" Gill laughed. "I know it's a lovely bracelet but it's not the crown jewels. Get that tea poured girl, I only have half an hour before picking up the kids but seeing you so happy has made my day – and I am certainly not leaving until I have said hello to the invalid and had a good look at great grannies bracelet up against that wonderful dress of yours!'

As the two friends enjoyed their tea and biscuits Carol - for the first time in her life - felt thoroughly content.

*****

CHAPTER FIFTEEN

"Not long to go now Lad!" Jeff straightened up, polishing cloth in hand and rubbed his back. The silver lady was now gleaming once again after hours of Jeff's loving care.

Tony stuffed his hands deeper into his pockets. "Not long at all my friend but it can't come soon enough for me." The young man's sparkling grey eyes gleamed with anticipation as he spoke.

"Well, at least you are standing upright." Jeff remarked. "When you first came off that catwalk and fell so awkwardly I had this sudden flash of us pushing you down the aisle in a bloody wheelchair!"

Tony's handsome face crumpled into a frown. "That would have been unthinkable!" He replied. "It still hurts to put my right foot forward but in two days time that should have improved greatly. Carol is insisting I do little or nothing which, I am sure, is a good thing but only in moderation. Today I had to tell one or two small lies to be allowed out and come here to supervising your cleaning!"

Jeff laughed. "I heard you insisting that a little gentle exercise would do you the world of good! But that's true anyway, you will only get stiff sitting about doing nothing. A little gentle walking often improves your aches and pains. Just don't overdo it and put yourself back – you know what the doctor said."

"Yes, Yes, a little at a time and make sure I don't lift anything heavy. Luckily Carol is not too heavy for when I carry her over the threshold." Tony said straight-faced.

"Carry her over the .... Hey, for one minute there I thought you were serious!" Jeff threw the polishing cloth at Tony's grinning face. "So there we are – all done!" Jeff threw his arm expansively at the two gleaming Globetrotters. He had polished the 'Flying Angel' to within an inch of her life. As Carol had said, the people at Gretna were being very understanding about having a truck parked at their prestigious venue in the first place so making sure the Flying Angel was spotlessly clean and gleaming was the least they could do and – as Jeff had pointed out - it was the wedding transport after all!

"Well, tomorrow off we go young Tony!" Jeff matched the younger mans slow progress as they made their way back across the yard towards the house. "Any worries or second thoughts you had better get them out of your head now or – as they say – forever hold your peace. Remember Carol is a very headstrong young lady. She will certainly never be the 'little woman at home' you know." Jeff glanced sideways at Tony's profile as they walked. Tony was, after all part Italian and Jeff knew well that Italian families had different values to English ones where family life was concerned.

Tony smiled. "No, my friend. No second thoughts or worries. Carol and I were made for each other I am sure. She is a lovely lady and I still cannot believe my luck that I found her. I realise what you are saying my friend but don't worry. I love Carol for who she is and would never want her to change. I could not see her easily stepping into the same role as Mamma, and I would not expect it of her. I think it is very wrong to meet someone and fall in love then expect that person to change. Carol does not expect me to change so why would I expect it of her?"

Jeff nodded. He was often surprised by how this handsome young man was wise beyond his years. "Well if she had been a different character then she would never have taken the chance on driving to Italy in that clapped out old Transcon in the first place so would never have broken down halfway up that hillside and never needed you to come to her rescue. It's all written in the stars mate – it's all fate I believe!" Jeff mused philosophically.

"I am as great believer in fate my friend." The young man replied seriously. "I just look at how Mamma and Poppa met all those years ago – who would have thought that they would ever meet and marry and be so happy. But they did and they are and I strongly believe that fate sent me into town that day so that I would find the broken down truck on the way back and meet my lovely Carol. As you say my friend, it is written in the stars."

Jeff nodded as he swung the garden gate open and made sure Bruno did not fling himself full weight onto Tony in his eagerness to greet them.

"Well, as we are being so philosophical right now." Jeff hesitated before opening the kitchen door where he could hear Carol and Gina chatting happily. "You know what they say. The road may be long and hard but it is the journey's end that is important. It's what makes life worth while.

"I agree my friend." Tony replied. "So if this is our journeys end then I know it has been one well worth the travelling."

Jeff did not reply. He knew that this quiet, handsome young man knew his own mind and was right now the happiest man on earth.

*****

Zhravko Markov held the box at arms length to judge the workmanship. It had taken many evenings to finish, and he was still not quite sure why he had taken on the task to begin with. Maybe it was the normality of being able to make something with his own hands as he had done so many years ago back in his homeland. As he had worked, cutting the pieces to size and dovetailing the edges to a perfect fit, he had been able to cast his mind back to his childhood. He had remembered his father in his work shed, cutting, shaping and smoothing what had once been rough pieces of wood into objects of beauty. Most of the men of the village took pride in their work. Not many of them simply made an object simply to be serviceable, but usually carved intricate patterns to distinguish their work from that of others. Pails for water would have woodland creatures, mice or rabbits carved into the handle's as would shovels and rakes. Markov remembered his mother cutting bread with a long knife, the handle fashioned into the shape of a wolves head.

His box was solid and well made. The hinged lid opened to reveal an inner layer divided into numerous compartments, each big enough to hold a number of cotton reels. This lifted off to reveal a base layer with more sections, suitable for scissors, needles and extra reels of thread. Underneath, hidden amongst the curves of the decoration a small catch was the only clue to the secret drawer which slid out from under the main body. The lid fitted perfectly and was intricately carved around the edge with tiny oak leaves in tribute to the tree which had provided the material to make the strong, but beautifully carved, box. A cluster of oak leaves and acorns adorned the centre of the lid and further tiny leaves tumbled down each corner towards the base leading on to further subtle decorative carvings. A tiny squirrel sat upright on the front of the drawer, its tail curving around the catch, an acorn clasped in its front paws. Markov was pleased. It was a finely crafted work of art of which his father would have been proud.

Markov could not remember the last time he had made anything with his own two hands. At first he had only attempted to make a basic box, just to see if he could remember the skills he had learned as a child, but as the work progressed he had become more and more involved with the intricacies of wood carving and had lost himself, evening after evening in the work. It was most therapeutic. He felt calm and relaxed as he worked, sitting at the kitchen table, his tools laid out around him as he cut, carved and joined the pieces into the finished article. He had told himself that a box would be a handy, and fairly easy item to make, but now it was finished he knew, that as he had worked, he had thought of the smiling face of Rhona Kirkpatrick and remembered the collection of brightly coloured reels of thread she had piled into the tattered cardboard box.

His trip to the library had proven interesting. He had pored over the Parish records and searched out all he could about Rhona Kirkpatrick. From what he could gather, it appeared she had been born in the next village and married a local man. The marriage had ended when she was widowed after a tragic incident at sea and she had moved into the small cottage where Markov had left her. Nothing seemed to be out of the ordinary, but even so, Markov had contacted Carter and asked him to make further enquiries. Carter had questioned the prudence of his acquaintance and had strongly urged him to make no further contact under the circumstances although everything seemed to point to Rhona Kirkpatrick being nothing more than she appeared to be: a widow living a solitary life.

Markov knew the advice to be sound. Under the present circumstances, a friendship, albeit a casual one, could cause complications and his better judgement told him to forget the sturdy bright eyed woman and concentrate on the task I hand. But something inside him had made him continue with his handicraft. Spending each evening painstakingly perfecting the wooden box to a thing of beauty. It made his life feel normal. Gave him a sense of peace as he worked, as any other man could work. In his own time in the security of his own home, passing the time with a pleasurable chore. But he was not a normal man and his life was far from that peaceful normality that other men enjoyed as their right. Even the short meeting, that day on the cliff-top, had immediately led him to investigating imagined dangers as his deep-seated suspicions had set in.

Markov had begun laying awake in his bed giving much thought to his scepticism. Was everyone he was ever to meet to be under a cloud of mistrust from the start, or would he ever be able to live a free life, speaking to anybody he wished to speak to and going about a normal daily existence.

Markov continued his solitary daily walks although he often found himself detouring to pass the little farmhouse where Rhona Kirkpatrick lived. He had seen her once, out in the garden tending her plants. She had glanced up as he strode by and had raised her hand to wave and he had waved back without breaking his stride, but noting that she was using a walking stick to help her get about. For a moment he had considered stopping and approaching the garden gate to ask after her health but had just as quickly dismissed the idea. It surprised him how much he had wanted to stop and speak to the down to earth woman with the twinkling eyes. A woman's company was not something he had allowed himself to think about for many years. And now, he reminded himself, was hardly the best of times to change his habits.

Markov turned the box on the table, examining it closely for any tiny errors that he could correct before beginning the final touch. He had purchased a large pot of beeswax on his last trip to town and now started to feed it into the wood. As he worked he felt relaxed and at ease. When all this was over - and if he was still alive - he would not let this remembered skill slip away. He had forgotten how much pleasure there was in taking a rough piece of wood and turning it into an item of beauty.

Working on the box helped him to feel free. Helped him to feel he was leading a normal, everyday life just as other men did. As he worked he could imagine himself taking a leisurely stroll over to Rhona Kirkpatrick's small cottage and presenting her with the gift. But deep inside he knew that this was a privilege that right now was nothing more than a day-dream. He knew that he could be putting the woman's life in danger by simply associating with her - and that was the last thing he was prepared to do.

*****

The spring sunshine was shining brightly as Carol eased the big truck through the wide gateway into what had once been the yard of an old mill. A huge mill wheel stood proudly at the entrance, reminding every visitor that this had once been a place of work and industry, but now was a tastefully arranged wedding village. The large cobbled yard was surrounded with small chalets that had once been stables and cottages but now were now housing happy couples who had planned a romantic getaway wedding. On one side there was a pretty tavern which welcomed visitors to sit and enjoy a glass of wine or local brew either relaxing in the cozy interior or at one of the many tables scattered outside.

Standing in the centre in pride of place was the wedding chapel. Tiny and quaint, surrounded by a pretty garden with a tinkling fountain where newlyweds could have their photographs taken to mark the occasion.

"I wish we had thought to book a professional photographer." Carol remarked as she eased the truck into what she presumed to be the most discreet corner and pulled up, clicking on the handbrake with a loud hiss. Bruno unwound himself from the foot-well and peered eagerly through the window, tongue lolling in anticipation and leaning heavily on Tony' legs. "But maybe we will have enough photos. Everyone seemed to be making a point of bringing their cameras."

Tony eased himself forward and stretched his arms over his head. "I am sure there will be plenty of pictures for us to remember Cara Mia." He smiled. "I must say I am glad to arrive. I am beginning to ache a little I must admit." He wriggled his feet from underneath the weight of the big German Shepherd.

Carol swung around to face him. "Oh, I am sorry darling. It has been a long old drive. I am glad that you manage to sleep for a while, but sometimes sitting feels better than lying down. So a little of each was probably the best way to go. Hang on while I go round to your side and give you a hand down."

Carol dropped down from the driving seat and slammed the door before running around to the passenger side. "It certainly looks like a pleasant venue Cara Mia." Tony swept a glance around the large cobbled yard and pretty buildings. "A lot more subtle than I expected I have to admit. I did have a sneaking feeling that it would be rather err…. well commercial, you know. But it certainly does not look that way"

Carol clipped Bruno's lead firmly into place before allowing him to jump down, then bade him sit while she supervised Tony easing himself down the metal steps out of the cab. "There's Jeff's car." She remarked pointing across towards the reception area. "Will you take a stroll over there and ask Jeff for help with the bags while I take Bruno for a leg stretch along the lane. Poor dog must be dying for a piddle by now." She laughed, making off past the big mill wheel and across to the grass verge for a short walk to stretch her own legs after the long drive as well as Bruno's

Jeff and Gina were beside the 'Flying Angel' by the time Carol and Bruno returned from their short walk and Jeff was manhandling the bags out of the cab. "Here comes the bride!" he laughed as Carol approached.

Gina was full of enthusiasm. "What a lovely place this is!" She enthused. It could not be prettier. Tomorrow will be lovely I am sure. Oh, Carol I can hardly wait for tomorrow, and I am dying to explore the area aren't you?"

"Well, you will just *have* to wait my darling!" Jeff reminded her. "Even you can't speed the clock forward, but if you and Carol want to go off and explore later on then feel free to do so – Tony and I will be happy to make use of that nice bar over there and keep Bruno company for a while.   Best thing for everyone I thing." Jeff knew how the girls loved to browse shops and exchange girly gossip and was perfectly happy to stay behind and relax with Tony in the bar.   Jeff was well used to long hauls in the truck, but driving almost the full length of the country by car was different. He was looking forward to staying put right now and Tony's painful back was excuse enough.

"Sounds good to me." Carol replied helping Bruno back into the cab and filling his water bowl from a large bottle.   "I am sure Bruno won't want to be stuck in here for too long and would enjoy sitting with you two while you enjoy the local brew." Carol wound the cab windows halfway down and shoved the sunroof fully open before locking Bruno inside.

"Yes, that would be nice.   Let's get settled in, have nice cup of tea then Carol and I can take the car and go for a browse around the village while you two relax." Gina was definitely up for exploring.

Carol glanced over to Tony as they made their way to the chalets. "You don't mind me disappearing do you darling?" she asked. "I feel so bad that you can't come and join in and if you want me to stay with you then I don't mind a bit."

Tony put his arm around her as they walked.   "I don't mind at all Cara Mia." The diamond eyes shone kindly at Carol.   "I am sure that I would have enjoyed discovering this historical area with you under normal circumstances, but I will be perfectly happy to join Jeff in the bar or even sit in the chalet for a while.   My only concern is that my back is in good condition for tomorrow – that is the important thing - so you and Gina go off and have a happy afternoon.   We can all enjoy a nice meal together this evening and........." he squeezed her shoulder. "After tomorrow we will have the rest of our lives to be together so please – go and enjoy your day."

Carol leaned towards him and kissed his cheek. What a kind and lovely man he was. Her world was a wonderful place right now and she felt that nothing could possibly happen that could dampen the happiness she felt right now.

****

The large gift shop was too much of a temptation for Carol and Gina. Although most of the items offered for sale were typical tourist souvenirs,

Gina could not resist buying a delicately carved letter opener. The silver blade was engraved with intricate Celtic detail and the handle decorated with finely crafted thistles. She decided against considering it a frivolity, in favour of regarding it as a particularly useful item that would not only save her fingernails from the ravages of letter opening but also serve as a suitable souvenir of her best friend's Scottish wedding. Taking all these reasons into consideration the item suddenly bordered on necessity. "Well, you can't visit a place and not buy a little reminder can you?" She announced with a wink, noting that the price was a little inflated but deciding to indulge herself nevertheless. "It would be almost rude not to."

Carol giggled at Gina's habit of excusing almost every purchase she made and followed her friend to the pay point, carrying a warm Aran style sweater in soft lambs-wool, the complex cable pattern a testament to the skill of the maker. "My excuse." Carol began holding the sweater up to eye level. "Is that I couldn't find the time or inclination to sit, night after night, going cross-eyed while laboriously knitting this!" She folded the soft woollen garment over her arm as she reached for her purse. "Life is too busy right now to indulge in sitting about knitting woollies, but Tony will love this in the cold weather, I'm sure."

"And of course it will always remind you of your trip to Gretna Green." Gina confirmed, handing her money to the smiling assistant. "There is a nice little tea shop over there too." She pointed out of the window. "Fancy a cuppa and a sticky bun?"

"Always!" Carol replied. She was happy to be out alone with Gina, browsing the village shops and behaving like tourists. Jeff had been happy to stay behind to keep Tony company and relax after the journey while the girls indulged in an afternoons sightseeing.

The two girls made their way from the temptations of the gift shop and strolled over to the tea rooms. A small, quaint building with bulging white washed walls and sturdy mullioned windows with a number of tables and chairs placed outside on the cobbles. Although the sun was shining down from a clear blue sky, a sharp breeze had caused most of the diners to head for the cosy nooks inside the small café, so Carol and Gina had no trouble in finding an empty table outside. "Feels almost continental sitting here." Gina remarked after ordering a large pot of tea and two huge scones with jam and cream to share.

"It always gives me that holiday feeling, sitting outside." Carol replied, leaning back in her chair, feeling relaxed and happy.

Tomorrow was her wedding day, she was sitting in glorious sunshine with her dearest friend and all felt right with the world. She was looking forward to wearing the gorgeous dress and walking down the small aisle in the intimate chapel to Tony's side. She was also looking forward to Katy's arrival and enjoying a relaxing evening with her dearest friends and her adored lover. Life could not have been better.

"Are you listening! Look will you!" Gina's voice eventually broke through Carol's reverie.

"Sorry, what?" Carol gave Gina a blank stare.

"Carol, you are hopeless – over there, look – that man – I thought it was Markov!"

"Who, where........? Oh, right." Carol turned and looked down the street to where Gina was gesturing. A tall, heavily set man with thick wavy hair was folding himself into a battered old saloon car. "You mean him." Carol whispered, not knowing why she was whispering. The man would have had to have been in possession of exceptional hearing to catch any conversation from so many yards away.

"Yes, him! I could have sworn it was him from the back, but when he turned around........."

"From the back?" Carol remarked wryly. "You didn't see his face then – just his back. Honestly, Gina, what made you think it was him?"

Gina pulled a face and poured the tea. "Mannerisms, stupid. You know. The way someone walks and all that, it just reminded me so much of, well you know, it was so much like the way he walked and held his shoulders......." her words trailed off. Yes, it did sound silly when she heard herself saying it like that, but she had thought, just for a moment.

"Well, I got a glimpse of the face." Said Carol, "And there was no beard."

"That means nothing. He could have shaved?" Gina pointed out, having no intention of letting go so easily.

"Yes, I suppose." Carol agreed. "But for the life of me I never imagined Zhravko Markov wearing an all-weather hill walkers jacket and moorland boots. That guy looked every bit the well-seasoned highland walker. And anyway, what the hell would Markov be doing here?"

"How would I know?" Gina raised her eyebrows. "But he would hardly be marching around a Scottish village in full Bulgarian – or Russian uniform would he?" She pointed out sensibly. "But anyway, I only said the guy *looked* like him, I wasn't trying to say it *was* him!" Gina decided to back down, it was hardly worth an in depth discussion on such a happy day.

"He certainly was the same size." Carol admitted, watching the man in question glance back over his shoulder before pulling out into the road and driving away from them. "An exceptionally tall guy, but I doubt we will ever see Markov again. He has probably disappeared into the dubious London underworld by now. Pass the jam pot please, these scones look delicious." Carol split the warm scone and spread butter onto each side, watching it melt into the soft cake before piling it with jam and thick cream. She did not want to admit it, even to herself, but the sight of the man had sent a jolt down her spine. Gina was right about the mannerisms. That was something that the most clever disguise could rarely hide. The face had been totally different from what she remembered of the bearded giant, but as Gina had pointed out. A man could shave. A man could also change his mode of dress within moments too. That was not outside the bounds of possibility, but surely it was far too co-incidental that he should be here. But something in the back of her mind reminded her of something he had mentioned. He had told her that he had visited Edinburgh. She had asked him, simply for want of conversation on the drive from Bulgaria, if he knew anyone in England and he had vaguely suggestion that he 'knew people'. He had also told her that he had visited Scotland. "I once went to Edinburgh" he had said. "It was a business trip, not a holiday." So maybe – just maybe...............

Carol shook the idea out of her mind. It was ridiculous. Besides, Edinburgh was miles away and Markov had also mentioned Portsmouth and that had a much more likely ring to it. Anyway, she had far more pressing issues to think about than whether a rather dubious immigrant was wandering around the borders of Scotland. Her wedding the following day for one and right now the scrumptious cream scone was calling for her full attention.

"Do you think we will ever see him again?" Gina was obviously not to be distracted from her train of thought.

"Dunno." Carol mumbled through a mouthful of cream scone. "Never know what can happen I suppose. Won't make any difference to us one way or another I don't suppose. I should imagine he just wants to get on with his life. He probably had some plan or other, I doubt he would have just come over here on a whim and then sat himself down wondering what to do next."

"Hmm, suppose you're right." Gina conceded. "But more importantly about tomorrow." She sat back in her chair her eyes shining with the anticipation of the following day. "You, my girl, are to do nothing!

Nothing at all. You get up in the morning and do whatever you want to do. Katie, Anna and I don't want to clap eyes on you until it's nearly time to get you down the aisle. We know exactly what we are doing and you Kiddo, are going to relax and just enjoy the day. Go with the flow my dear!"

"I know, I have been told!" Carol raised her eyebrows. She was under strict instructions that she and Tony were to do nothing other than sit back and enjoy the day, and if she were to be honest she quite appreciated having all the worries taken off her shoulders. Katie would be arriving with Andy and Anna some time in the morning and Spyder and his wife Suzy would also be getting there well before lunch time so as the wedding was mid afternoon it felt like there was plenty of time to arrange anything that had to be done – although Carol could not imagine what would need arranging. The chalets were grouped around an attractive cobbled square with less than a hundred yard walk to the tiny chapel with the pretty surrounding garden. Then a few strides would take them across the courtyard to the bar and restaurant where they would be raising a glass after the anvil was struck and the knot tied.

Of course Anna was bringing the cake. Carol still had no idea what it was like but had told Anna that she trusted her taste implicitly and as Anna knew her so well she was in no doubt that the cake would be perfect for herself and Tony. Carol had even refused a sneak preview when the cake arrived. What would be the point? She asked herself. Even on the slim chance that she did not like it at this late stage there was very little that could be done so she was happy for it to be a complete surprise. Carol presumed that the cake would be placed in the bar so that they could all enjoy a slice with a glass of champagne after the ceremony, but each time the subject came up Gina simply told her not to worry and that all was in hand, so Carol decided that she would do just that. Not worry about a thing and enjoy the whole day.

Carol leaned back in her chair. "You know this is just about perfect." She announced, gazing up into an amazingly blue sky. "Apart from the fact that poor Tony is still feeling a little delicate and can't come out and about with us I can't think of anything I would want to change."

Gina nodded. "Jeff is more than happy to stay and keep Tony company." She remarked. "In fact it's rather nice just the two of us wandering around here. Men don't do gift shops particularly well do they?" The girls giggled. It was true that Carol and Gina had thoroughly enjoyed their afternoon together exploring the village and admiring the shops. Carol felt she needed these few hours to relax after the drive and prepare herself for all the goings on of the following day. Katy would arrive full of energy, along with Andy and Anna and Spyder and Suzie were setting out early and would arrive by lunch time so her day would be filled with chatter. This peaceful time was to be enjoyed.

"In fact I would not be in the least surprised if Tony has not been able to stroll very carefully to that nice little bar and enjoy a glass of beer while we were out." Gina continued. "I know Jeff would be up for one or two!"

"I hope they have gone to the bar. I feel awful thinking that poor Tony is stuck in the room nursing his aching back and taking the tablets. The weather is so nice they can sit outside and have Bruno with them too. That way poor old Bruno won't feel so left out of things." Said Carol. "But looking on the bright side, we have had this one small disaster with Tony's injury so surely nothing else can possibly go wrong can it?"

"Well no, absolutely. I think it will be plain sailing from now on. A lovely cosy evening with a nice meal, just the four of us, then tomorrow you just relax completely for best part of the day. Katy and Anna and the rest of the gang will be here by then so just leave it all to Anna and me. Tomorrow is your day and you are going to enjoy it!"

Carol still could not think what on earth Gina and Anna had planned and what there was to arrange but she decided not to ask. She would do exactly as she was told. Relax and enjoy her day. Tomorrow she would become Mrs Antonio Copeland and that, as far as she was concerned, was going to be the start of a wonderfully happy chapter in her life.

*****

CHAPTER SIXTEEN

The early morning was grey with mist. There was not even a hint that the sun may show its face at any time today and a fine drizzle of rain drifted down from the overcast sky. Markov pulled the hood up on his thickly padded jacket and locked the door behind him as he stepped outside. His daily walking had become part of his lifestyle and the weather made no difference to his routine. There was a strong wind blowing in from the sea and a multitude of seagulls screeched in unison as they wheeled overhead, riding the currents with ease and grace. Some days they appeared noisier than others and today they were in full cry, wheeling and screaming over the farmhouse and swooping back towards the ocean.

Markov checked the driveway and the tall bushes out of habit as he strode towards the gate. He checked the latch before opening it, stepping through, carefully resetting it in a particular position, just slightly ajar with the edge directly over the oddly shaped piece of gravel that he had chosen. No man, not even a child, could pass through the gate without moving it and it would be virtually impossible to reset the gate exactly as Markov had left it. He could tell immediately if he had been visited in his absence. The daily task had become boringly monotonous, but Markov knew well that he could not drop his guard. Not now. Not after all these weeks of vigilance. Carter had put the wheels in motion. He had subtly leaked Markov's whereabouts and both of them knew it was only a matter of time before the leak spilled over and trickled towards the waiting ears of the hunter.

Markov strode out briskly. More briskly than he felt inside. He was getting tired of this game, of this waiting and not knowing. He wanted it over and done. He wanted to live a normal life, something he had not been able to do for so many years he wondered if he ever could.

He strode round the headland, passing close by the side path that led to Rhona Kirkpatrick's cottage but resisting the urge to walk down and see if she was out and about – although he felt that it would be highly unlikely at such an early hour and on such a damp day, but one never knew.

The sea was iron grey as it lazily rocked towards the gravel beach and back out again. Markov hunched himself against the fine drizzle as he walked, glancing up to the sky and noticing that it was starting to appear lighter and the promise of blue just might be there for later that day. He bent and picked up some pieces of driftwood that had been blown inland by the high winds. His hobby had taken a grip that had surprised him. Most of his thoughts were on what shapes he could conjure with whatever pieces of wood he came across and had almost taken over from the constant consideration of the assassin that was surely by now getting too close for comfort and certainly too close for him to let his guard down even for a second.

Holding his precious prize he turned inland and started his walk back down the muddy track towards his farmhouse. He would make a bowl of porridge, a dish he had become rather accustomed to and found sustained him for most of the day then go to his woodland and find some more pieces of twisted root to compliment his find and spend the rest of the day working his magic on them. It almost felt like a normal life.

Almost like a normal life but not quiet. Markov once more carefully checked the gate before stepping through onto the driveway and spent a moment sweeping his gaze around the house and beyond for any signs of change and making sure nothing was even the slightest bit out of place before entering the farmhouse and making his breakfast.

It was almost beginning to feel as though he had lived there forever. The peace and quiet of the place seemed to have a healing quality giving Markov the urge to lay so many ghosts from his past. He had spent many hours mulling over the events in his life. Thinking about things that he had banished from his memory forever – or so he had thought. Some of the memories were painful, but he had forced himself to think them through, to evaluate his past and try to put it into context with the man he had become today.

Echo's of his youth and happier times came flooding back as he worked with the wood and tools and he often found himself smiling at fond memories of family and old friends. He had even bared his soul to himself and considered the work he had taken on at an adult and the things he had done and ordered to be done in the name of – what?

Sometimes the thoughts made him weary. He wanted a peaceful life. He was sure that given a chance he would be perfectly happy to spend the rest of his days in this quiet and peaceful place, working with his hands and striding along the coastal paths, the only sounds the crashing of the waves and the screaming of the gulls. Fresh air in his lungs after far too many years being closeted away inside musty buildings.

His life's journey had been long and winding, taking different turns that he himself could never have envisaged in his youth, and he knew that one way or another he had reached that journey's end. How it would end was still hanging in the balance, but however it was going to turn out Markov knew that he would not have long to wait.

The big man finished his porridge, the hot cereal warming him through and setting him up for another venture into his woodland in search of interesting pieces to work with. The early morning mist had cleared and grey had almost left the sky and been replaced with a delicate shade of blue giving promise of a pleasant day ahead. But still, Markov felt a need for his jacket as he closed the farmhouse door and made his way towards the tangle of trees, the constant scream of gulls blotting out the usual woodland sounds of garden birds and scurrying creatures.

The woodland was like a treasure trove to him by now. Pieces of twisted root and broken branches offered themselves to him as though suggesting the shapes that they could become.

Some of his work had been useful items such as spoons with carved animals or flowers along the stem and some abstract pieces that could easily grace the most discerning of homes. He often found pieces of branch or root that immediately lent themselves to be sculpted into the shape of animals, fantasy creatures and human form. His skill had surprised even himself as the sculptures took shape. But work like this took time and patience and Markov had both in abundance. One small knotted root looked already mouse like as he pulled it from a tangle of bracken and brambles. Small pieces were almost more pleasurable than the larger pieces he often felt.

But above all his work box still took pride of place in his heart. Was it because it was the first piece he had made in his new life or was it the thought of the pleasure in Rhona Kirkpatrick's eyes if she should ever accept it that made it so dear to him. He was not sure, but he held the beautiful piece of work in high esteem and made it the catalyst for his other pieces.

Markov turned the small piece of root over in his hand. Yes, a mouse he was sure. Maybe he could carve a corn stalk with the tiny creature climbing up and clinging to the stem with a curled tail.

The gulls screamed overhead as he searched. He did not hear the car draw quietly to a halt on the lane outside, nor hear the soft tread of steps on the gravel drive. All Markov was aware of right now was the sound of birds singing with delight as the rain gave way to watery sunshine, the rustle of some tiny woodland creature scrambling for cover as he searched amongst the bracken and the soft swish of the ocean far in the distance.

*****

Carol stretched luxuriously as she lay, fully dressed, on the comfortable bed in the cosy chalet room. She and Tony had joined Gina and Jeff for a filling breakfast in the dining room and Carol was beginning to regret her indulgence. "I don't really feel like moving much but I think Bruno had better have a proper walk, stretch his legs and have a good sniff about." She called to the half open bathroom door where steam from Tony's shower billowed through into the bedroom.

"Poor animal must be feeling a bit left out, stuck in that cab all night by himself and only a quick trot over the road this morning." Tony replied, walking back into the room, still damp from the shower. "And anyway, we have plenty of time to do pretty much as we please don't we? The wedding being late afternoon is nice, plenty of time to prepare without any mad rush or panic and spend today relaxing."

Carol had done all her panicking days before. Right now she had decided that what had been forgotten would have to stay forgotten and probably wouldn't mater anyway. She had her dress, shoes and flowers and had remembered to bring the small silk jewellery roll that Gina had given her to hold her wedding finery so what else did she need. "How's your back feeling now Darling?" She enquired. "Still aching or did the warm shower help?"

Tony pulled a face. "Not as bad as it was but I can still fell it a little. Nothing serious though, I won't be hobbling down the aisle like an old man – hopefully."

"Thank goodness for that!" Carol smiled. "At one point I thought you may want wheeling down there. But I don't think you had better come out with me right now. I will take Bruno for his walk while you have a rest here. Can't chance making it bad again can we? You just take it easy and get yourself better for standing at the anvil, that's the most important thing Darling."

Tony eased himself onto the upright chair in front of the dressing table. "Yes, you're right Cara Mia, I think I will just sit here and read a book or see if there is anything of interest on this television while you are gone. It feels so much better now, I don't want to take a chance on upsetting it again. I haven't had to take a painkiller this morning so I will see how it goes. When the wedding is over it can do as it pleases, as long as I can stand up straight and say 'I do' then that's all that matters to me at the moment."

Carol swung her legs off the bed and slipped her feet into her trainers. "Well Katy and the gang should be here before long." She reminded him. "They left at the crack of dawn this morning so all being well everyone should arrive around lunchtime which will give us all plenty of time to get ready for the wedding without a mad rush. But Gina will sort everyone out, get them settled into their rooms and everything. She insists on taking all work off my shoulders for this day, which is wonderful. I can just concentrate on you my darling." She leaned over and kissed Tony, running her fingers through his thick black curls. "There is a hairdryer there if you need it." She added helpfully. "Not that you have to style it or anything, typical men – they have all the luck – we women have to spend longer to get the desired effect!"

Tony laughed. "You don't need any time at all my love, I think you are lovely at any time of the day whether you have taken time or not."

"Flatterer!" Carol laughed as she made for the door. "I hope you are still saying that in twenty years time when we are an old married couple!" She stuck her tongue out at Tony and left the little chalet to walk across to the 'Flying Angel' in the large car park. The morning had been completely covered in a soft blanket of mist which was now lifting, although a thin drizzle of rain was still coming down with little evidence of stopping. Carol crossed her fingers that it would dry out by the afternoon so that she could take the short walk to the tiny chapel without getting too damp.

Bruno was already at the cab window, ears pricked and tongue lolling with delight as he watched Carol approach, his nose poking out of the open gap at the top of the window. "Good morning again boy!" Carol greeted her beloved pet as she opened the cab door and stood back as Bruno bounded down and leaped around her legs for his morning fuss. "Let's get this lead on you then." Carol struggled to hold Bruno still enough to slip the chain around his neck. "No free walking around here puppy-dog," She announced. "Might be sheep and stuff and we don't want anybody even thinking you may be guilty of anything. You stay close to me now."

Bruno calmed down a little as Carol led the way to the road to walk along the grass verge, Bruno sniffing with intent interest at all the strange smells that needed investigation. As they made their way down the narrow country lane the drizzle miraculously eased off and a small patch of blue sky was beginning to appear as they strolled along heralding the possibility of a pleasant day. The road was fairly quiet as it wound its way into the Scottish countryside. The odd car passed by them. Swishing through the damp lanes as they walked along but there was no heavy traffic to mask the fresh smell of the countryside that Carol loved so much. A pair of curious highland cattle strolled idly towards the fence as Carol walked along, one pushing its nose over to investigate the big dog sniffing at the edge of the hedgerow. Bruno stepped back, never having seen such a creature before then tentatively approached to sniff noses with the strange beast, who quickly lost interest and lumbered off to join its companion further along the field. Carol felt happy and relaxed. Today she would become Tony's wife. She no longer had any doubts about it. This was what she wanted and was one hundred percent sure that it was the right thing to do. Ok, so they would still have a fairly unconventional lifestyle for a married couple. Both of them working and Tony away most of the week but many truckers' wives led a solitary life for most of the time and this held no fears for Carol. She had always been comfortable with her own company and boredom was not a word she tolerated or had ever suffered from. There was always plenty to do and since starting up Transcon Haulage there had never been a moment to discover the dubious delights of boredom.

Of course there was the wedding celebration in Italy to look forward to as well. A huge party at La Casaccia would be wonderful. Carol could picture it now, the balmy summers evening with lanterns on the veranda and Mamma Gina cooking up a storm. All the village would be there of course as well as all the family. Tuscan villages never had private celebrations Carol had discovered. Any celebration was shared with all and sundry within striking distance and the warmth and love that surrounded such occasions was wonderful to be a part of.

The morning air was cool on her skin and a breeze brought a little colour to her cheeks, blowing her mass of unruly curls about her face. As she daydreamed she hardly noticed the distance she had walked and didn't really care. It was nice not to be tied to time, racing for a ferry or desperately trying to battle through traffic to arrive at a delivery depot before closing time. She felt no urge to dash back to the chalet to check on Tony. She was sure that Jeff would have arrived by now and no doubt the two men would be deep in conversation about trucks and deliveries and her absence hardly noticed. She was enjoying the solitude. A time of peace before all the hustle and bustle of the wedding to come.

A small side lane caught her eye. The entrance overhung with trees and a tiny winding road, hardly better than a track, leading to – heaven knows where. "That looks interesting boy." She remarked idly to Bruno, checking that no cars were coming along before stepping onto the tarmac and crossing over and walking under the trees to investigate the little country lane. Carol revelled in the peace and quiet. A country girl at heart she had never developed a love of the city and here, walking amongst the hedgerows, she felt a pang of longing to spend more time in the fresh air and gentler lifestyle of country living.

The road swung away to the right. Carol could see over the hedge and could see that it re-joined a larger road some way up ahead. Just a small cut through maybe, she thought idly, almost disregarding the other small gated track leading off from the bend. She was vaguely aware of a car parked just outside the tiny track, almost hidden by the tress and just beyond, the corner of a stone built cottage, tucked away behind tall bushes with a gated driveway.

Carol was undecided as to whether this was a small public footpath or a driveway leading exclusively to the property and hesitated. She was just about to turn and keep to the path she was on when she noticed the second car parked down the driveway outside the house. Surely that was the same one that she had seen in the village. The one that Gina had imagined to be driven by Zhravko Markov. She peered down the length of the track. The car was not unusual in any way but her curiosity was aroused. It would do no harm to wander down the driveway and take a closer look. Maybe the owner would see her and demand to know why she was trespassing on his property and she would apologise and claim ignorance of the fact that it was private and turn and go on her way.

Emboldened by the sense of adventure she stepped through the half open gate onto the gravel of the driveway and strolled towards the house, Bruno tugging eagerly at the lead as he sniffed the bushes alongside the drive. There were no signs of life that Carol could see. The car stood locked opposite the long stone building. The windows and doors were closed shut and no appearances of activity were obvious. Beyond the house were two large stone buildings, the door of one slightly ajar. Bruno continued to sniff happily as they approached the buildings. A walk was a walk as far as he was concerned and the bonus of being in a completely strange place led to further delights to sniff and investigate to the full. Suddenly he stopped. All four feet planted firmly on the ground head raised ears alert. Carol noticed her pet's behaviour and stood still.

"What is it Boy?" She asked, her voice soothing. As she spoke she realised that she could hear sounds of activity coming from the copse of woodland at the rear of the property that she had not noticed until now. Bruno stared straight ahead. Was he staring at the barn or beyond? Carol could not be sure. A low growl emitted from the big dog's throat, his hackles rising like spikes on the back of his neck. "Hey now, come on, it's okay." Carol began to feel nervous. Bruno rarely behaved like this. In fact Carol could never remember a time she had heard him growl. After being spoiled by all from puppyhood he was far too friendly and laid back to notice any problems that may be going on around him. But Bruno stood stock still, his ears forward and his teeth beginning to appear from the now curled lips, drops of saliva forming around the snarling fangs. Carol involuntarily stepped back. This snarling animal did not even look like Bruno right now. She could see nothing of the lolling tongue and eager eyes that she knew and loved. "Bruno. What is it?" She repeated in the calmest voice she could manage right now. "Come on boy, it's OK, come on, back with me now." Her voice lacked the assurance that she had been hoping to impart on her pet as she tugged at the lead and began to turn back in the hope that Bruno would shift his attention away from whatever had alarmed him so, and follow her back to the road. Bruno flicked a quick glance in his owner's direction but still stood as though rooted to the spot.

Carol was feeling thoroughly uneasy by now. Bruno's behaviour was totally out of character and it seemed that the whole atmosphere of the place had taken on an ominous feel. "Bruno! Come on now!" She snapped. She had had enough, her curiosity was not as important as getting Bruno's attention and taking him and herself away. Whatever had upset her pet she didn't want to know and only wanted to get back to the chalet and the security of Tony's company. She stepped back and tugged firmly at Bruno's lead almost hauling him off his feet and it was at this moment she felt rather than saw the slight movement inside the stone building and at the same time saw the big man stride out of the woodland copse.

The man stopped dead for a split second as he saw Carol, then his eyes moved to Bruno, still snarling at the barn door. With amazing speed and agility he crossed the few yards of grass between them, dropping the piece of wood he was holding on one hand but keeping a firm grip on the axe in the other.

Carol felt her stomach curl as he reached her side and then suddenly push her violently into the shrubbery making her lose her grip on Bruno's lead.

The big dog did not hesitate and dashed straight into the barn followed by Markov. Carol heard a yelp of pain, obviously from Bruno and the sound of wood crashing to the ground. A tall wiry man came into view as the door swung wide. Carol could see he was holding a knife – a rather large knife - and his stance was one of a fighter, knees slightly bent ready to spring. There was no sign of Bruno and Carol's heart sank as she tried to get to her feet, the brambles catching on her clothes and her trainers slipping on the damp ground.

Markov came into view wielding the axe. The stranger ducked and lunged at Markov with the knife, slicing through the thick padded coat which suddenly started to seep red with blood. Markov swung to the side with an agility that belied his huge frame and hooked his leg under the man's knees sending him crashing to the ground. With no more ado Markov swung the axe. Bringing it down with great force and splitting the man's skull as though it were no more than a coconut.

Carol was stunned. Never in her life had she imagined she would ever witness such a scene. Somehow she managed to get to her feet although her legs had turned to jelly and she was totally incapable of putting one foot in front of the other right now.

"Get inside!" Markov snapped the command as Carol stood, rooted to the spot. Her head was swimming and she felt faint. Fear gripped her once again. Was this man going to kill her too? "Inside!" Markov grabbed her arm and propelled her towards the door, flinging it open and propelling Carol through into the kitchen and shoving her roughly into a chair. "Are you unharmed?"

Carol could hardly understand. It was as though she was in a completely different place and was watching the scenario unfold from a distance. Markov grabbed her shoulders and shook her. "Mrs Landers!" he demanded.

Carol had lost the power of speech. She was shocked to the core with the whole situation and also shocked that this man recognised her and she was known to someone who had minutes before killed a man. She stared into the big man's face, fear clearly showing in her emerald eyes. Her head was spinning, she was shaking from head to foot, her stomach had contracted into a tight knot and she felt sick. Part of her brain was trying to take in what had just happened while the other part was trying to deny it completely. "Drink this." Markov pushed a tumbler towards her lips and poured a fiery liquid into her mouth. Carol choked but managed to swallow. "Brandy." Markov announced, easing the glass into her hand. "You have had a shock, it will make you feel better."

A shock! The incongruity of the words filtered through the thick muddled fog of Carol's brain as she struggled to bring herself back to reality. She took another sip of the brandy, her hand shaking so badly that she spilled some down her chin. Markov pulled one of the other wooden chairs forward and sat facing her, clasping her free hand in his. "Mrs Landers. You must calm down. You are no longer in danger." His words settled on Carol's ears but seemed only to reach her brain in slow motion. Was she in danger or was she safe with Markov. She managed to focus on his face but was struck dumb by the enormity of what had just taken place.

"I know this had been a great shock to you Mrs Landers." Markov was speaking quietly, trying to keep Carol calm. "I doubt that you have ever found yourself in such a situation before. Drink your brandy, it will help."

Carol did as she was told and gulped down the last of the fiery liquid. It settled the turmoil in her stomach but did little for the reeling sensation in her head. A million questions were spinning around in her brain, but she was still unable to string any words together.

The sound of a whimper floated through the half open door. "I will find your dog." Markov announced as she sat transfixed, clutching her empty glass.

Bruno! Oh, my God he had been injured. Was he dying. The thought of Bruno lying dead in the shrubbery shocked Carol into semi-rational thought. "Bruno, Oh my dear Bruno is he badly hurt? Did that man stab him?" She managed to voice the words. Under the circumstances it seemed an odd thing to be worrying about right now, but Bruno was the only normal thing that seemed to exist in this whole fiasco.

Markov got to his feet, but before he could reach the open door Bruno appeared, walking with difficulty and obviously in some pain, but alive. "Bruno, darling!" Carol reached forward as Bruno made his way painfully across the tiled floor and flopped at her feet with a grunt, his head resting on Carol's lap. He looked dazed and obviously in some pain but managed to eye Markov with suspicion. "Oh, thank God he's alive. Are you hurt badly Boy?"

"Shh." Markov whispered then spoke quietly in his own language to the big dog, slowly reaching down his hand for the animal to sniff. He continued speaking gently while Bruno breathed in his scent then slowly began running his hand along the dogs neck and over his back. Bruno visibly relaxed as the soft words and gentle touch gave him confidence. Markov ran his hands over Bruno's, side. The dog winced but did not attempt to snap.

Carol watched with amazement as Bruno relaxed under Markov's touch. "No knife wounds I think. It looks like he was kicked and very violently but I think your friend will survive the ordeal." Markov announced, still gently running his hands over the dogs sides. "I suspect he has a cracked rib, or maybe two, but nothing that is life threatening. He was lucky. That man had the ability to kill a grown man with one kick or punch, your dog was very lucky Mrs Landers. I am glad he is not badly hurt as we probably both owe him our lives."

"What!" Carol spluttered the single word.

"That man hiding in the barn was going to kill me and despite all my precautions I have to admit that he had secreted himself there without my knowledge and would surely have been in a most advantageous position to take me by surprise had your dog not warned me of his presence." Markov said quietly, still stroking Bruno's ears. "And have no doubt Mrs Landers, had he succeeded in killing me then you would certainly have never been allowed to leave this property alive."

Carols emerald eyes widened with the horror of it all. It was like something out of a cheap black and white film noir B movie and nothing to do with real life at all. Any moment now Peter Lorre or Sidney Greenstreet would loom ominously into frame closely followed by Humphrey Bogart just in time to save the day.

"The main question right now." Markov continued, his voice cutting through the fog and confusion of Carol's brain. "Is what you have in mind to do about this situation. Do you imagine that you can tell anybody else about it?"

The words struck fear once again into Carol's heart. Was he going to kill her to keep her quiet. She had no previous experience with random killings and new nothing about what to expect from those who committed such acts.

Markov read her thoughts – the fear in her eyes. "Don't worry Mrs Landers." He softened his tone. "I have no intention of hurting you. You are safe with me, have no fear. The big man ran his hand once more over Bruno then sat up and met Carol's eyes. "In fact you are safer now than you have been for some time."

Carol was still in shock but the shaking had eased a little and she began to gather her wits. She did not know what to believe. Was he trying to lull her into a false sense of security before bludgeoning her to death with one of the array of tools scattered across the big kitchen table. "Mr Markov." Carol still could hardly believe that this was he, but there was no mistaking the huge man's voice. It was the same man that they had met in the Bulgarian prison. "What the hell happened out there? Who the hell was that man and what on earth are you doing here, of all places?" It all came out in a rush as Carol found her voice, although she still could hardly believe that she had just witnessed a killing, a murder even, and was sitting here in the killer's kitchen drinking brandy while he tended her dog.

Markov was obviously in no hurry to answer her questions. "Wait." He commanded, rising to his feet and striding out of the stable door.

Carol could hear scraping on the gravel and felt her heart leap once more as Markov re-appeared, dragging the body of their attacker behind him. She watched in shocked silence as Markov pulled the body across the floor and dumped it unceremoniously in the corner, and without giving it a second glance returned to sit on the chair facing her.

Carol felt sick at the sight of what was left of the man's head covered in congealed blood and the limp body, thrown casually into a heap, as though it were no more a human being than a bundle of old clothes. She could hardly believe what she was witnessing. Surely this could not be happening. Things like this did not happen in her life: to people like her. "The shed has no lock!" was the only explanation.

Markov sighed and dropped his head, staring at the floor for some moments before raising his eyes again and meeting her gaze. Suddenly, to Carol he looked old and weary. He took a deep breath. "The man's name is of no importance. The most important thing is that he is now dead and many people are now safe because of it." He sat back in his chair and reached for the packet of cigarettes off the table, lighting one and watching the smoke spiral towards the low ceiling and disperse into the air. "You, Mrs Landers are one of those people I believe."

"Me! Why on earth would a total stranger want to kill me?" Carol reached for the brandy bottle and poured herself another drink.

Markov sighed again.. He was not good at explaining such things. Explaining anything really. He had never had to. "This man was a trained killer. He worked in Moscow for many years, He killed on command, it mattered not who, as long as he had the orders, then he would kill." He leaned back on his chair. "I left Moscow many years ago but had made enemies. This man was sent to find me. He found me in Sofia so I had to leave. As you know, my entry into this country was not conventional."

"So it was you he was after." Carol was beginning to realised that this was not just a random attack.

"I was his primary target." Markov agreed, "But the fact that he was here, in this country is testimony to the fact that he knew how I arrived. You, your friend Mr Meredith and his pretty wife and also your young man and your daughter for that matter, would most possibly have been on his list of 'loose ends', as you say here, to tidy up.

Carol felt a shudder run through her body. Katy! Oh my God! Katy in danger. She felt sick. What the hell had she managed to involve herself in. It sounded like something from a cheap novel. "I can hardly believe what I am hearing." Her voice had steadied itself a little as the brandy worked its magic. "You mean this man would have killed us all without even having a conscience about it?"

Markov threw back his head. A deep-throated laugh filled the room. "Conscience Madame, is something this creature has been devoid of for many years. He carried out his deeds in a cold and dispassionate method. There was no human feeling left in this man's being." Markov spat the last words out with venom. "He has killed a great many targets over the years. Some he knew the names of, others he did not. It mattered little. He was programmed to kill so kill he did."

"You mean he was a robot of some sort." Carol's eyes widened. This was all too much to take in.

"Markov gave a dry laugh. "Mrs Landers. I do believe you have been watching too many movies. No, he was not a robot. Had he been, then he could have been re-programmed, no doubt, to behave in a better manner. No, I am afraid he was as human as you and I. Simply – what is the term - psychotic I think it is known as. Killing was not just a job for him, it was a pleasure. He killed because of the power it gave him.

The power over life and death is something that some human beings cherish above everything. It gives them exhilaration to wield such power. That...."

He gestured towards the crumpled body. "....was one such person. Gladly it is over with."

Carol shifted in her seat slightly, her hand still on Bruno's neck, the big dog was still lying with his head on her lap feeling very sorry for himself. "But what are we going to tell the police?" She asked. Surely they were expected to do something. What did anybody do when they had just killed, or witnessed somebody, kill a person. Surely not sit drinking brandy over the body.

"Nothing." Markov snapped the words. "The police do not have to be informed. It will be dealt with. But you, Mrs Landers, are an inconvenience in the matter. You should not have been here, you should not have been involved or witnessed what you did. So I ask you again. Do you imagine you can discuss that matter with anybody else?"

Fear ran through Carols being. Markov had spoken so openly about himself – about his past. Was it because it did not matter what she heard? So why was he asking her whom she was thinking of telling? She had not thought far enough ahead to consider speaking about the incident. This was a unique situation. She had no idea how she was going to deal with it, she had not had time to give it any thought. Speaking about it had not yet entered her head. From somewhere deep inside, Carol's fighting spirit found its way to the surface. "Do you plan to kill me to keep this quiet Mr Markov!" She spat the words out in defiance. She might as well go down fighting although somehow she felt she was in no danger from this man.

Markov looked into her eyes. His expression was almost painfully sad. "Please, Mrs Landers. Don't insult me!" He stubbed his cigarette and immediately lit another. "There has been too much killing over the years of my life. I simply want peace. The people I know in this country will clear up all this and leave no trace. If you do speak of it there will be nothing that the police will be able to discover, it will just make things more ...... public if you like and maybe even attract unwanted attention from sources that we would prefer not to hear about your involvement."

Carol tried to force her brain to think straight amidst all this mess. "So what happens now? What on earth are we going to do?" She realised that she had inadvertently used the term 'we', but maybe that was appropriate. Was she implicated in the killing in any way? Was she involved? Oh, she was involved all right. She was sitting there with the killer in the same room as the body, she was involved in the worse possible way. At the very least she could be prosecuted for her involvement in the killing - or at worse, she could never leave here at all.

"For the sake of everyone, Mrs Landers, including yourself, I ask you to speak to no-one about this incident. When you read about an incident at this cottage in the papers, if it does indeed reach the national papers, keep your silence. Say nothing to anybody. It is for your own safety as well as mine, and that of your friends."

Unbelievable as it seemed, things started to make sense to Carol as she listened to Markov's calm explanation. Markov was not going to kill her and why indeed would he, it would only serve to complicate matters further surely, in fact all he was asking for her silence - and why not? This killer, it seemed, would not have stopped before he had

murdered not only Carol herself but all who were involved with her. It did not bear thinking about, so why go to the police? This man would have hurt Katy so was better wiped off the face of the earth.

"But what of you?" Carol suddenly felt a pang of sympathy for the big man sitting before her. A man that seemed to have carried the weight of many tragedies on his shoulders.

"Me?" Markov fixed her with his gaze again. "I am now dead Madame. There lies the body of Zhravko Markov. Dead and gone. Assassinated by the killer who has sought him for more years than you could imagine."

Carol gasped. "You are going to pass this person off as yourself!" Suddenly things began to make sense. The mysterious flight from Bulgaria. Markov appearing in the middle of nowhere and that awful man with the cold eyes lying dead not a yard from her feet.

"You mean this man has been after you for years?" Carol asked, feeling braver now.

"Many, many, years Mrs Landers. In the end it was pure hate that drove him on. He would have eliminated anybody that had ever been in contact with me."

"Why did he hate you so Mr Markov." Carol's curiosity was getting the better of her.

Markov hesitated. Why did he have to answer these questions? He didn't have to, but suddenly he wanted to. Wanted to clear the past from his troubled mind. Maybe cleanse his soul. "I was the one who saw him for what he was in the beginning and approved his training for the work he was to undertake. It was I who sent him on his 'errands'." He took a deep breath and rose from is seat, casually running some water into a bowl and placing it before Bruno who lapped thirstily. "Shock will have dehydrated him." he observed simply.

Carol felt ashamed that the thought had not occurred to her and was once again surprised by this mans train of thought.

"He was ideal for the work that was required. He took a delight in it and conducted his missions with the greatest of pleasure. Too much pleasure, I often presumed and I had misgivings. The whole system was corrupt and I began to question it. It was then that I realised that I too was in danger. Nobody was ever allowed to question the chain of authority in those days. The Cold War I believe you referred to it in this country, a situation that lasted much longer than was popularly believed."

"Who *are* you Mr Markov – really." Carol could hardly believe what she was hearing. Things like this just did not happen in her life. Surely this must be an elaborate story to explain the astonishing events outside: but something in Markov's demeanour made her believe that there was at least, a grain of truth to what she was hearing.

Markov sighed. He had borne the weight of immeasurable problems on his shoulders for too many years. Maybe now it was time to release his soul from the burden. "I am Nikolai Vladimir,Dmitri Zakharov. I was born in a small village north of Moscow. My father was a woodsman, a carpenter you might have called him. A maker of many useful and beautiful things. He was a fine artisan of his trade. I too could have followed him in his line of work, but I was young and headstrong, I followed a different path."

For the first time Carol noticed the wood carvings scattered about the big farmhouse kitchen. Intricate pieces of work that obviously had been made with love of the trade.

Markov seemed far away as he spoke, remembering his life, his family, his childhood. "I travelled to Moscow and began getting involved with politics. Most young Russians were passionate about politics then." Carol said nothing, sitting before him, her hand on Bruno's neck she realised that his man was divulging intimate information that had been kept locked away for many years.

"I worked my way up to a strong and powerful position." Markov continued. "No man challenged my word. If they did, I had the means to silence him." He glanced over to the body, then turned back to Carol. "Yes, Mrs Landers, I sent this man and others like him, on their errands." His voice was bitter as he spoke, the word *errands* taking on a whole new meaning to the simple term that Carol used in her everyday - now seemingly mundane - life. "But life changes, Mrs Landers. I began to doubt the way of life I was leading. Doubt the rules that I had learned to live my life by, rules that had been set by others. Why was I following them when in my heart I had stopped believing? That was when the danger to my own life began."

"So you ran to a different country and changed your name?" Carol spoke bluntly to simplify things. She could see the big man was struggling with his words and somehow felt that she wanted to hear no more. There was too much going on in her brain to take in any further information.

Markov nodded. That was certainly the simplified explanation.

"And suddenly you had to move on again. That would explain your unorthodox exit from Bulgaria with Jeff and the truck." Carol was starting to believe that this was indeed all true and not an elaborate story to guarantee her silence.

"I had not realised how deep was this man's hatred of me - but I should have. I held the position that he coveted and also.........I married the woman that he wanted."

"You have a wife Mr Markov?" The thought that this mysterious man could have a family had been the last thing that Carol had considered.

"I had." Markov said bluntly. "He killed her!" He spat the words with venom, his eyes turning for a moment to the still body, slumped with no dignity, on the kitchen floor.

"Good God! He killed your wife!" Carol began to realise how deep this thing was. How dangerous the situation had been.

"It was then that I knew I had to leave Moscow. Go as far away as I could in the hope of being out of reach." Markov continued. "I left Moscow, taking nothing with me, changed my name to suit the country and was given employment by an old acquaintance at the prison."

"Bulgaria." Carol understood now.

"Yes. That is where I fled and lived for many years. There until you met me, Mrs Landers."

"Well, I am glad that we did meet you Mr Markov." Carol answered, "We all owe you a great debt for how you helped Jeff and released him from that awful prison."

"You owe me no debt." Markov admitted candidly. "It was at that time that I discovered that I had been tracked down and had to leave. I needed a way of leaving the country and took my opportunity. Your friend was simply the means of my escape."

At least he was honest, Carol thought. He could have told her anything right now but the simple truth in the words rang true. Rang true enough for her to believe the whole story.

"What had you planned to do when you reached England." She asked. Surely he had not expected to end up in this situation.

Markov decided it was not prudent to mention his connection with the British Government department. He had said more than he would have preferred to in any case. "I had some tentative plans but they have changed since I entered your country."

Carol nodded. He obviously still needed to keep certain things to himself. "So now you are dead, is that it?" she asked, her overloaded brain beginning to grasp the situation and unbelievably start to deal with it.

"Yes, you will understand it is the best way, the only way that this thing can be over and safest for those around me. I must try to lead some sort of life that is as far removed from what I used to be as possible. I just regret that you have had to witness this event. It must have been very distressing for you."

Carol realised that had stopped shaking and her brain was now beginning to function. "I still find it unbelievable that I met you here and as for what happened, I still can't take it in, but you have my sworn word that I will say nothing of what has happened here. But lord knows how I am going to explain why I have been away so long or what happened to Bruno."

Markov suddenly realised that he had not asked exactly why Carol was there. "But why are you here Mrs Landers." He asked. "I had not expected to ever meet you again, especially here."

"Well, I thought I saw you in the town, getting into your car." Carol admitted. "And then I saw the car outside the cottage and decided to be nosy." It sounded rather lame under the circumstances.

A flicker of a smile played round Markov's mouth. "Ah, the feline curiosity of women." He noted. "What is it you say in this country. The enquiring mind of kittens leads to death?"

"Curiosity killed the cat!" Carol replied ruefully. It had certainly nearly been the end of her that day.

Carol suddenly remembered. "There was another car. Tucked into the hedge just outside the gate. Will that not be his?" She gestured over to the body in the corner, trying not to look at it. "It will have to be hidden, or disposed of in some way. It could be traced you know!"

"Ah, thank you. Yes. I will look into it." Markov seemed to be perfectly calm and slightly amused at her comments. Carol doubted that his pulse rate had risen at all throughout the events of the last hour. "But what I meant." He continued. "Was what are you doing here in this place, in this part of Scotland. I believed you to live in London."

"Ah, I see. Well, believe it or not." Carol said wryly. "I am getting married today, not far from here. So today is actually my wedding day. Jeff and Gina are also here and Tony too of course, and my daughter." As she spoke she doubted the wisdom of informing him of the others also being there but it was said now.

To her amazement Markov threw back his head and laughed out loud. "What a strange situation we find ourselves in Mrs Landers." Carol noticed that his coal black eyes had a charming sparkle when he laughed. "Fate has a way of throwing us together has it not?" He got to his feet. "It is your wedding day today and here you sit in my kitchen. I must keep you no longer." It sounded as though two old friends had been spending time visiting and he was excusing her to go about her business as on any other normal day. "May I suggest that you say there was an incident with a car. Maybe a speeding vehicle glanced your dog and you could not report anything about it due to shock."

"I smell of brandy." Carol remarked almost calmly.

"A friendly passer-by, a walker, stopped to help and offered you a drink from his flask to calm your nerves." Markov suggested. It sounded as good as anything she could have come up with. It was simple and uncomplicated. A hit and run with a helpful passer by stopping to help. It was perfectly believable. She looked up at Markov. She realised that this man was more complex than she had ever imagined. He had killed the assassin without a second thought, but had shown kindness and gentleness to Bruno. He had spoken quietly to her and explained the situation as best he could and was now calmly sending her on her way with a corpse in his kitchen. Carol realised he had hardly given it a second glance after dumping it in the corner like a sack of rubbish.

"I will drive you to your destination Mrs Landers." Markov reached for a set of car keys off the window ledge. He saw the hesitation in Carol's eyes. "You are not in a fit state to walk and I presume it is the wedding venue about two miles from here is it not?"

Carol nodded but stood her ground. "I feel the walk will fare me better Mr Markov. I am made of stronger stuff than you may imagine and apart from

that I think a walk to clear my thoughts and get my head round what has just
taken place will be good for me."

Markov nodded. He admired this strong young woman and felt that his
secrets would be safe in her hands. "But you forget your dog is injured Mrs
Landers.' He pointed out and once again Carol felt ashamed for not
remembering Bruno's injuries. "I will take you most of the way and leave
you discreetly within walking distance." There was going to be no further
argument about it.

"What will you do now?" Carol asked as she got to her feet and helped
Bruno to his. She almost said 'what are *we going to do now':* She felt
equally involved in the whole sordid situation. As deeply embroiled as
Markov himself almost.

"That, Mrs Landers is not your affair." Markov told her bluntly. "But you
will no doubt hear of my demise in the coming weeks. Remember, say
nothing. I believe you are a strong woman and can keep this secret to your
grave if need be."

"Oh, believe me Mr Markov, I have no intention of incriminating myself in
any of this, and as you say, I have my family to consider. My daughter's
safety is the most important thing in the world to me and if keeping this to
myself will keep her safe then nothing would drag it from me!" The fire I
her voice as she spoke left Markov in no doubt that she was speaking the
truth.

"I will escort you to the car." Was the only answer.

Markov helped Bruno onto the back seat then drove slowly out of the drive
and turned onto the leafy lane. As they past the assassin's car, Carol felt a
chill run down her spine. She could have been dead, lying on the cold floor
where the assassin's body now lay, possibly with the body of Markov next
to her. It was not so much that thought that chilled her to the bone, it was
the thought that her beloved Katy could have been in danger. Certainly she
would keep the secret of this last hour at all costs. She would take it to her
grave without a doubt. There had been a horrid incident with a hit and run
driver. That was what had happened and poor Bruno could not contradict
her story.

*****

CHAPTER SEVENTEEN

"Are you sure you feel okay Mum?" Katy asked, still very concerned after Carol had related the story of the reckless driver that had come so close to knocking them down. "I feel so mad to think that lunatic did not even bother to stop!"

Carol unwrapped her hair from the big fluffy towel and reached for the hairdryer. She was feeling much calmer now she had bathed and checked Bruno over yet again and done her best to explain as casually as she could the reason for Bruno's limp and her own rather shaken and dishevelled appearance.

"I am fine darling." Carol's calm tone belied her inner feelings. "Honestly, Katy the only thing I was worried about was Bruno. I just landed in the bushes in rather an undignified heap, but I was worried that Bruno may have been injured internally and I am just so glad that the emergency vet could see him straight away." The carefully rehearsed lie tripped off her tongue. If she repeated it often enough she could even start to believe it herself.

Carol had arrived back at the chalet and immediately told the tale of the hit and run driver and at once called the emergency vet that was listed in the phone book. She thanked all that was holy that the wedding had been arranged for late afternoon so there was plenty of time for the vet to check Bruno and pronounce him bruised but otherwise okay.

Carol had insisted that Tony stay behind once more and accepted Jeff's offer of a lift to the vet. No point in undoing the good that had already been done in making Tony feel better by overdoing things now, she had pointed out.

Secretly she had worried that if she were alone with Tony she may have been tempted to spill out the whole story, and what good would that have done, she asked herself. The sight of his gentle, worried face when she had returned was enough to still her tongue and the nightmare that every one of them had been in danger from that madman had been a spine chilling thought that pushed the words further away.

The vet had administered a shot for Bruno and had kindly advised Carol to call into the nearby chemist and buy herself some over the counter painkillers after hearing her story. Carol had taken his advice and had wisely taken one of the strong pain killers after noticing the start of a stress headache coming on. A hot soak in the bathtub was the best way to ease her aching muscles so she made sure that she had lain in the soothing water for as long as she could. Taking time to relax her mind as well as her body.

Delayed reaction had set in as soon as she tried to relax and wind down. She had locked herself in the bathroom and vomited violently, retching until her stomach was empty. She had run the taps noisily so that Tony would not hear as she stayed locked in until the waves of sickness eased and she was able to act as normally as she could. She was determined that nothing would spoil this day not just for herself but for Tony and Katy and her special friends who had travelled so far to join in with what should have been the happiest day of her life. And why should it not be a day of celebration? She asked herself. There had been a terrible danger lurking in the background that she had not known about and now this danger was over. Katy was safe and there was nothing to threaten their lives or their happiness any more. The morning's events had taken care of that. She should be happy about it and be thankful that it was over. But of course it was not quite that simple. But she would act her way through it. She was sure that the shock would soon fade and she could forget the whole terrible incident.

In fact the hit and run driver story was related so convincingly to everyone time and again that she herself began to wonder if the events of the morning had all been a bad dream that she and Bruno had actually been skimmed off the road by a speeding driver.

"But don't let's think about it any more Sweetie." She reached out and took Katy's hand. "We are all okay and apart from poor Bruno being a bit sore and dopey from the painkillers things could have been a lot worse so let's look forward to a lovely afternoon, yes?"

Poor Bruno was certainly very subdued right now, lying half asleep with his head on his paws on the rug at the side of the bed. Carol had completely disregarded the 'no dogs in chalets' rule and settled her beloved pet to recover in comfort from the shock events of the morning. Nothing was too good for her darling Bruno, especially now. His actions had not only saved her own life this morning but the life of Markov too. Not to mention Katy and Jeff and Gina had that evil man lived.

How true that things could have been so much worse. Once again Carol pushed the terrifying thoughts out of her mind and switched on the hairdryer, hanging her head down and swishing the hot air through her scalp, whisking her auburn curls into life once more.

Katy was already dressed for the occasion in a pretty black dress covered in red roses. She wore black kitten heeled shoes and a black mesh hat trimmed with a red ribbon, complimenting Carols own ensemble. She was bustling happily around the small chalet, taking Carol's wedding dress out of the layers of wrappings and laying out shoes and jewellery. Carol glanced at her lovely daughter and filled up with emotion. Katy was happily unaware that anything had been amiss and Carol was determined that she would stay in blissful ignorance.

Tony had been bullied to dress much earlier and then take a slow stroll round to the small bar a short step from the chapel to spend an hour with Jeff and Andy while the girls got on with preparing the bride.

"Yoo Hoo it's me!" Gina arrived looking perfectly groomed in a stunning royal blue silk dress which cleverly disguised her growing bump and a glamorous Hollywood style creation of a hat perched on her blonde upswept hair, trimmed with swansdown which floated gently around her face.

"Anna has decided to stay with the boys in the bar?" She announced. "She wants to enjoy the first sight of you walking down the aisle in your full glory and has been so busy all morning I think she deserves a drink anyway!"

"What on earth have you two been up to?" Carol queried. Ruffling her hair into its trademark tumble of curls and slipping off her bathrobe. "You certainly have been very secretive together."

Katy passed her mother the carefully chosen underwear for Carol to slip into. "Well, Anna had to bring the cake didn't she?" She put in innocently. "So she had to make sure it was taken care of before leaving it of course." She glanced quickly at Gina as she spoke and Carol could not help but notice the conspiratorial glance between the two.

Thinking better of making any further remark on the subject Carol took out her make-up bag and continued with her preparations. She had known Katy and Gina far too long to be fooled by such innocent expressions.

"But how do you feel now Kiddo?" Gina enquired. "That must have been awful for you being knocked flying like that. Bloody idiot drivers!" Gina announced indignantly as she walked around the bed to stroke Bruno who managed to raise an ear and flap his tail in a half hearted attempt at greeting.

After being smuggled back to the chalet to rest, and still dopy from the pain killing injection, it had been decided that he would be excused from walking down the aisle with Carol and would be far better left in peace to sleep off the effects. In truth he was certainly not taking any interest in events as Carol prepared for her wedding. Far better to leave him to sleep and recover in peace.

At last Carol was ready to slip on her sparkling silver shoes and step into her dress. She breathed in a little while Katy tugged up the zip.

"Perfect!" Gina announced stepping back to admire the finished effect. "Oh, Carol, you look so lovely! Bring the bouquet Katy let's see the full picture – where is the camera, I will take photograph of the two of you just here. Wedding preparations and all that!" Gina was in her element.

The girls spent a few happy moments taking casual snaps of each of them with the bride as the sound of bagpipes heralded the fact that Tony and the guests were being escorted to the little chapel.

"That's my cue to leave." Gina announced, kissing Carol quickly on the cheek and dashing towards the door. "See you in there Kiddo and make sure you enjoy every moment!" Gina left in a flurry of silk and swansdown leaving Katy and Carol alone.

Carol gave herself a last minutes check in the full length mirror. She had to admit she was happy with the reflection that greeted her. The silver jewellery glistened in the light and the stunning rubies of Gills bracelet flashed like fire, complimenting the beautiful red dress as it floated around her ankles skimming the silver shoes. The discreet silver and diamante tiara nestled amongst her auburn curls and the bouquet of pure white lilies cascaded almost to the floor contrasting perfectly with the startling red dress.

"Mum you look wonderful!" Katy announced, standing back to check that nothing was even slightly out of place. "I am so proud of you and I just know you will be happy with Tony. He is a lovely man and I can't think of anyone better that I would rather have you married to."

"Thank you darling!" Carol spontaneously pulled Katy to her and hugged her tight. For a moment the events of the morning flooded across her mind. She could have lost Katy. Her precious Katy could have been in danger but now all was well. Thank you Markov, she whispered silently: Thank you and God speed to you whatever your plans are.

Katy gasped for breath. "Easy Mum, let me breathe!" she laughed. "Anybody would think you would never see me again!"

Carol fought back a tear. "That my darling will never happen. We both have very happy futures to look forward to!"

A rap on the door interrupted Katy's reply. "That will be Maggie, the wedding organiser." Carol announced, a small flutter of anticipation running through her. "So it looks like it's time – here we go." Katy grabbed the tiny red satin cushion bearing the wedding rings and opened the door.

As Carol and Katy stepped outside the chalet door they were met with bright sunshine and blue skies. "Well now, were you not the lucky ones choosing an afternoon wedding. Not a cloud in the sky!" The cheerful smile of the efficient Maggie met them as she took charge of the chalet key and locked the door. "Oh my, and don't you look stunning young lady!" She admired Carols dress as she briskly arranged Katy onto the correct side and nodded to the kilted piper to strike up his pipes and lead the way to the chapel.

A warm breeze fluttered her hair as Carol took the short walk with a spring in her step and a lightness of heart towards the tiny chapel. The sun shining on the old weathered stone seemed to be welcoming her on her journey to her new life with Tony.

Katy squeezed her mother's arm as they walked and gave Carol a mischievous grin. "What does the best man usually say at this point?" She whispered. "Something along the lines of this is your last chance to run away. Run or forever hold your peace or something." She giggled.

Carol Laughed. "I don't think I could run in these shoes if the devil himself was after me." She replied light-heartedly, but as she spoke a small icy stone hit the bottom of her stomach as a flashback of the mornings events ran through her mind. Surely the devil himself had already crossed her path this day. No! She would not allow herself to think about it. She would bury it in the back of her mind and not let anything spoil her wedding day.

As they arrived at the chapel gates Carol was delighted to find a photographer waiting outside, a surprise gift from Gina and Jeff: wedding photographs for her and Tony to treasure.

"I knew you would be pleased about this." Katy smiled happily for the camera as Mother and daughter posed in the pretty chapel garden, the breeze fluttering Carols dress in gentle waves. "I got to hear all about all the secrets and surprises and couldn't want to see your face light up when you discovered them." Katy leaned in towards Carol under the photographers instructions.

"You mean there is more?" Carol asked, trying to make sure she did as the photographer asked, standing close to Katy and smiling happily.

"Aha, you won't get anything out of me that way!" Katy giggled as they had their close up cheek to cheek. "I am the worlds master at keeping secrets, my lips are sealed!"

Carol thanked the photographer as he finished his session. Oh, Katy my darling, she thought silently, you have no idea what a real secret is: and once again she had to shake the thoughts out of her mind.

At last she and Katy arrived at the chapel door. Maggie beamed and flung the door open to allow the piper inside, striking up in full flow as he led the way down to the anvil.

Carol saw Tony turn, saw his face light up as he saw her as she took a deep breath and walked down the aisle, arm in arm with her lovely daughter towards her handsome Italian lover. Today was the start of her new life and she held her head high as she walked towards her future.

*****

CHAPTER EIGHTEEN - EPILOGUE

The stars were out in abundance, glittering like diamonds in a deep velvet sky. Carol pulled her padded jacket around her a little more tightly as she stepped outside the kitchen door and took in deep breaths of the sharp fresh air, Bruno walking carefully beside her. Still a little subdued and sore, Carol needed to make sure he did not forget himself and attempt to bound down the length of the garden as he usually loved to do, but Bruno seemed to know his limits and was content to sniff amongst the ivy growing under the old privy shed.

An owl hooted gently, the swish of his wings disturbing the night air as he swept by like a phantom as Carol escorted Bruno around the garden. Although Bruno was probably perfectly capable of attending his own needs in the familiarity of his own garden Carol was glad of a moment alone and a breath of fresh air.

Carol could hear happy chatter coming from her large living room. Everyone had insisted on stretching the celebrations to the hilt and were all happily re-living the events of the wedding, poring over the photographs and opening more champagne to enjoy with slices of Anna's rich fruit wedding cake which was being demolished at a rate of knots.

The events of the last few days had been a whirlwind of activity to say the least. Starting with the long drive in the 'Flying Angel' over the Scottish border with Tony at her side and Gina and Jeff driving ahead by car, all happily anticipating the wedding. Andy and Anna, Spyder and Suzy and of course Katy arriving full of excitement in a flurry of activity on the day of the wedding. And of course the terrifying attacks that Carol had desperately tried to push to the back of her mind so as not to arouse the suspicions of her guests.

The event of the wedding morning had taken on a dreamlike sequence to Carol as she had tried her best to maintain her usual demeanour so as not to provoke too many awkward questions. Questions she certainly did not want to answer. Strangely, the more she thought about the terrible happening the less she could bring herself to voice it.

Not that she ever had any intention of telling a living soul a word about the attack. She had promised Markov that she would say nothing and Carol was a woman of her word.

Apart from that Carol had never been the type of person who felt the need to discuss every little thing with others. Not that this could be classed as a little thing, but all the same, Carol always believed that a secret shared was a secret no longer, and this was surely the biggest secret that she had ever been asked to keep safe. And although it seemed strange, as long as she kept her thoughts to herself, Carol felt much more able to handle the situation. She could not bear to face questions that she would find difficult to answer.

What if she had confided in Tony? How would he have felt knowing that Carol had walked unknowingly into danger, while he himself was relaxing not far away. Tony would have felt dreadful about it so why burden him with it? Why give him an unnecessary worry. No, apart from her promise to Markov, it would not have been fair to do this to Tony, far better he continued to remember his wedding day with pride and pleasure. Carol loved him enough to spare him the turmoil she herself was struggling with.

And of course there was no way she could have unburdened herself to Gina. No way she could have given her friend such a terrible secret to hold, especially as she was so happy right now and looking forward to the birth of her baby.

No, Carol could hold the dreadful event in her head and mull it over alone until it lost some of its gravity. She was sure the whole incident would fade with time. Well, at least she hoped it would. It was not as if she had witnessed an innocent person being murdered after all. Already she had counted her blessings time and again that the man was dead. It was terrifying to know that he had been so close for so long. Know that he would have without a doubt killed Markov had he been able to and then, if Markov were to be believed – and Carol felt sure Markov had been open and honest with her – the assassin would have come after Carol herself and all others that were connected however loosely to Markov. Katy – her precious Katy, could have been in danger.

After such an unbelievable morning the rest of the day could not have been more different. Her wedding day. A day full of happiness and celebration and many surprises.

The wedding itself had been a delightful occasion full of surprises. Carol had been taken aback when she realised that Marco was standing there, right next to Tony as she walked down the aisle in the wake of the piper. Tony's brother had flown in the day before, having arranged a business meeting nearby and had hired a car to make the journey to the Mill so as to stand next to his brother on his wedding day. Tony had been moved almost to tears at Marco's unexpected appearance, but as Marco had jokingly pointed out, someone had to report back to Mamma Gina that the deed had not only been done but done properly under a consecrated roof by a true man of the cloth.

Things like this were important to Mamma. She had wept copiously down the telephone to the newly married couple until Poppa Copeland had managed to prise the receiver from his wife's hand and send his own congratulations to his eldest son. Now Mamma could happily start to make lavish plans for a magnificent occasion at La Casaccia in a few weeks time, where the entire village would be involved. There would be music and singing and dancing – and of course plenty of Mamma's food. In fact most probably the celebrations would last a good few days.

Both Carol and Tony had been delighted with the surprise reception that had been Andy and Anna's gift to them. A room above the bar had been hired for a buffet and champagne reception, Anna's triumph of a cake standing in full splendour on its own special side table.

Anna had surpassed herself. Three pure white iced cakes, trimmed with scarlet rose buds, arranged on a silver stand bound in scarlet ribbon. Instead of the traditional black and white bride and groom topping the highest tier, Anna had fashioned a bride in a scarlet dress in almost an exact copy of Carols own, the bride and groom seated in an old American car. Scarlet ribbons cascaded down the sides of the cake tumbling amongst the rose buds in artistic waves that only Anna could have thought to create. A one off creation as Anna herself put it.

It was clear that Gina and Anna had been busily arranging the reception room for most of the morning. The table and the decorations were a work of art and certainly proved well worth the hours of effort that the girls had lovingly put in to make Carol and Tony's day one to remember.

Bruno snuffled in the bushes as a hedgehog busily waddled out of sight into the shrubbery, making his way through the hedge and into the woods beyond. Carol glanced across the haulage yard and down the deserted country lane and was immediately reminded of the country lane leading to her fateful meeting with Markov. She had set off so cheerfully that morning with Bruno, a spring in her step and not a worry in her mind; never for one moment could she have guessed what would happen on that short walk.

She wondered how different things might have been had Tony not been injured and had gone with her. Maybe Tony would have tackled the man and been knifed, possibly killed or maybe the killer would have kept hidden if he had seen another person – especially a man – and may have waited until they had left. In that case what would have happened then? Might Markov have been off guard when the killer approached and been killed himself? And if that had been the case would then the killer have gone after Carol and Gina and Tony and Jeff and – God forbid – Katy.

A shudder ran down Carol's spine at the thought of Katy being in any kind of danger. Right now Katy was happy and laughing with Tony, Jeff and Gina. She was happy and safe and Carol prayed that she always would be. She dearly loved Tony and knew there was nobody else that she would rather spend the rest of her life with, but a mother's love is the strongest emotion in the world and it would always be Katy's safety that would come first for Carol. Anything bad happening to Katy had always been Carol's greatest fear.

Carol shivered slightly despite the mildness of the evening. There were far too many 'what if's' to consider and even so, no amount of running it back and forth through her mind would change what happened. She was alive and well so that was all there was to remember and be thankful for, and there was no longer any hidden danger for the future. She fervently wished that the recurring thoughts of that terrible morning would stop flashing into her head. Maybe in time they would fade away and she could live each day without spending a few moments dwelling on what happened. She knew that all brides would remember their wedding day forever, but there was that part of her own that she would prefer to forget.

"Come on boy, let's get you back in the warm and me back to my guests." Carol mentally pulled herself together and clicked her tongue to Bruno who willingly turned from his sniffing expedition and followed her quietly back to the house and the comfort of the thick rug that had been laid for him in the kitchen.

Carol made sure he was settled and stepped back outside for a moment, looking up at the myriad of starts twinkling in the sky. Those same stars would be twinkling over Tony's family home in the Tuscan hills, and also over the farmhouse down the twisting country lane in Scotland.

For a moment she wondered what Zhravko Markov was doing right now. Was he burying the body, digging a grave in the moonlight as if in some black and white horror movie, or had he called in help like one reads about in spy novels.

No - She had to stop thinking about it. She pushed the dark thoughts firmly away once again, took a deep breath and mentally shook herself into action. The worse had happened and she had survived it. She was now Mrs Antonio Copeland. She was married to the most wonderful man in the world who loved her to distraction. She had the most beautiful daughter that any mother could wish for and had the very best of true loyal friends. She had a beautiful home and her business was going from strength to strength. There was nothing more she could wish for. No point in dwelling on what might have been. She would look forward to a bright future and enjoy the rest of her life.

No more dwelling on what might have been, she told herself. It's over so look ahead. Yes, she had been in danger but fate had been with her and Markov had saved her life. 'Bless you Zhravko Markov.' She whispered.

She closed the door with an air of finality, ruffled Bruno's ears and held her head high as she walked towards the sound of laughter, towards her new husband, her new life and the warmth and security of her family and friends.

*****

Zhravko Markov pulled on his walking boots and padded jacket and walked over to the table where the rosewood box gleamed in the morning sunshine. He was once again filled with a sense of pride as he picked up the intricately carved piece and laid it gently in a sturdy carrier bag. This morning his walk would not detour past Rhona Kirkpatrick's house but lead him straight there. There was no need now to hold back: No need to guard his every move and watch his every step. The small piece of news in the paper had told of a freak car accident. A man had been killed. A visitor to the area whose name had been Nikolai, Vladimir, Dmitri Zakharov.

Oliver Carter had dealt with the details. The 'accident' had been given little prominence in the local papers – simply another tragic occurrence on the winding country lanes. The unfortunate driver had obviously been travelling far too fast and the car had careered off the road and burst into flames, the driver standing no chance of survival. Oliver Carters men had taken charge of the body and arranged the inquest as to the cause of death. The local police had gone through the proper channels and were satisfied that all had been handles according to the book.

The very small piece in the local paper had told of the tragedy and the incident was forgotten, apart from the fact that some thoughtful soul had placed a spray of flowers at the roadside where the scorch marks of the burned out car still lay in evidence of the incident. The news had, however, been leaked to other news agencies where the name would not have gone unnoticed.

Markov felt like a free man at last. The brisk morning air filled his lungs as he strode out, his steps light on the springy bracken path as he made his way towards the headland and the little side path that led to Rhona Kirkpatrick's house. There was plenty of time to think about his future.

The farmhouse was rented for a number of months ahead and there were negotiations already in place for the purchase of the property, the present owners being given such a generous offer for the place that it was highly unlikely they would refuse the sale. Oliver Carter had been grateful that his family was safe and had pulled many strings to secure Markov's ownership of the property. The old man had not long to live, he knew that well, but now the threat to his family was over all he needed to do was repay his debt to Markov and he would die a happy man.

Markov had made it clear that his life had taken a turn in a totally different direction and he would be happy to stay exactly where he was, carving his sculptures and taking his daily walks along the headland, so the farmhouse would be Carters gift to his old friend, a safe haven for him to live out the rest of his life in peace. The only other thing he had left to give was a small piece of paper with a name and an address written on it. It was the name of a young man that was currently studying botany at Moscow university. A young man that one day Markov may wish to contact – his son.

Markov turned down the muddy path, his back to the headland and a brisk breeze blowing him on his way. Rhona Kirkpatrick's door was open and the lady herself was in the pretty front garden struggling to place a plank of wood under a decidedly drooping gutter in order to shove it back into place. She looked up as Markov approached the gate and waved as best she could with her free hand. This time Markov did not walk by, he stopped at the gate and raised his hand in greeting.

"Well don't just stand there gawking man!"   Rhona Kirkpatrick called briskly. "Come away in and help why don't ye!"
Markov smiled. This invitation was just what he had been hoping for.

*****

(Many people who have witnessed or been involved in a traumatic experience find that they suffer from flashbacks to the event. If symptoms persist for more than a few weeks, professional help should be sought.

Printed in Great Britain
by Amazon.co.uk, Ltd.,
Marston Gate.